AVSTRALIS – Trouble and Triumph in the West Indies

AVSTRALIS

The Search for the Lost Southern Continent

Book 1

Trouble and Triumph in the West Indies

Written by Brandon T. Scholes

All rights reserved. No part of this book may be reproduced, scanned, or distributed in any printed or electronic form without permission. Please do not participate in or encourage piracy of copyrighted materials in violation of the author's rights. Purchase only authorized editions.

ISBN 978-0-692-72001-1

2nd Edition

Printed in the United States of America; Rochester, New York

Copyright © MMXVI   by Brandon Scholes

www.avstralis.org

brandon.scholes@avstralis.com

Foreword

Trouble and Triumph in the West Indies is a fictional story that takes place in the non-fictional context of the 18th century age of sail and has been written for middle school aged children. The story highlights the boldness required to venture forth into uncertainty to answer a seemingly impossible calling; to persevere in faith through trials and set-backs; and to put first the Kingdom of Heaven by issuing grace, love, and forgiveness.

This book is dedicated to my children Emma, Natalya and Levi; and to all still young at heart. May your lives be filled with exploration, discovery and peace as you go forth to love and serve others as Christ Jesus has loved and served us.

I am forever indebted to all those who encouraged and equipped me to cross state borders, national borders, and oceans in order that I may discover the world and bring the Gospel of hope to those who dwell in distant lands.

To God be the glory!

Table of Contents

Chapter I - The Scorpion and The Platypus

Chapter II - Beyond the Horizon

Chapter III - Porky Finds his Sea Legs

Chapter IV - Close-Hauled on the Open Sea

Chapter V - Breakfast with Unexpected Company

Chapter VI - Friend or Foe

Chapter VII - Porcupine Overboard

Chapter VIII - Singing in the Brig

Chapter IX - A Lonely Trunk

Chapter X - Breakfast in the Sand

Chapter XI - The First Night on Land

Chapter XII - Mr. Shelton Express

Chapter XIII - A Grand View

Chapter XIV - War Drums

Chapter XV - A Captain of a Different Feather

Chapter XVI - The Plan

Chapter XVII - Thunder on a Starry Night

Chapter XVIII - Royal Company

Chapter XIX - One Hour to Rescue a Nation

Chapter XX - Surrounded

Chapter XXI - A Narrow Escape

Chapter XXII - Rescue or Run

Chapter XXIII - A Leap of Faith

Chapter XXIV - Humility and Freedom

Chapter XXV - Mid-Morning Muskets

Chapter XXVI - Hosting a Princess

Chapter XXVII - Papers Unravel the Spanish Navy

Chapter XXVIII - Greetings, Stories, and Fights

Chapter XXIX - Dining in Good Company

Chapter XXX - Cornered by a Spanish Goliath

Chapter XXXI - The Best Way to Stop a Broadside

Chapter XXXII - Dastardly Diplomacy

Chapter XXXIII - Burial at Sea

Chapter XXXIV - A Bold and Secret Mission

Chapter 1

The Scorpion and The Platypus

The sky was clear and the air was crisp on this particular early spring morning. Porky the Porcupine rubbed his eyes and stretched out his arms and legs to start a new day. After ruffling out his quills to a more comfortable assortment, Porky looked up to the sky and saw that the stars were retreating from the light of dawn. A flutter of excitement churned in Porky's stomach as he considered all the new adventures the rising sun was ushering into the new day.

The first light of morning always excited Porky. As the eager young critter did almost every morning, he put on his satchel containing both his journal and his Bible which Porky's Grandfather referred to as 'The Compass of his Heart'. He would say to Porky, "Do not attempt to sail into a new day without first setting a proper course! Your heart, your mind, and your Compass must all be in agreement!"

Porky heeded his grandfather's advice and consulted his 'compass' first thing every morning. Perhaps more so out of hope that someday it and circumstance would guide him to the place where his heart would come most alive; to a place where all his days he could do exactly what he was created to do.

Porky lived with his father and mother in an old hollowed out pine tree on Moose Island's sunrise-side not far from the Grandmother Pine, which was the tallest tree on the island Porky knew of. Porky scurried down from his moss-covered pine tree and set off running atop the forest floor, which was still wet with the cool dew of the morning. His footsteps churned up, from the rock littered soil, a wonderful piney and earthy smell. Just minutes before the sun crested the horizon over the great waters surrounding Moose Island, Porky, being an excellent climber, effortlessly ascended the Grandmother Pine.

Being one of the few creatures that could reach such lofty heights, it was Porky's duty on Moose Island to locate and identify ships approaching and to alert the lighthouse keeper accordingly. Porky could never predict when a ship would appear, but when the sailing ships did come in to Moose Island Harbor, he loved to meet the sailors and listen to their stories of adventure and peril from distant lands! Porky treasured these stories up in his heart and was eager to discover all that awaited him beyond the furthest horizon of Great Waters.

Porky stood tall on his hind legs atop Grandmother pine and read aloud from his 'compass' as he faced the rising sun, "If I rise on the wings of the morning, and dwell in the furthest parts of the sea, even there Your hand shall lead me, And Your right hand shall hold me fast."

 When Porky finished reading, he closed his eyes and let the rising sun warm his face. The cool air, carried on a moderate easterly gale, smelled of freshly melted snow. A faint sound likened to that of a brass bell reached Porky's ear. Porky rubbed his eyes as they were watering quite a bit from the wind, and he refocused on the lake attempting to look aside the glaring orange morning sun. Porky also took note of some fairly angry looking clouds moving in quickly from the West covering up the sky above him. The Sun had just appeared out from below the horizon and looked as if it would disappear just as quickly above the clouds moving in!

The rigging of what looked to be a Top-Sail Schooner came into view now clearly silhouetted by the light of the rising sun. "A Ship!" Porky shouted to himself. Porky looked behind him to the West. Over the top of his head he perceived angry looking clouds which often arrive without warning over the great waters. "A ship and a storm!" he said to himself realizing the situation at hand.

The lighthouse, which could be seen down shore to the north, had no lanterns lit inside and no smoke coming from the chimney of the keeper's house, "I've got to wake up Ol' Man Henry and get that beacon lit!"

Porky shoved his journal and bible into his satchel, slung it over his shoulder, and dashed down Grandmother Pine with instinctual skill. As soon as Porky's feet hit the forest floor, he tore off running with all of his might towards the harbor, leaving behind him a whirlwind of pine needles and leaves.

When Porky reached the harbor, he noticed that the sun was getting darker and that the pine trees were whistling in frightening chorus from the increasing easterly gale. Porky's heart became startled when the wind would gust making the trees roar like mighty rushing waters.

Porky ran quickly to the lighthouse and scurried up the door post to pull the bell. After a few rings he heard some faint shouting and the tumble of a chair, "I'm coming!" Ol' Man Henry's voice was becoming clearer, but it seemed to take forever for the lighthouse keeper to open the door. Along with the clouds that were racing to cover the sky, the Great Waters surrounding Moose Island started to make a constant and increasing thunder as angry white-capped waves crashed into shore.

The old man was adjusting his service hat as he opened the door. The wind ripped the door knob out of the lighthouse keepers hand and slammed it open against the outside wall. Porky noticed that Ol' Man Henry's uniform jacket was inside out which distracted his thoughts for a moment.

"Good morning Mr. Henry!" exclaimed Porky. "Sorry to bother you. I was atop Grandmother Pine, and in haste I ran here to make known to you that there is a ship on the Eastern horizon! A Schooner is approaching!"

Ol' Man Henry took note of the sky, "Oh my, look at the weather." The wind blew the lighthouse keepers hat off his head and forcefully blew his hair opposite of his part making it stand straight up. Not taking any note of his missing hat, he concluded, "We had better get the beacon lit. Now let's see here…"

The man was fumbling around trying to light his oil lamp, and when he lit the lamp after the third match was struck, he noticed that his lighthouse service jacket was inside out, "Oh goodness, this won't do!"

Ol' Man Henry stood there for a long minute just getting the first button undone. Porky could not stand to wait any longer. The old lighthouse keeper's senses had been dulled by age and he didn't notice Porky dash up the lighthouse tower. Porky just loved running up its tight spiral stair case.

Once to the top, Porky wound the mechanism that turned the massive lamp and reflector mirror. He checked the timing to make certain that it made a full turn every ten seconds. Porky suddenly realized he should have lit the lantern before he wound the giant mirror up to make its rotations. This wasn't the first time that Porky needed to hop on the lantern while it was spinning to light it. He always seemed to miss a few steps in the process when he was excited.

Once the lamp was lit and Porky recovered his vision from being blinded by its light and thundered back down the old wooden stairs of the lighthouse tower. Porky was about to tell Ol' Man Henry not to bother continuing in his present efforts, but he was busy mumbling to himself trying to unbutton his inside-out overcoat. Porky left him to his task and ran out of the keeper's house down the shore to a point where large rocks jutted out from the island diving down into brownish-orange water of the harbor.

There he sat, wedged behind a stone keeping an eye on both the light beacon and the great expanse of the increasingly angry waters to the East. Porky had to intermittently take cover behind his rock, for every time a wave would strike the shore the strong east wind whipped the icy spray inland. The spray of the crashing waves was extremely cold and traveling so fast that the water drops felt like pebbles being whipped against his face on the occasions that he failed to take cover in time! Porky ran down the shore a little more to the point where the breakwater met the calmer harbor, and he peered keenly at the point where the giant rollers crested.

The wind, which seemed to be growing stronger, created a mist atop the wave crests making it difficult for him to see the ship. The island's rocks jutted sharply out into the great waters and settled just under the surface in many irregular locations. The ship's captain had to perfectly navigate his vessel into the protected waters of the harbor or face being broken up along the unforgiving shoreline. This unfortunately was the fate of many ships before the lighthouse was built.

Porky wiped the cold spray of the waves from his face and refocused on the rollers. At that moment, the noble bow of a ship exploded through the crest of a massive wave only to dive down and disappear between the swells. For what seemed like a longer than desired pause all that could be seen was the two masts with their sails taught full of wind. Suddenly the ship shot straight up in the air again slicing through the crest of another rolling wave which sent a sheet of white water flying straight across the tops of the waves powered by the wind. As the hull of the ship disappeared yet again in the trough between the waves, Porky could see that the top square sail had ripped and was snapping violently in the wind. No man dared to tend to it.

As the ship neared the harbor, Porky could now begin to see all of the sailors scurrying about the deck in vigilant effort to keep the ship upright against the wind and the waves. They were sopping wet. The orders of the captain could be heard as he shouted above the thunder of the great waters. It looked as if the ship was on course to make it safely into the harbor. Porky started dashing over the rocks down along the harbors edge towards the beach landing.

Porky looked over his shoulder and saw that the captain had smartly guided the ship into the safety of the calmer sheltered waters. The sails on the weathered schooner were being lowered, the ripped topsail was furled, and the anchor splashed down into ten fathoms of water. The wind swung the Schooner's stern around to face the landing beach and Porky read aloud the name of the ship, which was freshly painted on its stern, "Scorpion".

Not much time passed before some of the schooner's crew was rowing towards shore in a skiff. A group of men came out from a lakeside cabin to greet them and receive them ashore. The schooner was clearly a merchant ship delivering a fresh order of supplies to the island. Porky was about to head toward the shelter and warmth of the log cabin trading post to hear what stories the sailors had brought, but an odd thing caught his attention.

A small raft with a storage tote on the top secured by a leather strap seemed to be moving on its own exactly towards where he was observing the morning's events on the beach. As it got closer, Porky could see that the small raft with a crate on top was being pulled towards shore by a rope that disappeared into the water. It was almost within a rocks throw from Porky when he could read the letters 'P.P.P.' on the side of the crate in tow. A very strange creature, the like of which Porky had never seen before, emerged out from the frigid water.

He looked like some type of beaver but with a bill like a duck. He was clearly older than himself, and he wore a vest with many filled pockets giving him the appearance of an explorer. The creature had the appearance of preferring to dwell in the water as it had smooth light brown oily hair, webbed feet and a large tail. Before Porky could collect his thoughts, the creature billowed out with a strong cheerful British accent, "Good day young Sir! Quite splendid to be ashore again!" The creature took a deep breath of the cool and fresh morning air and patted his chest with rejuvenated delight, "Well my boy, mind lending me a hand with my parcels?"

He spoke to Porky as if he was expecting him to already be there. They both took hold of the rope and heaved the raft to shore. The strange guest pulled a pair of sopping wet bifocals from his vest pocket and adjusted them onto his bill. He reached out to shake Porky's hand, "Nice to finally meet you, and thank you kindly for the help. The name's Pastor Peter

Platypus, and you must be the porcupine I've heard so much about."

Staring half stunned at the unexpected guest Porky replied with a bit of delay, "Porky, yes. Porky the Porcupine."

"Great! Quite nice to finally be able to put a face with the name. Thank you for coming to meet me so promptly." Pastor Platypus carried on, "Well, let us not waste any more time in the gale jibber jabbering. Go ahead son. Take my supplies, and let's get going." Pastor Platypus pointed to his crate and motioned to have it brought into the woods.

Porky, puzzled by the interaction, started to load the pastor's crate onto his back, and by the time he looked up, the pastor was heading in to the woods shouting through the wind, "Well, come along now. Let's get going!"

Porky was stuck between wanting to look at the new ship that came to Moose Island and the new visitor who emerged from the water with a seemingly urgent agenda. He reluctantly stepped away from the shore slipping and sliding on the rocks as he tried cumbersomely to handle the luggage crate of his odd looking guest, "Wait, Pastor! I'm coming!"

Finally catching up, they trudged together for a few steps through the thick pine forest. "Well, which way do we go now?" inquired Pastor Platypus with his strange accent which still distracted Porky.

"I thought I was following you Pastor Pus-a-plat," replied Porky a bit confused.

"It's 'Plat-a-pus', now what is the meaning of this. Look at us, we are both freezing, tired, and hungry. Are you going to take me to Mr. Paul J Porcupine are you not?!"

"You know my father?! You mean you are here to see him?" asked Porky quite stunned.

"Yes of course!" Pastor Platypus informed. "Didn't he send you to collect me from the harbor?!"

Before Porky could answer, he heard his mother calling out his name in the near distance, "Porky, oh Porky!"

"There you are Porky," she half scolded not yet seeing their new guest. "Your father and I have been looking all over for you. Why didn't you come in for breakfast after your time up on Grandmother Pine?! We have an important guest coming that you were supposed to......and what is that you are carrying?!"

At that moment Pastor Platypus came into view on the trail behind Porky. "Oh, Pastor Platypus, you did make it!" Pricilla Porcupine celebrated. She nearly knocked Porky off the trail getting to Pastor Platypus to give him a warm heart-felt hug, "Oh my, you are soaking wet and cold as winter. Come along now, we have breakfast on the table and a very inviting fire to warm your fur."

Pricilla Porcupine and Pastor Platypus started off down a path together towards their home. Porky lagged behind struggling to navigate the pastor's supply crate down the rock laden path to Porky's tree side cabin. He was more curious than ever to find out what the matter at hand was! Paul Porcupine eventually caught up with Porky, "Son, where have you been?! Of all mornings...," Paul paused as he saw Pastor Platypus, "and yet you managed to find our guest. Well done my boy, well done!"

"Sorry Pa, I was doing my reading at the top of Grandmother Pine and I saw a ship in the distance and a storm movin' in, so I ran off to the harbor to light the beacon in the lighthouse tower and to watch the Schooner come in!"

"That's enough, son, I'm just glad it all worked out. Let's head in and warm our quills up a bit. Here, let me help you with this crate," offered Porky's father.

Porky and his father followed not far behind Pricilla Porcupine and Pastor Platypus as they traversed the piney trail to Porky's home to host their newly arrived guest.

Chapter II

Beyond the Horizon

Smoke gently rose from the top of a large hollowed out pine tree. At the base of the old pine, Porky's father had built a cozy log cabin for his family. Inside there was much talking around a warm crackling fire over which patty cakes were rising on the griddle. Porky thought the patty cakes were an excellent reason to have what he really enjoyed most, maple syrup. Porky had many great memories collecting maple sap and cooking it down to syrup every spring with his father.

Porky's Pa and Ma were jabbering on like old friends with Pastor Platypus about what sounded like a lot of wonderful shared moments and memories from the past. Porky was going in and out collecting sticks and logs to keep the morning fire going strong. He was feeling a bit frustrated because he didn't quite understand exactly what was going on. It seemed like Porky's parents knew that this Pastor Platypus was coming on the supply schooner, but Porky could not figure out why they had been secretive about expecting his arrival.

As Porky was carrying the last awkward bundle of wood into the cabin, he froze in his steps when he overheard Pastor Platypus conversing with his parents and remained out of sight.

The Platypus carried on in his strong British accent, "Your minister here on Moose Island has sent three letters across the Atlantic to me at Portsmouth England over the past year concerning the young Porcupine. It sounds as if you have raised him well. A fine young porcupine he has become!"

Pastor Platypus pulled a folded letter out from his pocket, unfolded its crinkled pages, and glanced at it through his bifocals, "Now let's see here: cleans the church every Saturday evening, assistant lighthouse keeper, blacksmith's apprentice, directs children's Bible studies on Sundays, and recipient of the 1765 Moose Island Student Achievement Award in Physical Sciences. Not to mention 'very polite', 'heart of a servant', 'full of cheer', and 'longs to explore the world more than all the rest'."

Pastor Platypus folded the letter back up and placed it in his vest pocket and looked directly at Porky's parents for a couple of silent seconds, "That is precisely why I have taken a bit of a detour by venturing into the American colonies to find you all here at Moose Island in order that I may present to your child a magnificent opportunity which history has not yet offered until now."

The platypus handed a different letter to the trembling claw of Porky's mother. The platypus continued his proud proclamation, "I have come to implore you to allow your son to join me on a great and significant journey. It is rare to find such maturity, knowledge, and selflessness in a young creature. And it is rarer yet to find one who would be willing to venture to the ends of the earth!"

Pastor Platypus paused to take a deep breath. Porky's parents and the platypus sat down next to the warm morning fire. You could hear the wind howling outside which seemed to make the fire that much more inviting. Porky's father broke the wax seal of the letter given to him by Pastor Platypus as he sat atop a chair by the fire.

Porky set the firewood down and sat against a wall and covertly listened to the conversation about his possible future. Porky thanked the Lord over and over again in little whispers realizing that the fulfillment of his dreams was upon him!

After a deep sigh, Pastor Platypus continued with his strong British accent, "There is much talk back in England about a distant unknown land commonly referred to in Latin as 'Terra Avstralis Incognita' meaning quite literally 'Unknown Southern Land'. You see, there is a vast unexplored portion of the world towards the southwestern most reaches of the globe. It is assumed by all the leading scientists and cartographers that there exists a great continent yet to be discovered in the vast unmapped area of the South Pacific Sea."

Pastor Platypus adjusted his bifocals, "England searches her out for its gold, sugar, coffee, spices, and dare I say slaves for new plantations which they will establish. King George seeks only what is best for his kingdom, which I suppose is his duty. He stands in competition with his French and Spanish neighbors to discover and claim new found lands all around the world. That is why I have come to the American Colonies, to call upon those who seek independence from such monarchies. To find a new generation that is interested in building God's kingdom as well as making fantastic new geographical and scientific discoveries not just for the benefit of a few wealthy English noblemen, but for the benefit of all! To embrace, love and serve peoples of distant lands, not to conquer them!"

Pastor Platypus leaned in over the table, "But as you can see, I am not as young as I once was, and it is for that reason that I have traveled deep into the American colonies via the great waterway to your Island. I have done this in accordance to the recommendation of your pastor here on Moose Island in order that I may commission your boy as my First Mate and Pastoral Apprentice on this very significant and grand journey! What do you say?"

Porky's parents were speechless for a moment or two attempting to comprehend all they had been informed of. They were wide-eyed at the passion and vision of Pastor Platypus. Porky's mother was the first to tactfully delay the momentum of the conversation, "Pastor, why don't you sit down at the table over here and enjoy your patty cakes and syrup, you've had such a long trip to Moose Island, and in such poor weather." She was trying to hide her sadness and fear with her duties of hospitality, and for the time being it was working quite well. Porky's father asked, "How long do you suppose the boy will be gone in search of the lost southern continent?"

Pastor Platypus lovingly responded, "With work such as this, the journey may very well take years if not a life time. But, I do know this: If it is God's will that Porky join me, if this is the calling upon his life, then God's peace will strengthen and comfort your hearts as the purposes of your son's life are fulfilled."

Porky's mother started to cry, but she tried to hide her immediate sadness. She knew in her heart even before the question was asked that Porky was called to go. It had been revealed to her in a dream before Porky was born; A dream which she had hidden in her heart since that time. Still her heart broke, and she felt like the days with her son had passed far too quickly. She felt also a peace and sense of pride in the fact that her son had been called to a mission of such grand significance.

Porky thought this was a good time to make his entrance as to smooth over the moment. Porky pretended he didn't hear a thing Pastor Platypus said even though his heart was pounding in his chest nearly ready to explode with excitement and anticipation.

Porky's father expressed to Pastor Platypus, "This decision carries with it great significance and great consequences be it good or be it bad; My wife and I are going to need to pray about this and have a discussion with our son. When it comes to life-changing decisions we like to sleep on it, even if we think our minds are made up."

"This is very wise of you, and I respect your need for time," Pastor Platypus replied. "But I'm afraid tonight is all you have. I would like nothing more than to offer you more time, but the storm delayed us much more than we would have liked."

The Platypus was half out the front door buttoning up one of the pockets on his vest after placing his glasses in it, "The Scorpion will be resupplied today and Captain Hopkins intends to weigh anchor and shove off tomorrow morning should the weather permit it. The ship's carpenter will be mending the top sail through the night."

Pastor Platypus stepped out into the rain unaffected by its arrival. He turned back to peer into Porky's house with the front door open, "Your son is just the man I need at my side for a journey such as this. I have a lot of peace in my heart about our duty Mrs. Porcupine, and I know that God's provision will far outweigh any fears we may have. I have lived a full life and I am prepared to lay it down. This young man has his entire life before him, so whatever your choice, I will not pass judgment. I'll be by later this evening. I still have many duties to tend to as we make ready the schooner for the open sea. Good Day Mrs. Porcupine and thank you for opening up your home to me during my short stay here on Moose Island."

"You are very welcome Pastor, and do come back before sundown in time for supper," invited Mrs. Porcupine as she waved goodbye.

The platypus gently shut the door and started off down the trail towards the harbor. Just as the door latched shut, Porky looked at his mom and dad as if to say, 'What was that all about?!'

Porky's dad put his arm around him, and started walking towards the table, "Come here son. We've got a lot to talk about today, but first let's start the day off right with some hot patty cakes and a game of chess."

Porky's mother joined them wiping a few tears from her eyes, but Porky thought that just for a moment he saw a gentle smile emerge at the corner of her mouth. They all folded their hands and bowed their heads to pray. Steam continued to rise up from their patty cakes releasing a glorious smell. During prayer, Porky peeked out of the corner of his eye through the window just in time to see Pastor Platypus scurry down the trail towards the shoreline to help his crew replenish the Schooner.

During breakfast prayer, the peace of God surrounded and comforted the hearts and minds of Porky's family. They set aside all of their work and duties to spend the day just simply being together as a family discussing the journey and mission proposed by Pastor Platypus.

Chapter III

Porky Finds his Sea Legs

It was the morning watch, about two and a half hours, or five bells, before sunrise. Porky's eyelids were heavy, but his heart was filled with excitement. With legs stiffened by fatigue and cold, Porky strained to scrub spots of tar from the rising and falling foredeck of Captain Hopkins' smartly rigged top-sail merchant schooner named Scorpion. He was given a scrub stone and a bucket of sand to work the tar out of the deck. The tar had fallen from the rigging. Porky couldn't necessarily see the tar, but the officer of the watch assured Porky it was there.

It helped to keep busy. It kept his mind from getting too troubled about leaving his family for the first time in his life.

After an hour of scrubbing, the 'Holystone' as they called it felt like it weighed fifty pounds. It was black as pitch out and the deck of the Scorpion was tilting and rolling with unpredictable force. Porky dug his back claws into grooves of the deck boards the best he could, but just as stability was achieved an ice–cold wave would plunge over the bow sending Porky rolling and sliding across the deck. The outside starboard wall of the forecastle cabin stopped Porky from sliding clear across the ship deck.

Porky was trying to orient himself desperately to the position of the deck. He could not make out any horizon line and was becoming quite dizzy and ill having completely lost track of what was up and what was down. Porky eventually caught sight of the stars which would rise and fall as if the ship was still.

With little warning another frigid wave crashed over the bow smacking Porky in the face unannounced.

Pastor Platypus shouted from out of nowhere, "What makes it all the more fun is that you can't even see the waves coming before they hit you. Just you wait until they are laden with salt!"

"I'm not sure I'll survive this journey Pastor!" shouted Porky over the whistling morning wind.

Pastor Platypus encouraged, "Worry not my friend! With every sunrise God will renew your strength! The darkest hour is always just before the dawn. Life at sea has a way of making an hour seem like a year, and at other times you will look back and a year will have passed like an hour."

"That's fantastic, but can your words bring back the feeling in my arms?!" inquired Porky with a forced smile.

He didn't really hear what Pastor Platypus said in response, but when Porky smiled he felt a feeling somewhere between victory and rest surge through his body. It felt powerful to smile. Porky felt like he had defeated the waves, the cold and the darkness.

A lantern approached. It was the officer of the watch. Porky was clinging to the trim of the forecastle in an effort to not fall off the ship. The officer was standing holding on to nothing seemingly unaffected by the movement of the ship and the freezing water which was saturating his stately but worn overcoat.

With water dripping from his weathered face and green stained copper lantern, he smiled in a most uninviting way, "Not sure guardin' the fo'c'sle was part o' yer duties this mornin'. The spindle jib and the flying jib need to be made fast. By the sound o' it they're flappin' loosely in the wind. Cap'in Hopikns don't take kindly to that sound. The men aloft report the fore royal stay has lost all tone. Lay to the bowsprit and belay the sheets a' once. We was havin' a devil of a time with the dolphin striker yesterweek, so my best recommendation is to well inspect the martingale stay and the bobstay."

"Aye-Aye", replied Pastor Platypus. And with that the Officer of the Watch disappeared into the darkness of the early dawn.

"I didn't understand a single thing that came out of his mouth," admitted Porky looking wide eyed at Pastor Platypus.

Pastor Platypus quickly informed his friend, "The bowsprit, and the Jib boom make up the large spar that sticks out from the bow of the ship which serves to secure the bottom of the front triangular jib sails. The dolphin striker sticks straight down from the bowsprit. It is called the dolphin striker because it plunges into the water where you will see dolphins swimming with the ship. But because it plunges into the water so frequently it puts a lot of stress on the martingale stay and the bobstay which provide the downward tension to even out the pull of the jibs which force the bowsprit up. One of those stays must be loose and we must belay it. That is to tighten it. Make sense?"

"A little. It would sure be a lot easier to understand if the sun was up," observed Porky.

"Come along now, I'll show you the best I can. It's much more fun to learn in the dark anyhow, but we do need to get this fixed before Captain Hopkins himself comes along. Follow me," instructed Pastor Platypus.

The two scurried up to the bowsprit. The light of the setting moon illuminated the task before them.

"You have got to be joking, we are climbing out on that!" exclaimed Porky.

"We'll make a sailor out of you yet! Now let us not delay any longer."

Porky climbed atop the base of the bowsprit just in time to see the portion needing mending plunge into the water only to be ripped out again as the ship rose above the swell. Porky turned and looked wide eyed at Pastor Platypus.

Pastor Platypus warned, "Hold Fast! It means hold on tight to your rigging and life lines as you go about your work lest you be claimed by the sea."

Porky was still speechless.

Pastor Platypus replied with a smile holding his arms straight out to his sides, "Who ever said answering to one's destiny would be easy? Your life may be asked of you a bit earlier than you expected, but at least you will be among the few to have truly lived! Listen, It's much better to spend your morning out on a bowsprit fully alive, than up on a tree top with a deadened heart! Is it not?!"

Porky took a deep breath and gave Pastor Platypus a small grin, "Hold fast." And with that Porky made his way out onto the bowsprit and was soon atop the jib boom. With the bow of the Scorpion behind him, it felt as if Porky was flying over the water like an eagle. As the ship plunged forward Porky and Pastor Platypus would go from being just inches above the rushing water to being thrust upward to about 20 feet above the water.

It was absolutely exhilarating. Porky forgot all about his aches and pains. He forgot about the cold and about his life. The sky was starting to become brighter making the water simply brilliant as it passed by. It was the most amazing feeling Porky had ever experienced in all of his life put together. He let out a shout as if atop a cantering horse, "Yee Haw! This is amazing!"

Pastor Platypus agreed, "Isn't it wonderful! Do you see any obvious insult to the rigging?"

"Do I ever!" replied Porky. "The stay going from the end of the jib boom down to the bottom of the dolphin striker is draggin' and floppin' in the water."

"Yes. That would be the martingale stay. Think you can manage to belay it back in place?"

Porky replied with a renewed sense of mission, "Do I have a choice? The Officer of the Watch commanded us to fix it and fix it is what we are going to do!"

"Fine by me, Porky. Take your time. On the open sea haste is a killer," warned Pastor Platypus.

Porky being an excellent climber transitioned to a sturdy hold onto the upper portion of the dolphin striker and slid down wedging himself in the angle where the bobstay attached itself. Porky held on with one arm to the dolphin striker and reached with the other for the martingale stay which was being dragged along through the water.

The bow of the Scorpion took its rhythmic plunge after cresting a swell and in a moment the dolphin striker dove under the water with Porky holding onto it. The force of the rushing water was immense, and Porky received an unwelcome morning bath.

The bobstay behind Porky is what kept him from being washed under the boat and the cold is what kept his attention!

The bow shot up out of the water giving Porky just enough time to catch his breath only to be submerged again. The icy water was so shocking he couldn't even recall the task at hand. Pastor Platypus shouted down to recover his focus, "Grab the martingale! Its right next to you!" The next plunge Porky took into the water the martingale stay came right up under his right arm. He grabbed hold without a thought. The next two swells were small enough to keep the dolphin striker on the dry side of things.

On his third attempt, Porky belayed the rigging to its proper place restoring the tension of the jib sails. The next thing he realized was that he was sitting safely on the deck of the bow. He had instinctively retreated from the bowsprit to safety only to look up and see the Officer of the Watch towering above him with the light of the morning sun shining against his smiling wrinkled face on which a match could be lit.

"Well done Mr. Porcupine," congratulated the officer with a gruff weathered voice. He turned and walked off just as Pastor Platypus arrived at Porky's side.

"I would have to agree with that!" expressed Pastor Platypus reaffirming the compliments of the officer.

Just then, the quartermaster rang eight bells which meant the watch was over.

"Come along now," directed Pastor Platypus, "Let's make our way below decks for a bit of breakfast. I believe you have well-earned your rations of coffee and burgoo."

"Burgoo?" inquired Porky

"I think you'll like it," encouraged Pastor Platypus, "It's a hot oatmeal porridge of sorts…. nobody actually knows what's in it except our cook Muffins who says he doesn't have the heart to tell us. It does have kind of a fishy smell."

"Don't worry Pastor, at this point anything warm sounds wonderful."

They both laughed and took one more look at the taught jib sails which were now glowing pink from the rising sun.

Chapter IV

Close-Hauled on the Open Sea

The Scorpion and its crew were navigating through what the French and English called the Northwest Passageway. The weeks passed like days aboard the Schooner. Porky avoided homesickness by remaining focused on learning his role as a member of the crew.

The entire twenty-four-hour day aboard the Scorpion was divided into seven watches. Out of the seven watches total, Porky tended to his sailing duties every other watch. When Porky was off duty, he spent his time writing in his journal, reading his Bible, and refreshing his navigational skills.

Porky and Pastor Platypus shared a hammock in a very cramped forecastle with the other members of the crew. The officers slept in a more accommodating aft cabin which they did not yet have the privilege of seeing. The forecastle at the front of the ship was no castle at all. It was a small room in the bow of the ship that seemed to house twice as many men as it was built for. It tumbled up and down, and to and fro with the waves. It was dark, cold, and felt wet all the time. Hammocks had to be shared with the opposite watch. During the day all the hammocks were folded up or hung out to dry.

The officer of the watch shouted through the door of the forecastle, "Out of your cots and muster your spirits! We'll be headin' into the open sea this fine mornin' and Captain Hopkins wishes to make a change of course at once, so hop to it and lay aloft to adjust the gaff sail rigging! The ship isn't going to sail itself!"

Porky rubbed his eyes, rolled out of his hammock, and dropped to the deck with a thump. There was much activity as the fatigued men of the middle watch were being replaced by the morning watch. Porky was stumbling quite badly trying to get his bearings straight.

Only a couple of dim oil lanterns provided light below deck. The ship seemed to pitch and roll with more force and magnitude than the past few days. The air smelled different too as it howled through the portholes. Porky stretched his quills and noticed he could almost see his breath as he tried to rub and warm up his stiff limbs which were not accustomed to so much work. Porky quickly unhooked his hammock, folded it up, and placed it near his personal belongings satchel which hung by the corner frame near the ceiling which was the bottom of the upper deck.

The sky was still dark and would not be lit with the light of dawn until four bells into the watch, which is two hours. The Schooner was just exiting the fresh water sea-way of the Americas and the crew aboard the ship teemed with great excitement knowing that they were entering the vast salty sea that is the Atlantic Ocean!

Porky and Pastor Platypus scurried to the stairs and climbed to the upper deck with about ten other men. The stars and moon were still out. The air was cool and the wind was brisk. Even though it was not Porky's duty to navigate the ship, for his own awareness, the first thing he did was locate Polaris, the unmoving and ever-faithful North Star, before it was snuffed out by the light of day.

The Captain was giving orders to the Boatswain, but Porky was not listening as his mind was immediately captivated and somewhat concerned about the enormity of the waves. "By God, what is this?!" asked Porky taken back at the tremendous movements of the ship.

"Welcome to the mighty Atlantic Sea Porky!" answered Pastor Platypus smiling and rubbing his chest as he took a deep breath of the salty and fresh morning air. Porky was holding on for his life and marveled Pastor Platypus who was standing on his back two legs holding onto nothing as if the ship wasn't moving at all!

Pastor Platypus galloped and leapt down the rolling deck towards the bow thoroughly enjoying the movements of the ship. "Huzzza!" Pastor Platypus shouted, "How I love the open sea!"

Porky was in absolute awe at the massive size of the swells. Walls of water were before them. They weren't frequent and choppy as was the case inland, rather they were massive, rolling swells that would take some time to ascend and descend. The movements of the ship were grand but smooth.

The wind was southeast by east at a moderate gale, clear weather overhead, but hazy on the horizon all around. Captain Hopkins shouted out to the Boatswain with stern pride and a hint of an English accent, "I want full sail this morning Mr. Junak." Turning to his quartermaster he ordered, "Mr. Williams, run her close to the wind baring south south-east. I want all the speed we can get out of her!"

The Officer of the Watch echoed the orders to the crew as he strutted across the deck, "You heard the captain! Lay aloft with you and belay these gaff sails to run close to the wind!"

At that the men went about the work seemingly unaffected by the large waves and almost enjoying it. You could hear it in the way that they were singing. It was a bit livelier than other mornings.

Porky's job was almost always to scurry up to the top of the mainmast to make adjustments to the top sail. He was an excellent climber and was the perfect critter for the job. The officer of the watch approached Porky with specific orders, "You heard the captain, we'll be sailing close-hauled! Now, lay aloft and take in a reef on the top sail, we don't want the canvas to rip again in this gale."

"Yes, Sir. Gladly, Sir," replied Porky.

The officer of the watch grinned, "It is sure wonderful to have you aboard. Such an excellent climber with such an agreeable attitude. I wish we had more like you." The smile quickly left his face, "Now quit jabberin' and get up the main!"

Porky was a bit bewildered at the officer's statements, but he had learned not to read into their emotions too much. The work aboard a ship was simple: listen and obey, do exactly as you are ordered, and ask no questions! It was nearly the same approach that brought Porky on his amazing journey. Learn to hear the voice of the Good Shepherd and follow with trusting obedience.

The masts were very high above the deck; they were no taller than Grandmother Pine back on Moose Island. The only difference was on the open sea the main mast swayed back and forth with the tremendous movements of the ship. Porky eventually learned to relax and become a part of the ship anticipating its movement.

There was rigging called shrouds, which the men preferred to climb, that could bring a person to the top of the main mast, but

Porky felt more comfortable climbing the mast itself. During his assent he found himself tightly hugging the mast as he went up. As the ship lurched over the waves Porky felt as if a force was trying to rip him sideways off of the mast in both directions. It was slow going, but it eventually proved to be quite fun after he realized he could trust his claws to hold him.

When Porky reached the top of the main mast the topsail was fully set and taught full of wind. He took a moment to close his eyes, stretch his cramping paws and take a deep breath. The wind that was whipping through his quills up and over his back was quite overwhelming. The white flag, with thirteen red stripes of the american continental navy atop the jack staff, snapped in the wind and Porky's quills made all sorts of dissonant whistles. He opened his eyes to see a vast array of morning stars in a giant canopy above him. The moon was giving way to the sun, and Porky remembered the tree which he perched atop of every morning back on Moose Island.

The helmsman made his course adjustment to bring the bow of the ship as close to the wind as the sails would allow putting the schooner in a position to achieve its top speeds. Porky found himself clinging tightly to the spar for dear life as the ship suddenly listed far over to port. It felt like the ship was going to heal right over into the sea. No more did he see the outline of a ship below him; he instead was staring down at the lively sea in the light of early dawn.

Porky looked over his shoulder down to the quarterdeck to see the first mate giving the helmsman orders and pointing in every direction at the men on deck to adjust the rigging. The helmsman was turning hard to starboard bringing the bowsprit to point south by west. The canvas sails flapped loosely and violently with the change of wind direction. The masts seemed to stretch and groan under the immense strain as the men adjusted the rigging and made tight the sails to catch the wind. As the ship turned south, she began to cut through the massive swells at a rate of speed Porky had never seen before. The ship righted itself after the fore and main gaff sails were adjusted.

Porky, remembering his duties, recovered from the change of course and began to reef the top sail to reduce the amount of canvas that was exposed to the high winds as to lessen the stress upon it. The sun was peaking over the horizon and Porky was able to see the last sliver of land disappear. Now all that could be seen in every direction was nothing but water. It was an overwhelming sight.

Porky fastened three gaskets on both sides of the yard arm which effectively secured the top sail in its new position. He adjusted the sail filling it tightly with wind. The main mast groaned even more under the added force of the new sail position. The Scorpion caught hold of the wind and took off like a horse out of the gates. The schooner was heeled so far over that the edge of the main deck was right at the level of the sea. Porky was suspended over the Atlantic flying through the sky like an eagle atop the main. It was as if the schooner came alive. It leapt and bounded over the giant swells slicing though the water with a speed and rhythm which Porky had never felt before.

Pleased with his work and quite unsettled about his lofty position, Porky made a quick descent to the main deck by sliding down the mainmast backstay which is taught rigging that runs from the topmast cap down towards the deck. With these rough seas, Porky thought he might use the reverse route to ascend the main at the next order to adjust the sails. It was challenging to move across a deck that was tilted at least thirty degrees. Unless of course you're Pastor Platypus who was lying down on the leeward rail dragging his hand in the sea as it rushed by. The Scorpion's course change was now complete and Porky reported to the Officer of the Watch who relieved him for morning meal rations.

Chapter V

Breakfast and Unexpected Company

Porky smartly made his way below deck down a slippery and crooked ladder and let out a sigh of relief as Muffins ducked low through the doorway from the galley to bring Porky his morning meal.

"Callops today with Scotch Coffee!" celebrated Muffins in a loud jolly voice. Muffins gave it to Porky grinning from ear to ear with one silver tooth on the bottom and one whitish tooth on the top. Muffins was a simple and very large man, but Porky could tell his heart was kind. Muffins just stood there frozen with a giant smile plastered on his face waiting for a response of satisfaction from Porky.

Muffins broke the silence as Porky continued to stare at his food, "Yup! The Lieutenant ordered a special meal this morn b'cause we was now in open sea! Callops! Salted pork and eggs heated together."

"It looks wonderful!" reassured Porky. "This will be my first morning not having Burgoo in about two weeks! It's just that I think I will pass on the scotch coffee and just have regular coffee. I like to keep my mind clear so I can learn and not lose my balance aloft. "

"Oh no no Spike, this doesn't have real scotch. They just call it that, but no one has told me why. We actually ran out o' coffee," clarified Muffins.

Porky asked a bit confused, "Well, if it's not coffee and it's not Scotch, what exactly is it?"

"Oh that's easy," answered Muffins, "Ye bring a pot o' water to boil, then ye know those bunch of biscuits I burned black yesterday?"

"Yes Muffins," Porky recalled, "It was hard to miss all the smoke. We thought the ship was going to burn up. I heard the Lieutenant yelling quite a bit at you. I'm sorry that happened."

"I didn't mean to fall o'sleep. The big waves rock me to sleep like my mama used to," Muffins stared out the porthole thinking about his mother. "Yeah, I miss mama."

Porky thought this moment was a bit odd coming from a man of twenty stone who could single handedly hoist the anchor, but he sympathized with Muffins anyway, "I know how you feel. I was used to seeing my mother every day, and now I don't know if I'll ever see her again. For now, we talk to each other in our prayers."

Another odd bit of silence passed, and Porky thought he saw muffins wipe a tear from his eye. Porky had a feeling that if Muffins started to cry that it would be quite an outpouring, and for that reason he quickly changed the subject back to the Scotch coffee, "What exactly do you do with the burnt and blackened biscuits?"

Snapping right out of his thoughts about his mama, Muffins boomed with a prideful grin, "Well Spike, ye put them all together, like a big happy family, and ye throw em' all in the boiling water, and keep stirring until all the lumps are gone. Then we have Scotch Coffee!"

Porky wanted to gag just thinking about it, but it actually didn't smell all that bad. Nodding his head in acceptance Porky said, "Thank you Muffins, I will be happy to try it."

Muffins grabbed the cup and pushed it up to Porky's mouth, "Here Spike, let me help ye try a sup o' it." Muffins began to tip the cup into Porky's mouth. Wide-eyed Porky took a giant unwelcomed gulp and pushed the cup away struggling to swallow. Porky spoke through a coughing spell, "Thanks Muffins – It's not too bad."

"Aww, I knowed you'd like it!" grinned Muffins from ear to ear. "I'll learn'ee to make the best o' things here Spike! Are ye and the beaver goin' somewheres special by orders?"

"Actually the pastor is a platypus," corrected Porky, "and we are on a grand adventure to find the lost southern continent Australis."

"Well ain't that the end o' our luck!" exclaimed Muffins, "None o' me mates had the mind to tell me we lost a whole continent! Cap'n ain't goin' to take well the news!"

Porky's hunger overcame his desire to further explain his mission. He politely changed the subject, "Is your name really Muffins?"

"It's a long story Spike, I'll share it to ye sometime later today," boomed Muffins in a deep raspy voice and a giant cheeky smile.

One of the sailors shouted across the deck, "He fell asleep with two half eaten muffins sticking out o' his mouth whilst we was dining with the Cap'n in his quarters the first night he made his acquaintance!"

The room full of sailors having their morning rations erupted in laughter.

"Speak plain truth for once!" pouted Muffins, "I met the Cap'n once afore that dinner!" Muffins stuck out his tongue as the sailors, ducked back into the galley, which was billowing out more smoke than Porky thought the oven should produce.

Porky never drank coffee, or Scotch coffee for that matter, until his new adventure began. It proved to be a wonderful drink to bring him from cold and tired to warm and awake! On Sundays each sailor was given two cubes of sugar which Porky saved for his coffee. Porky always finished his meals quickly, and he was never quite full.

One of the other sailors named Jenkins shouted from another table, "Spike! I'm impressed the waves didn't knock ye off the yard arm this mornin'! Not bad for a stinky lil' spike ball!"

Another sailor sitting next to Porky, named Scottie, spoke up on his behalf, "Harken to me Jenkins! Just be thankful it's not ye who lays aloft to reef the top sail whence under this heavy gale!"

Jenkins stood up and challenged, "Aye, one half-crown says ye could n't hoist ye're own walrus butt halfway up the main to save ye're own skin!"

Scottie retorted in jest, "Are ye suggestin' that my hind quarters is shaped like a Walrus! Leave all that! Perhaps ye're own stench be foggin' up those buggy lil' eyes o' yer's!"

Mr. Jenkins standing up now shouted gruffly across the galley spitting chunks of his breakfast out of his mouth as he spoke, "Ye're hind quarters may have not the appearances o' a Walrus, but during the middle watch whilst ye slumber in ye're cot, it sure does make some mighty sounds which are likened to a Walrus!"

The room erupted in laughter and another sailor shouted above it, "Me thinks I'd rather sleep next to a Walrus at low-tide than down-wind of Scottie that's for sure!"

Scottie shouted back with a stern Scottish accent, "That can be arranged!"

"God be thanked for that!" celebrated Jenkins with great laughter.

At that moment, Pastor Platypus tapped Porky on the shoulder and motioned for Porky to promptly follow him. Porky was happy to leave his Scotch coffee behind, but he brought his bowl of collops with him which left a trail of steam behind him as they walked aft across the heavily listed gun deck, "Your timing couldn't have been more perfect Pastor."

"Yes, lots of head-strong men in close quarters can lead to some entertaining moments Porky, both for the better and for worse."

As they were making their way across the gun deck towards the stern, the ship heavily listed causing Porky to spill the remainder of his collops all over the floor. "Drat!" Porky proclaimed, "What a sad ending for this morning meal." Porky did his best to put it all back in the bowl, and decided to take a few bites anyway as he followed Pastor Platypus.

Pastor Platypus led Porky up a small and steep ladder-way. They arrived at a door beautifully decorated with carvings looking to be the seal of the american colonial navy. Pastor Platypus knocked on the door.

"You may enter," authorized a stern voice from within.

"Good to have you aboard Porky!" bounded Captain Hopkins as he stood up to greet his newest member of the crew, "The name is Hopkins, Captain Esek Hopkins at your service. I trust Pastor Platypus and my officers made you feel welcome."

"Yes Sir, very much so," nervously replied Porky.

The Captain's eyes were wild and blazed with intense focus which did not exactly agree with his tone of voice which was far more cheerful. His chin was square and face well weathered and darkened by the sun. Long brown and wavy hair came out from the sides of his tricorn captain's hat, and a dark blue overcoat with gold buttons and white trim well established his authority.

 He seemed to pause in thought looking down at some papers on his desk and continued, "I have been to every quarter of the earth as a privateer, and I believe this is the first time I have had the good company of a Porcupine aboard one of my ships. I witnessed your skill and agility as you reefed the top sail this morning. I have not yet had an able-bodied seaman who has been able to single-handedly manage the top-sail in such high winds, and running close-hauled at that! You have helped the Scorpion reach a new top speed! Well done!"

"Thank you Captain," answered Porky trying to find a way to more respectfully hold his breakfast bowl. Porky hissed in a whisper at Pastor Platypus, "You could have told me we were going to meet with the captain! I would have left my breakfast behind!"

The Captain muttered to himself as he strolled over to look keenly out the starboard window, "You have proven to be very useful on this voyage, not to mention those magnificent quills….

44

I shall find a use for them yet as long as we don't find them stuck in our feet."

Porky was startled by the captain's bounding reentry of words, "Be sure to do as you are told! Work with honor and with joy, and you shall do well on the open sea. But remember, we all must work as one, or the ship will unravel before our very eyes…. our greatest weapon aboard this vessel is and shall always be unity and a love for true freedom!" he bounded as if giving a victory speech.

"I would like to extend an invitation to the both of you to dine with me and our officers tonight as our guests of honor. At that time, I should like to hear more about this mission you both have set out upon. I know that Pastor Platypus sympathizes with the efforts of the American colonies and therefore you shall always have the support of…"

The captain's conversation was abruptly interrupted by the Officer of the Watch barging through the door into the captain's quarters shouting out of breath, "Captain, Captain…"

Captain Hopkins cut him off, "Mr. Diggs, can you not knock before entering the captains quarters!? I refuse to run this ship as strict as the British Royal Navy, but I do require some degree of order! Now whatever is the matter!?"

The Officer of the Watch recovered his professional composure, "Sails Sir, spotted off our stern to the east north east and closing. Your presence is requested on the quarter deck."

Captain Hopkins sat down at his desk staring at Mr. Diggs and remained silent for what seemed an unusually long amount of time tapping his fingers on his desk as he stirred cream and sugar into his coffee. The captain's right eyebrow raised as something came into his remembrance, "Mr. Porky, it came to my attention that you do not fancy Scotch coffee. I happen to have a bit of the standard issue coffee left. Would you like some?"

"Why, yes, that would be wonderful," replied Porky with a bit of hesitation trying not to let his eyes wander to look out the stern window for the ship that was sighted.

"Would, you like cream and sugar?" asked the captain, "It's goat's cream, I must warn you."

"Just sugar will do for me, thank you."

The Captain looked at the platypus, "And how about for you Pastor?" The pastor kindly replied, "No thank you, I'm quite settled for the morning, and you know how I prefer tea."

The Captain responded apologetically, "Tea, yes of course. How rude of me. I despise what Britain has become, but I do still like to have some tea from time to time."

The captain gestured to the Officer of the Watch who was still standing in the doorway, "Mr. Diggs, would you mind getting Pastor Platypus some tea."

Mr. Diggs replied with a bit of urgency and frustration, "Captain, the ship. Your presence is requested on the quarter deck."

Captain Hopkins' face grew suddenly stern, "Well how long before she is upon us, and what flag does she fly Mr. Diggs! What is her distance?! What is her sail configuration!? What is the wind speed and direction!?"

"My apologies Captain," answered Mr. Diggs knowing that he wasn't permitted by the captain to ever answer 'I don't know'.

The Captain was irritated at his report which lacked information, "Well, while you fetch the pastor some tea, why don't you find out!"

"Aye-Aye Captain", and the Officer of the Watch turned to walk out the door.

The Captain sternly interrupted his departure, "Oh and Mr. Diggs!"

"Yes, Captain," sweat and nervousness were all over Mr. Diggs' face.

Captain Hopkins was looking down at his map making a quick calculation with his calipers. Having never looked out the stern window since the Officer's arrival, he stood up from behind his desk and began to walk slowly towards Mr. Diggs with his voice increasing in intensity as he went, "She is a Man of War flying two large spirit sails off her bowsprit making her a 1st or 2nd rate of about 60 guns. She flies the Spanish flag and will be upon us in three bells. The wind changed from southerly to easterly and is strengthening to the same degree the barometer is falling."

The captain was now right in Mr. Diggs face almost growling through gritted teeth, "So keep us close to the wind heading southeast by south, beat to general quarters, and next time, for the sake of God, do not wait so long to inform me of a man of war bearing down upon us! She was visible at first light, why do you think our masts are buckling and we are flying with full sail!"

Mr. Diggs involuntarily thought aloud, "But, how did you..."

Captain Hopkins interrupted, "I am not blind! Now do as you have been ordered!"

"Aye-Aye Captain," the Officer of the Watch ran out and shouted in a very loud and urgent voice, "BEAT TO GENERAL QUARTERS!" Drums began to roll and every man aboard created a thunder of well rehearsed activity.

Captain Hopkins continued to lightly stir some sugar into his coffee with a silver spoon and he looked at Porky with a most calm and bright face, "I do apologize for the interruption, my honorable friend. Mr. Diggs hasn't seen much action yet and tends to get a bit excited."

Pastor Platypus commented, "Very clever Captain. That is why you called for the change of course and full sail at sunrise. And you kept quiet to test your officers as to learn their degree of attentiveness. Very clever indeed. Do you suppose that the Spanish intend to be hostile toward an American merchant schooner?"

The Captain soberly replied, "The last it was made known to me, we had a treaty with Spain to help us stand against England, but I have a feeling it isn't so that the american colonies can be free! The only thing Spain cares about is Spain."

The captain looked out one of the stern windows of his quarters with his looking scope, "Now we just came out of the Seaway of Saint Lawrence two days ago, and as soon as the sun came up today this ship was upon us. This was no coincidence. The Spanish know that ships coming out of the seaway are loaded down with supplies from inland. I believe she wishes to catch us as a prize and relieve us of our stash of supplies. This is the reason why I did not allow any of the Scorpion's cannons to be off loaded. All we have to do is evade her until nightfall. We will keep close to the wind. For that reason, they will be forced to tack back and forth to follow us. That would be the preference anyhow. Be it day or be it night, I know that this Schooner can out maneuver a square rigged Spanish Man of War. This schooner was built for speed and maneuverability. The sky, wind, and barometer also tell me we have quite a storm that will soon be upon us which we must figure a way to use in our favor."

Captain Hopkins lowered his scope, "We cannot allow them to have even one broadside on target lest we be sent straight to the bottom!"

Porky spoke up, "What would be the point of that Captain Hopkins? They would lose the supplies they wish to attain."

"Right you are Porky! You are sharper than I thought! If and when you hear the order to clear the deck for action, I want you both at the quarter deck close to me. Understood?!"

Pastor Platypus, pushing his bifocals back snug up upon his nose looked seriously at Porky, then back at the captain, "Captain, if you don't mind, could I say a prayer for you and our crew."

"Yes, I welcome the offer; we will need all the help we can get should that Man of War catch up to us." As the Captain's cabin swayed and creaked with the bounding ship which now accelerated and heeled over even more with the strengthening wind, Porky, Pastor Platypus, and Captain Hopkins bowed their heads to seek the favor of the One who created both man and the sea.

Chapter VI

Friend or Foe

Porky was high aloft in the rigging adjusting the sails and tightening the ropes trying to capture as much wind as possible in the canvas. It seemed, however, that every time Porky looked off the stern the Spanish Man of War was getting closer. It was the biggest ship that Porky had ever seen, and he marveled in fear and in awe at the sight of it.

Captain Hopkins never seemed to be pleased with the setting of any of his sails. He was always demanding more speed. His best Lieutenant, John Paul Jones, was on duty forcefully ensuring that the crew quickly and correctly executed that which the captain had ordered to be done. Porky always loved when Lieutenant Jones was Officer of the Watch. He marveled over how the lieutenant led his men with such ardor and zeal. Porky felt courage seep into his bones when Lieutenant Jones spoke, and felt that, if given a sword and an opportunity, that he could single handedly cut down the approaching Spanish Man of War.

To make matters worse, a storm seemed to be developing on the southern horizon. It was now nearing noon and the sky was getting darker. The storm seemed to be pouring more life and energy into Lieutenant John Paul Jones who welcomed and embraced the intensifying wind and waves as if they were long lost friends. The direction of the wind was becoming very irregular and every time the wind changed the captain wanted the rigging of the sails adjusted.

Porky began to appreciate the never ending list of orders given by the captain. Trying to complete them to his satisfaction at least kept his mind off of the approaching Man of War from the North and the impending storm from the south.

Porky zipped down the mainmast backstay and ran up to the quarter deck to report to the captain. "Ahh, there you are Porky!" announced Captain Hopkins, "I was just looking to teach you a bit about sailing." Kneeling down to Porky's level, Captain Hopkins went on to educate Porky, "You see Porky, a schooner's sails and rigging are such that we are able to sail more into or towards the wind. A square-rigged frigate such as the one just off our stern here will have a terrible time sailing into the wind because it is not able to adjust its sails at enough of an angle to capture the wind head-on. What the Captain of the Man of War will have to do is make tremendous back and forth zig-zags to follow us. He may still catch us, but it will take him more time than he likes and his crew will be well fatigued! It takes a tremendous amount of work to frequently adjust the sails of a full-rigged frigate, and if we must fight them, I'd rather they be good and worn out! So you can see this storm may actually work in our favor. Presently our efforts are two-fold. We are trying to avoid getting sunk by both the storm and the Man of War! Good fun, isn't it!"

Porky wasn't exactly comforted by his tutorial. The captain laughed a bit and stood up to reassess the situation when suddenly the wind gusted violently against the topsail causing the top of the main mast to snap. Immense stress came upon the rigging and the ropes began to break with the most terrible whipping sound. The top of the mainmast remained attached and hung down greatly hindering the functioning of the main sail as it flapped violently in the wind.

"Lay aloft and cut those ropes away!" shouted Captain Hopkins desperate to regain the functioning of his ship as quickly as possible. He tossed Porky a knife and shouted, "Cut away those ropes and secure the topsails!"

Porky placed the knife in his mouth and ran down upon the pitching deck to the base of the main mast dodging waves which were starting to wash over the deck of the Scorpion. Porky smartly ascended the mainmast shrouds. Loose ropes snapped all around him, and the giant lower yard arm for the top sail was swinging loosely in the wind slamming against the main mast with frightening thuds.

The rain started coming down in sheets all of the sudden. The masts and the hull of the ship was buckling and groaning as the Schooner bounded over the ever growing waves. It sounded as if the whole ship at any time would snap in half.

Every time Porky got startled by the violent movements of the ship he would notice how precisely and swiftly his shipmates were carrying on with their duties which gave him great courage and focus. Porky could barely hear Lieutenant Jones shouting orders above the wind and rain.

The wind howled through the ropes and the rigging began to whistle an eerie symphony. The schooner had to slow down considerably to make quick repairs.

Porky looked down to see waves crash over the deck of the low lying schooner causing some sailors to lose their footing and nearly fall overboard. Ropes, called lifelines, had been slung the long way across the deck from bow to stern prior to the storm's arrival so that the sailors could hang onto them as they went about the business of sailing the ship.

Porky looked down at the Scorpion which had taken in the gaff sails and left only the stay sails and the jibs which greatly reduced the stress on the masts and rigging but still enabled Captain Hopkins to have some forward movement and control over the schooner. Porky looked back and saw the Spanish Man of War about a musket shot off the stern on the starboard side. She was scudding before the wind with bare-poles. All of her sails had been quickly furled and only her main fore course was set.

Porky was clinging to the main topmast being pelted by wind and rain and began to pray under his breath, "Lord help us in this desperate hour. Deliver us Lord, deliver us."

When he opened his eyes after his prayer, an air splitting whir flew right by Porky's head. His ears popped and Porky lost his footing as the Spanish Frigate's warning cannon shot whizzed right by Porky's head. The Man of War was just off their stern insisting with her cannons that Captain Hopkins surrender.

Things went from bad to worse. As Porky was dangling by his front claws from the ropes high above the deck. The schooner smashed through a giant wave knocking Porky clean off of the slippery yard arm. Suddenly everything went quiet.

The ropes stopped howling, the wind stopped blowing, the rain was not beating against his face, the shouts of the sailors could not be heard, and his movements seemed to be in slow motion. For a moment Porky thought he had died or at the very least was in the process of dying.

Chapter VII

Porcupine Overboard

Porky's eyes started to burn and bubbles left his mouth as he exhaled. He quickly realized he was under water, salt water in fact, and that he had fallen into the sea from atop the broken mainmast. Porky didn't have time to be afraid. He clawed with all his might at the underwater portion of the wooden hull of the schooner that was quickly passing him by.

Porky bumped and tumbled down the starboard hull of the Scorpion straining now to hold his breath. All was suddenly calm again as Porky floated in open water. The schooner had passed him by. Porky gasped for air, gagging on the terrible tasting salty sea water. He watched in shear panic as the schooner left him behind. Porky could see Captain Hopkins and Pastor Platypus standing with the helmsman on the quarter deck smartly navigating through the storm trying desperately to recover control of the ship after losing the top of the main mast. The schooner's stern lantern all too quickly disappeared into the sheets of rain.

Porky suddenly had another terrible feeling that made him look the other direction behind him. His body shuddered in panic as he saw a mountain of a bow smashing through the sea.

A determined maiden, who was carved atop the frigate's bow, seemed to glare angrily at the schooner before her. Both she and the bow exploded though the crest of the swell Porky was floating up to. Before Porky could even shout in fear the bow crashed into him pushing Porky down into the sea. Porky managed to immediately dig his claws into the hull.

The next time the bow lurched out of the water Porky scurried up the ladder built into the side of the Spanish hull. Determined to survive, he quickly crawled for his life up into the Man of War!

He heard and felt the Spanish cannons exploding as they fired at his friends. He could hear the Spanish sailors laughing and taunting at the seemingly perilous state of Captain Hopkins and the Scorpion which was no match for the storm or the frigate. It was like watching a cat toy with a mouse. Porky laid on the deck of the forecastle up against the side rail and let the rain hit and refresh his face as he caught his breath and regained his composure.

As Porky peered over the rail he saw the anger and cruelty of the Spanish men and quickly realized that he had to do everything he could to stop their attack. Something deep inside Porky's heart kicked in which seemed to drive away all fear allowing him incredible focus on the situation at hand. His senses sharpened and courage flowed through his sopping and quill-covered body!

The business of the Spanish ship mixed with the rain and high seas made it easy for Porky to sneak around the massive deck. He clamored to the top of the forecastle at the bow of the ship which put the schooner into view. It was strange to see the situation from the Spaniards perspective, because Porky could have sworn that a minute ago he was looking at *their* ship from atop the schooner's main mast.

To Porky's surprise, he saw what looked like a captain directing the cannon fire; he was much statelier and more decorated than Captain Hopkins.

The Spanish commander was in close proximity to the sailors who manned the forward cannons. They were giant compared to the schooner's cannons. Porky saw the captain grin and snicker as he peered through his looking glass, and as he took it away from his eye he pointed directly at something and began giving firm orders in Spanish. Porky couldn't understand much, but he heard the captain say "Fuego" which he knew meant 'fire'.

The explosion knocked Porky off of his feet and he fell into the barrels he was hiding against. He stood up to see the mizzen mast of the schooner crack and fall into the sea. The schooner was now set adrift with almost no sails in working order as she was almost completely demasted.

Captain Hopkins began to return fire with his stern cannons. Porky could feel the thuds of the Scorpion's cannon balls hitting the bow of the Spanish Frigate. But the shots seemed to have no effect on the ship.

Porky could see clearly over the shoulder of the men tending to the cannons as they adjusted them to what seemed to be a perfect shot to hit Pastor Platypus and Captain Hopkins squarely on the quarter deck. Just as the Spanish sailor was about the light the fuse to fire the cannon, the splash of a wave came over the deck causing the sailor to slip and slide away from the cannon.

The Spanish captain himself picked up the matchstick, re-aimed the cannon, and was reaching to light the fuse on what appeared to be a devastating and final bow to Pastor Platypus and Captain Hopkins. Porky picked himself up and ran with all of his might turning and sliding over the wet deck, then 'BAM!' Porky nailed the Spanish captain in the back of his leg with the full brunt of his quills. The captain shrieked and fell upon the back of the cannon causing it to point in the air as it fired! The recoil of the cannon tossed the captain back into the base of the foremast knocking him senseless.

The unconscious and injured commander caused all the men who were tending the cannons at the bow to leave their positions to help their leader. Porky dashed to each cannon snuffing out their fuses with his wet paw and scurried off into a hiding place.

After catching his breath in the shadows of the Spanish war ship, it came to his realization that he may have saved Pastor Platypus' life, as well as that of Captain Hopkins and perhaps even prevented the schooner from receiving its fatal blow. If he hadn't fallen into the sea his friends would all be at the *bottom* of the sea! Porky quickly realized that what seemed like a terrible thing, falling overboard, was actually probably a part of an answered prayer to save their lives! Realizing more than ever that God was truly in this battle with them, he regained his focus yet again and scurried up the foremast of the Spanish Frigate up to the lower yard to better reassess the situation.

The rain had let up quite a bit and Porky could see clearly that Captain Hopkins had steered his ship hard over to lee attempting to get in an advantageous position on the Spanish ship of war all the while running with the wind. The Spanish ship seemed at bit paralyzed at the absence of their commander. Porky could see some Spanish sailors carrying their leader below deck. The sailors looked confused not knowing immediately who to take orders from.

Hopkins had brought the Scorpion close along-side the Man of War and delivered a full broadside into the Spaniard's hull right at their moment of greatest disorder. It did not cause much physical damage, but it kept the Spanish crew flustered and disorderly. Hopkins brought the Scorpion in closer to deliver another broadside right at the water line of the Man of War hoping to cause as many leaks as possible. The Spanish sailors tending to the cannons would then have to go below decks to repair leaks. This would provide, for Captain Hopkins, a window of escape.

Flying only two jib sails and one stay sail Captain Hopkins navigated the schooner in close to the Man of War which had also turned to run with the wind. Suddenly a giant ocean swell lifted the Scorpion up and into the Spanish ship with a great crash. The timbers rubbing together made an eerie deep and guttural vibration. Porky could see from the yard arm that some of the rigging on the Scorpion became entangled around the massive anchor hook of the Spanish ship.

A number of officers giving different commands to the same men caused much confusion among the Spanish sailors. This effectively thwarted the efforts of the Spanish Man of War for the time being.

"No unity," Porky muttered to himself.

Soon enough, another stately Spanish officer, most likely a 1st Lieutenant, arrived on deck fiercely resuming command of the men and the vessel.

At that moment Captain Hopkins' ship let off a broadside at point-blank range right into the hull of the Man of War. Splinters of wood shot up from in between the entangled ships.

Spanish sailors approached the new officer on deck and reported to him water coming in on the lower decks. Porky could hear him giving commands in Spanish to fix the leaks.

Porky suddenly had an idea to wreak havoc on the Spanish Man of War. Porky slid back down to the deck of the forecastle and grabbed the knife out of the belt of a sailor close by. Porky held it in his mouth dull side in and dashed up the mast with all the strength God gave him. He made his way out on each yard cutting as much rigging as he could!

Soon the main forecourse, the only sail unfurled, was flapping violently in the wind. He worked his way up the foremast cutting away the supports for the yard arms and spars causing them to fall with a tremendous crash. Rope and rigging fell all over the deck where the lieutenant was standing.

Then, knife in mouth, he crossed over to the main mast scurrying along the top sail brace which is a rope going from the foremast to the main mast.

Porky came to the top of the main mast just above the crow's nest where a couple of Spanish sailors were firing upon Captain Hopkins and his schooner. Just as the Spanish sharpshooters took their shots, Porky cut the straps holding their powder horns causing all of their gun powder to spill into the wind. After which he dashed around to the other side of the massive main mast and went right up the ratlines towards the summit of the top main-mast.

It was now getting dark and the cannon fire lit up the night in such an amazing yet frightening way as both ships fired on each other at close range.

The schooner seemed to be floundering after taking the fire of a tremendous broad side from the Spanish Frigate which had three gun decks. The schooner was in so close that the upper two gun decks could not aim their cannons down far enough to even hit the Scorpion.

Porky heard the Spanish Lieutenant call over to Captain Hopkins, "Did you call Quarters?!" Meaning, 'do you surrender'.

One of the crew members on the Scorpion thought Captain Hopkins to be dead and was yelling, "Quarters!" over and over again. Porky could see clearly from his lofty position that Captain Hopkins was slightly wounded and being tended to on the quarter deck, but he certainly was not dead.

The officer of the watch aboard the Scorpion, Lieutenant Jones, assumed command and attempted to shoot the sailor yelling 'quarters' on the basis of treason. Surrendering in battle without the authority to do so was the same as desertion at sea and was punishable by death. But the gun did not fire and he, in the stead of it, threw the pistol at the sailor hitting him squarely in the head rendering him silent, and Lieutenant Jones proudly shouted back to the Spanish Lieutenant, "We have not yet begun to fight!"

Porky was astonished at the perseverance of Lieutenant Jones and at his refusal to surrender. Porky continued to work his way up the main mast sawing through as much rigging as possible. The Spanish marines in the crow's nest, whom he had just snuck by, were suddenly gone.

"That's strange," Porky thought to himself. He turned to look for the missing sailors. Suddenly, the knife was knocked out of his hand, and Porky found himself with a sack thrown over his head! He fought for a moment, but it was no use. His quills couldn't penetrate the canvas entrapment.

He heard some angry Spanish words as a rope was tied tight at the top. The men in the crow's nest must have caught on to his rope cutting scheme. Porky felt himself being zipped down quickly towards the deck of the Man of War. Porky landed sharply. The canvas zipped against the wet deck boards as Porky was dragged across it.

BAM-BAM-bam-bam-bam -thud, Porky was hauled and dragged down what were surely stairs. This happened three more times. Porky braced himself the best he could.

Then the sack was loosed and Porky was dumped harshly onto a dirty, wet, and cold floor almost unable to move from pain. He looked back just in time to see an iron jail door slam shut upon his cell in a dimly lit room with one small swaying lantern which cast nauseating shadows. An unshaven and scrawny Spanish sailor knelt down to look at Porky eye-to-eye. In angry and broken English he said, "Welcome to el San Carlos", then he left to go above deck to finish the fight.

Chapter VIII

Singing in the Brig

Porky lay curled up with closed eyes attempting to mentally subdue his physical pains. The dulled thunder of cannons exploding in sequence jolted Porky's thoughts. It sounded like a well-coordinated broadside from the Spanish Man of War. He could hear the entangled schooner slam and rub against the side of the frigate. An overwhelming feeling of helplessness consumed Porky's heart.

The movements of the ship on the stormy sea caused Porky to slide back and forth across his small cell. After a few moments the cannon fire stopped and there was a very uncomfortable silence. After what must have been at least a quarter hour, Porky could hear men shouting in Spanish, and a great commotion was happening on the deck just above the brig.

Lanterns that the Spanish sailors were carrying illuminated the gloomy brig enough for porky to see a few American colonial sailors from the Scorpion being forced into other dank jail cells. Porky couldn't see much, but his heart was comforted when he could hear Muffins. It was clear that their schooner had been captured. From what Porky could see, about ten of his shipmates were thrown into different cells in the Spanish brig, but no sign of Captain Hopkins. Porky assumed he fought to the death, was still fighting, or went down with his ship. Captain Hopkins wasn't exactly the giving-up type.

A Spanish sailor opened Porky's cell with a primitive key and another sack was thrown in. It lay still for a while as a lump of canvas against the corner in a pool of rotten and cold sea water.

Porky scurried over and slowly undid the tie not quite knowing what to expect.

To his great surprise Pastor Platypus poked his head out! He was a bit tattered and torn, but they were both alive and together again! He looked up at Porky and concluded, "I do think that is enough excitement for one day."

"Boy, am I glad to see you!" Porky celebrated.

"Thank God *you* are alright," sighed Pastor Platypus. "You saved Captain Hopkins and a great deal of the crew with your quick thinking!"

"Quick thinking?" Porky inquired.

Pastor Platypus was quite impressed, "Yes! It was magnificent how you snuck aboard the San Carlos and diverted the fire coming from their forecastle! Well done I say! What unbelievable courage in the midst of chaos!"

Porky replied, "I don't exactly know where all the courage came from; it was all sort of an accident actually, you see I…."

"Yes, yes," Pastor Platypus interrupted, "Now how to get out of here." He paused in thought for a moment studying the door, then he suddenly had an idea, "Oh, I forgot, I have something of yours I managed to recover from the Scorpion. Quite a fight broke out whence the Scorpion locked up with the San Carlos. Sailors from both ships were crossing the wreckage, it was simply a mess. It was like a bit of David against Goliath out there. Goliath wasn't expecting so much trouble from David you see, and we ended up in Goliath's belly." Pastor Platypus rubbed his bill with one hand in thought and tapped on the jail bars with his other hand speaking to himself as he looked down

63

to the deck, "No no, that would be the story of Jonah in the belly of a whale. His disobedience landed him a whale's belly and our obedience landed us in Goliath's belly."

Porky tried to regain his attention, "What of mine did you have Pastor?"

"Porky!" bellowed out the Pastor looking back up, "We're going to have to let that metaphor go."

"What metaphor?" asked Porky quite perplexed at the Pastor's train of thought.

"The David and Goliath metaphor, and the fact that Captain Hopkins in his little schooner is giving this Spanish Man of War a strong fight, and us now being in Goliath's belly. Haven't you been paying attention? That, my boy, would be mixing up two different stories! It makes no sense at all!"

Porky concluded, "Well, I would have to agree with that! But if we stick with the Jonah metaphor, all we have to do now is find a way to get this ship to regurgitate us after three days!" Porky had a big dumb grin on his face.

Pastor Platypus looked at Porky quite seriously, "My good fellow, ships do not regurgitate."

They stared at each other for a moment or two.

Pastor Platypus spoke first, "As I was trying to tell you before you interrupted me, I found…."

Porky retorted in his own defense, "I didn't interrupt!"

"Ahhh ha!, See! You just interrupted again! My boy, I'm going to put in a request for a new jail mate if you don't learn to restrain yourself." Pastor Platypus smiled brightly in the dark cell, "No worries mate! I'm sure in time you'll make a great cell mate. Now let's see what we have here."

Pastor Platypus reached into the canvas sack and pulled out Porky's satchel and handed it to him. Porky couldn't believe his eyes, "How in God's great sea did you manage to retrieve my supplies! What happened?"

Pastor Platypus continued, "Captain Hopkins brilliantly kept the Scorpion close enough to the San Carlos so she could not sink us with cannon fire. When our ships were locked up, the muskets came alive on both sides. Captain Hopkins sustained a minor wound and was brought below decks. Most of our crew were captured. That's when I ran below to grab our supplies which is where I saw Lieutenant Jones dressing Muffins up as the captain! Captain Hopkins bandaged up his wounds and put on the uniform of a midshipman and hid in the gun locker with Lieutenant Jones. When the Spanish demanded surrender, incredibly they accepted it from Muffins! Or shall I say Captain Muffins! His overcoat was far from being able to be buttoned if I do say so myself."

Porky interrupted to ask, "Did the Spanish find Jones and Hopkins?"

Pastor Platypus beamed with excitement, "No! It took the entire Spanish raiding party to bring us onto the San Carlos and once aboard, Lieutenant Jones and Captain Hopkins cut away the entangled Scorpion, and the gale immediately took hold of the jibs and off she went! The Scorpion was well off to the lee of the San Carlos before a shot could be fired. The storm did well to hide her quickly!"

"Wonderful!" Celebrated Porky, "So Jones and Hopkins are off and running!?"

"That's right!" confirmed Pastor Platypus. He put his hand on Porky's shoulder, "Porky, with God, all things are possible. Obedience has brought us to this situation, and I know that this will not be our end. Of course this is not what I had in mind, but at least we are alive, and as long as I have breath in me I refuse to lose hope! I'm certain the ardent tenacity of Lieutenant Jones and Captain Hopkins will see them safely to port, after which they will of course mount a rescue."

There was a moment of silence, if you could call it that. The ship was buckling and groaning. The imprisoned sailors of the Scorpion, to include 'Captain Muffins', were shouting at the Spanish sailors, yet the storm and the shouts all seemed to fade to normal.

"We should pray," decided Porky. Porky had memorized a lot of prayers that his family would always say at the dinner table, but this situation was different. They had never needed God like they did now. They both got on their knees, bowed their heads, and Porky prayed, "Lord see our situation. We did what we thought was right and I hope that you are pleased with us. Please Father, do not let us die in this lonely and horrible place. According to your power set us free. I know that you are able. Please guide Captain Hopkins and Lieutenant Jones to safe harbor. I praise you because you are able to do anything. Nothing is impossible for you, but if you do not calm the storm, we will still praise you. Amen."

A tinge of peace started to replace the fear in Porky heart now comprehending that the situation was in God's hands. Pastor Platypus remembered, "You know what I like to do when I'm frightened? I like to sing songs of praise to God, songs about his power and of his faithfulness."

That is exactly what Porky and Pastor Platypus started to do. Their singing started out low, but grew and grew in fervor. Porky suddenly found himself filling up with joy about who God *is* rather than feeling sorry about the undesirable situation they were in.

The song was one that was joyously sung by some of the sailors as they would go about their work setting the sails. In no time, all the rest of the American sailors in the brig were singing along in joyful defiance of both the storm and their Spanish captors! The singing filled the entire brig and echoed through the lower decks! It deeply bothered the Spanish sailors. A few came down and shouted at the prisoners to keep quiet, but the singing only grew louder.

"These could be our last moments," shouted Pastor Platypus to Porky over the singing, "We might as well exit this life and fold our tents in glorious song and praise!"

The Spanish were simply puzzled at the unity and the joy that the American sailors displayed. They gave up on quieting their newly captured prisoners and quickly returned to the upper decks to tend to their ship in the strengthening storm. One Spanish guard remained, and the singing continued. Some of the American sailors were even dancing! It seemed as if fear ran away and that peace instead flooded their hearts.

Suddenly the Spanish ship was struck by a giant wave from the port side. The hull of the ship warped so much that Porky and Pastor Platypus' cell door popped open! The sea was rushing in quickly down the stairwells and the Spanish Man of War was knocked down almost completely onto its side. Porky knew they were in trouble and moved quickly out of the cell. The Spanish guard was scrambling up the stairs against the rushing water to save his own life. Sailors seem to know when a ship cannot be saved.

Pastor Platypus shouted in Spanish, "Los llaves por favor", which means, "The keys please!"

The guard hesitated for a moment in the middle of fumbling up the stairs to escape the rising water. Even though they were enemies, compassion for his fellow men of the sea won out and he threw the keys towards Porky's cell. The keys hit the bars and fell into the water. Now all the lamps had been snuffed out, it was dark as pitch, and the men in their cells were shouting desperately for help.

"I'll get the keys!" Pastor Platypus shouted. Then he dipped below the sea water which was flooding the dark and cold brig. He came up with them almost right away.

"That's amazing! How did you do that!" Porky inquired.

"I can see fantastically underwater in the dark. Well, I can't really see them with my eyes….it's hard to explain, let's just get out of here."

Porky shouted back, "Incredible, now let's get these men out of their cells!"

"Quite right!" Pastor Platypus refocused.

Pastor Platypus swam quickly and precisely from cell to cell unlocking his fellow ship mates. The ship righted itself to about thirty degrees when the sea allowed it to. The freed sailors all made it out of the brig and up the stairs. Pastor Platypus and Porky floated up through the hatch. "Here! Take this rope! And hang on tight!" ordered Pastor Platypus.

Porky didn't know where Pastor Platypus got the rope but he held on tightly. The Platypus swam swiftly with his powerful tail and webbed feet through the heavily listing corridors which were filling up with rushing water. He pulled Porky behind him who was clawing past all the floating debris with every bit of strength.

Pastor Platypus made his way to a staircase which felt more like a waterfall. Porky was operating in complete darkness trusting the guidance of Pastor Platypus. Suddenly, a fresh wind hit Porky's face. They were emerging out of the belly of the heavily listing ship. The main deck was a scurry of chaos.

"Come along now!" shouted the platypus. They ran slipping and sliding towards the stern of the frigate. Men were falling into the sea all around them. Porky could see that almost all of the life boats had been jettisoned over the side. They took refuge at the base of the mizzen mast just as a giant wave swept across the deck. Then with the tug of the rope Pastor Platypus lead Porky right into the main cabin most likely the Captain's Quarters.

"We haven't much time!" Pastor Platypus informed as his eyes quickly gazed around the room as If looking for something.
"What do we need?!" Porky asked.
"Supplies my good man! We won't be waiting around to see whether or not this ship will stay afloat," the Platypus shouted.

It looked like the cabin was empty of people. "Quickly now! Find the compass and a chronometer if possible! I already have the sextant," ordered the platypus as he started to empty a large trunk of the majority of its contents.

"Chronometer! What's a chronometer!" shouted Porky over the wind which was howling through the cabin portholes.

"You see Porky, there is a fantastically brilliant Yorkshire carpenter by the name of Mr. John Harrison back home who has been in fierce competition, on behalf of the Board of Longitude, to invent a chronometer, or clock if you will, that will not require a pendulum to function so that it can be used in ships to determine one's longitude on the Earth! He has been successful in doing so! His latest chronometer, the H4, has produced a reward of 20,000 pounds from the Crown of England."

Porky replied in growing desperation, "That is fascinating and all, but let's just focus on getting off of this ship!"

Pastor Platypus dashed across the room and grabbed some maps, a flask of water, a partially eaten loaf of bread, a looking scope, and a few other smaller items, all of which he literally threw into the trunk.

Porky was scurrying through loads of debris on the heavily tilted floor just below where the compass was, until finally he took hold of it! "I've got it!" shouted Porky.

"Fantastic! I also found a chronometer in this trunk! Come along now!" Pastor Platypus urged as he started to drag the chest to the stern balcony, "Pull for all your worth!" They both managed to get the chest across the junk covered listing cabin floor out onto the stern balcony.
"Alright then! Jump in!" The platypus ordered.

"The sea?!" urgently questioned Porky.

"No! Get in the trunk now!" commanded Pastor Platypus.

Porky looked at him a little puzzled, but followed the orders anyway. Pastor Platypus jumped in just after Porky, shouting, "Yee Haw!", and closed the trunk hatch tightly behind him. With the very next mighty wave, they were swept into the sea safely sealed up inside the newly supplied admiral's trunk which managed one full flip before plunging into the ocean. It disappeared under the water for just a moment, then popped up and slowly drifted away from the San Carlos.

Chapter IX

A Lonely Trunk

The trunk bobbed and floated smoothly along with the stormy ocean swells. The rain and wind pounded against the hatch. "It actually pleases me to hear the rain falling on the lid of the trunk," remarked Pastor Platypus.

"Oh, why's that?" asked Porky.

"It reminds me that we have not yet sunk," answered the Platypus with a grin which could not be seen in the dark trunk.

"Sunk...are you expecting us to sunk?! I mean sink?!" questioned Porky.

"My dear friend, look at what we already have survived!" the Platypus pointed out with a slight chuckle, "If the Lord has sustained us thus far, I do not think that our story will end here in this lovely trunk."

Porky took a deep breath and let out a long sigh of relief, "I guess you're right. And, thank you for that fantastic rescue back there. I just can't believe we made it off of that Spanish Frigate alive! It seemed like just a moment ago I was on the Schooner trying to furl the top sail." Porky reflected, "I pray the rest of the sailors survive the storm."

"Oh, yes Porky," answered Pastor Platypus, "Men of the sea are quite resilient, always finding a way to survive. Not only that, but the storm started to calm itself shortly after we shoved off in this fine vessel. I wouldn't be surprised if both the San Carlos and the Scorpion managed to stay on the starry side of the sea."

A bit of silence passed. The waves lapped up against the sides of the chest and rain pitter pattered on the top. Porky could sense the trunk moving up and down, but the movements were so smooth and weren't at all unpleasant.

"What is all this stuff in here!?" Porky asked after noticing that he couldn't move very well on account of his being surrounded by quite a lot of clutter.

"I'm not too certain Porky. We'll have to take a careful look at what we have in the morning. I do hope that at least some of it will prove useful. I didn't have much time to pack you know, and I don't think you should complain so much. I'm crammed up against the Admiral's piano! Talk about uncomfortable!"

"A piano!?" asked Porky quite perplexed.

Pastor Platypus laughed heartily, "Just kidding ol' chap! A piano! Ha! How do you suppose I should have fit it in this trunk you silly porcupine!" Pastor Platypus went on talking more quietly to himself, "Not to mention, it was out of tune. I never like to travel with out-of-tune pianos. It bothers me so."

Porky thought this was a bit strange for Pastor Platypus to be making jokes in a situation such as this, yet he found himself chuckling along with him. Porky half-jokingly asked, "You didn't happen to accidently drink a bit too much sea water during our escape did you?"

"Well, Porky, I've never really liked the taste of salt water, but that doesn't mean I didn't drink any!" Pastor Platypus chuckled softly, "I do believe I shall retire for the night; I'm terribly exhausted. I can't get much of a navigational reading from the stars in this storm seeing as how they are hidden by clouds, and besides that, the trunk is closed. So, I might as well rest until all this excitement lets up."

There was a loud rustling and commotion as Pastor Platypus shuffled around to find a comfortable position for sleeping, "Just let me know if we start taking on water, I'd like to have a bit of a snack before we sink. Good night, and well done today. All we can do now is hope that this trunk is making its way towards Cape Horn."

Porky hesitated a bit, "Thanks..." Before Porky could say good night Pastor Platypus was already snoring. Porky was puzzled at how the Pastor could sleep in the midst of this predicament.

Porky also allowed his body to rest finding a comfortable position amidst the tight quarters of the trunk. He walked through the events of the day in his mind recounting all that happened. Porky thought also of his family back home, and all of the wonderful sailors he made friends with aboard the Scorpion. Somehow he knew that they'd be alright in the end. Porky's fatigue was enough to overcome his concerns and he fell fast asleep. And even though Pastor Platypus' foot was resting square against Porky's head having a mildly foul smell, Porky slept quite soundly.

Many hours passed and Porky awoke to fresh morning sunlight and to the sight of Pastor Platypus standing tall in the trunk with the hatch open looking through a telescope out over the sea. Porky rubbed his eyes and carefully stood up in the somewhat wobbly trunk to see the clear blue skies and the calmed sea.

Pastor Platypus lowered his telescope and refocused his eyes keenly on the horizon, "If I take the wings of the morning, and dwell in the uttermost parts of the sea; even there thy hand shall lead me, and thy right hand shall hold me fast. Psalm 139 verses 9 and 10. Do you believe that Porky?"

Porky was a bit taken back, "Yes Sir I do. It was actually the verse I read aloud atop of Grandmother Pine before I saw the schooner Scorpion bound for Moose Island."

"Good, then you shouldn't be disappointed when I tell you that I haven't spotted the least bit of land anywhere," reported Pastor Platypus tossing the collapsed telescope into the bottom of the trunk having no regard for where it landed.

"Nothing at all?" asked Porky.

"Nothing. But the good news is this," continued the platypus lifting high his right eyebrow and pointing his finger aimlessly into the sky, "The water is getting warmer, there are Magnificent Frigate Birds circling overhead, and look there…. plants of some sort floating in the water. All sure signs that land is close! You can almost smell it!"

"But not close enough to see," clarified Porky.

"Right! But with a little prayer and patience, soon enough Porky, soon enough," reassured Pastor Platypus.

"How are we not tipping over right now with this trunk hatch wide open to the side like this?" inquired Porky.

"Ah! Great question my boy! Quite observant of you. You see, I tied this end of the rope to the trunk latch and the other end to the brick of gold which I dropped into the sea as a counter weight. We must throw out the gold when opening the trunk and take it in when closing the trunk hatch. Do you understand Porky, or shall I say it again?"

"Gold!?" exclaimed Porky quite astonished, "There was a block of gold in this trunk!? And you are using it as a counter weight!?"

"Well it was the heaviest thing I could find! And yes, in fact there are five more blocks like it in the trunk which proved to be effective ballast for us in the storm yester-night."

Jaw still dropped Porky asked, "We have six blocks of gold in this trunk!?" Porky quickly sifted around using the fresh new daylight and found a block.

Struggling to take it up in his hands, "Gadzooks, I can barely lift this thing!" Porky examined the gold block a bit more carefully, "Look at this seal, it has some inscription around it, and some lions holding up a crown."

"Yes, that would be the seal of King George III of Great Britain. I highly doubt the Spaniards were just *borrowing* the gold from King George. For now, it shall remain as ballast, but I will be ridding us of these bricks as soon as possible!" Pastor Platypus continued, "I'm going to take a reading with the sextant once the sun is at its zenith here, which shouldn't be more than a quarter hour away. My hunch is that we were pushed quite a bit to the south. Do you have that chronometer available?"

"You're not just going to toss the gold aside as rubbish are you?!" asked Porky.

"Porky, the only things that comes from gold are troubles and death! Now look and see if we have any maps aboard, and we would greatly benefit from a chronometer as well."

"Look! I did grab the maps, even though they're a bit crumpled, I'm sure we'll be able to make some sense of them," concluded Porky as he was trying to unfold the giant map.

"Now Porky, you can put the map away, we won't need it until I take the reading." Pastor Platypus leaned over the edge of the trunk to run his hand through the sea water a bit, "With this warm water, I believe we are floating southward and that is quite fantastic seeing as how we set out to find Terra Australis Incognito which is thought to be found, well, precisely in the South somewhere."

A few moments of silence passed as gentle waves lapped up against the side of the trunk.

"I'm pleased we are drifting south," Porky strained in thought, "but are we not adrift in the Atlantic Sea? And isn't the lost southern continent thought to be in the South Pacific?"

The Platypus sifted around in the ballast of supplies at the bottom of the trunk as if to look for something specific, "Yes, Porky, there is that. It may take us a bit of time in this trunk to get around the Horn of South America. At our current rate of drift, ah here it is." Pastor Platypus peered keenly at the chronometer he had just found, "I suspect that we should be in the general vicinity of Terra Australis Incognito in approximately thirty-five years."

Porky looked at Pastor Platypus with a perplexed sort of smile then burst out laughing. They both began laughing quite heartily! Porky had an unexplainable peace wash over him, and had a feeling deep within that everything was going to be alright, eventually.

With Pastor Platypus still keeping a sharp lookout on the horizon he spoke without adjusting his gaze, "What else did we come away with from the captain's cabin?"

"Well, there is a small locked chest that seemed to be in here to begin with. Without the key, I don't think there will be any getting into it. It does however have some letters carved on the bottom."

"What does it say?" asked the platypus.

Porky brushed away some grime from the bottom of the chest and used one of his quills to prick some mud out of the engraved letters, "C..L..E..M..E..N..T.. I.. N.. E."

"Clementine!" said Pastor Platypus, "Hmm, well that's interesting."

Porky suddenly got excited, "And would you look at this! A harmonica!"

"Ahh, that should help to pass the time," sighed Pastor Platypus.

Porky went on to play a melody which seemed to almost flow with the gently rising and falling swells that carried the trunk along in the middle of a vast, never ending, and yet beautiful sea.

Pastor Platypus took his reading with the sextant believing the sun to be at its highest point. He peered through the small looking scope holding it level to the horizon line, then adjusted the mirrors until the split mirror brought the sun's reflection to the point where it looked level with the horizon line. He secured the slide and waited for the sun spots to leave his eyes.

He handed the sextant to Porky, "Can you read the number in the small window there?"

"It looks to be half way between 21 and 22," reported Porky.

"21 degrees North Latitude! That is further south than I thought!" celebrated the Platypus.

The repetitive bobbing of the trunk, the lapping of the waves, random squawks of gulls and frigate birds lulled Porky's mind into a calm peaceful state. The warm sunshine-filled wind blew squarely against his face. Pastor Platypus settled in on a pile of random items in the corner of the trunk. He took a turn at playing the harmonica while Porky kept watch for land or ship. This went on for hours as the sun gently fell towards the western horizon.

Pastor Platypus soon fell asleep and Porky gave up his search for land. He sat and rested as the stars and moon began to fill the sky on what was proving to be a clear night with fair breezes and becalmed seas. He was careful not to wake the platypus as he would be taking over watch at midnight. When darkness had fully set in, the waves and Pastor Platypus' snoring both kept a steady rhythm.

Porky was simply awestruck at the vast array of stars which overwhelmed the presence of the sea. There seemed to be more stars than there was black space between them. The beaming and nearly full moon made the waves shimmer and dance. Many stars also twinkled, and others streaked across the sky.

Then something happened that made Porky's heart flutter. Around the floating and bobbing trunk appeared swirls and swarms of bluish-green glowing clouds just under the surface of the water. When Porky looked closer he saw what looked like tiny glowing bugs all swimming together. The overall sight was simply magnificent; it was like he had entered another world of heavenly wonders.

The most terrifying experience had brought Porky to the most awe-filled moment in his life. Porky truly comprehended for the first time how awesome God's creation is and recalled the verse that God's thoughts towards his children outnumber the stars in the sky. Porky felt like he caught a special glimpse of the Creator himself revealed in the majesty of the stars, the moon, and the glowing sea.

After a few hours into his watch, fatigue crept through Porky's body and the lights of the night seemed to whisk Porky's mind off to a dreamy place. His eyes grew heavy. Breathing in deeply the crisp sea air with both his mind and spirit refreshed, Porky hoisted in the gold-bar counter weight, closed the top of the trunk, and proceeded to nuzzle himself into a deep sleep.

Chapter X

Breakfast in the Sand

The smell of smoked fish was slowly pulling Porky out of his slumber. For a moment he thought he was back in his tree on Moose Island. The next thing Porky realized was how incredibly hot he felt. The second was how many strange and awkward objects were poking uncomfortably into his body.

Porky managed to wrestle himself up to his feet. "Ah there you are young man! Top of the mornin' to you! I thought you'd never wake up. You must have really stayed up late," announced Pastor Platypus, "Here, Porky, I cooked you up some splendid cuts of fish which I had the pleasure of catching this morning."

Once Porky's eyes moved completely to the awake position, he perceived a beautiful beach with Pastor Platypus cooking over a fire in the sand. "Land!" Porky celebrated, "Praise the Lord!"

Porky leapt out of the trunk and started to bound and roll down the beach. He scooped up two paw-fulls of sand and threw it up into the air. Porky did ten summersaults in a row back to where Pastor Platypus was cooking, "Look at these amazing trees and all these incredible shells!"

"Quite fantastic aren't they!" agreed Pastor Platypus. "I do believe we have found ourselves in the Caribbean tropics; Most likely an island in the West Indies. Presently there's no telling how large or small it may be from this point of view. Now, Porky, take some of that excitement and help me pull this trunk ashore a little further so when the tide comes in it won't wash it back out to sea. I've had enough swimming for the day."

Porky pulled and the Platypus pushed as they relocated the trunk up to a dryer portion of the beach which was right about the time that Porky realized his paws were burning in the sun scorched sand. He quickly scampered back to the sea to cool them off again. "Oh my, that sand is incredibly hot!" shouted Porky.

"Yes! As we get closer to zero degrees latitude, or to the equator rather, the sun will become more powerful. Now come on over here Porky and let us have some breakfast and discuss a few things instead of running around this beach like a dog that lost its stick."

"Fish never tasted so good!" celebrated Porky. "What kind of trees are these that have sheltered us from the sun? They are magnificent! I've never seen anything like them before!"

"Ah yes! I believe what you are referring to is a plentiful gathering of Cocos Nucifera," informed Pastor Platypus.

"A gathering of what?" asked Porky looking up at the giant segmented green leaves which were flowing beautifully with the wind.

"They may be more commonly referred to as palm trees and or Coconut Palms," clarified the Platypus.

"How did you get this fire started, and how did you catch all this wonderful fish?" asked Porky on a deep exhale as he patted his contented belly.

Pastor Platypus explained, "I went for a bit of a swim to rid myself of the not-so-pleasant gun powder smell from all the fighting aboard the ships. I saw all sorts of magnificent fish which looked suitable for eating. Quite motivated by hunger, I resolved to partake in a sub-marine fishing expedition."

"Good show and well done I say!" encouraged Porky smirking as he tried sounding British in his reply.

"Yes, thank you. It is quite magnificent down there, like an entirely new world just under the surface of the water. It will not be like anything you have ever seen before. More colors than you can imagine! The strangest creatures you have ever set your beady little eyes upon. You do have to get used to opening your eyes in salt water, and you must get accustomed to the strong currents as the sea flows in and out from shore. But, once you decide not to let the burning of your eyes bother you it is quite tolerable." "Then the fire," Pastor Platypus continued, "the fire was quite easy. You see the closer we get to the equator the more intense the rays of the sun become."

"Yes, I believe you already mentioned that," corrected Porky.

"Quite right. I used the curvature of the glass in this telescope to arrange the rays of the sun's light to powerfully assemble its energy into one tiny spot." "You see here," the Platypus continued in demonstration, "You take some of this fluffy scruff off of the trunk of the coconut tree and set it upon the sand surrounded by some twigs. Then you hold the telescope above the ground a bit to bend the light concentrating it on the palm scruff."

A few moments passed. Porky questioned, "Aside from hurting your eyes a lot, when does the fire happen?"

"Well, you are not supposed to look directly at the spot, and it does take a bit of time young man, which is something we have quite a bit of now," retorted the Platypus.

They waited a bit. Smoke started to rise from the ball of palm tree fuzz. Then with a poof, it burst into flames!

"Amazing!" exclaimed Porky quite impressed.

Pastor Platypus was struck with a thought, "Porky, we ought to get started on building for ourselves a shelter to sleep in and for storing supplies. Not to mention the storms. As you might remember from the past few days, the weather around these latitudes can be just as unpredictable as Captain Hopkins' moods whilst under sail."

Sadness crept into Porky's heart, "Do you suppose anyone survived the storm."

"Only God knows Porky, but I shall say 'yes' without a doubt in my heart until proven otherwise. As we keep watch on the sea, we should sharpen our eyes to anything that might be adrift in the water. If we washed ashore here, others may be floating this way as we speak. God help them, if anyone be adrift by tomorrow, for lack of fresh water, their souls shall soon be escorted into the heavens, and their bodies to the depths of the sea. But, dare I say, I believe it might have been possible to recover both ships."

"God be with them," prayed Porky. "But If I do not find anything to drink soon, I may be joining them up in the heavens!"

"Look up there Porky – up in the trees. Do you see those round things up there in a bunch? Those are coconuts, and they are filled with the most marvelous and refreshing water you will ever taste! Swimming I do well, but I will leave the climbing to you."

Porky climbed the tree with great ease. The view at the top was quite incredible compared to being at sea level for the past couple of days.

"Porky!" the Platypus shouted, "What do you see? Anything at all?"

"The view is magnificent! Unfortunately, it is simply more of what you see down there –the sea and these wonderful trees. The elevation seems to rise quite sharply as one would move inland," reported Porky.

"Can you see the masts of ships down the coast line? Anything at all?" shouted back Pastor Platypus.

Porky took a more careful look. "Ah-ha!" Porky exclaimed, "There is an odd looking group of large fish that keep surfacing together blowing water up into the air! They have smooth triangular fins on their back!"

"Marvelous!" shouted back Pastor Platypus, "Those would most likely be porpoises! I haven't had the chance to speak with a porpoise since I was a child aboard an English vessel in the South Sea. They can do the most splendid tricks and they love to follow ships just before the break water. That is why they call the small spar that sticks down from the bowsprit the dolphin striker. They actually are not fish at all, they need to breathe air like you and me. That is why they surface so frequently. Are they close? I may try to swim out and meet with them. They are most intelligent and will probably know of any ships in the area!"

Porky sighted them in again, "I am afraid they are quite a way off, much too far to swim. You would never catch up with them."

"Alright then, send some of those coconuts down to the earth if you please!" the platypus commanded.

Porky chomped and clawed a few down to the warm and sandy earth.

Pastor Platypus who had been in the tropics before demonstrated to Porky how to open a coconut and get to its life-giving water. They sat together and very much enjoyed their treat from the trees.

"How wonderful that the Lord has placed for his creatures such wonderful things in the trees of this beach for haphazardly wandering souls such as ourselves," reflected Porky.

"Wandering!? My boy we are moving with a purpose! It just so happens that we have rarely been in control of which way we are moving. Porky, the hand of God will not send us to a place void of His provision and protection," encouraged Pastor Platypus. "Do not worry about tomorrow for today has enough troubles of its own. I honestly do not know what will come of all of this. If we are intended to bring the hope and guidance of the gospel of Christ Jesus to Terra Australis Incognito, then we must believe that it will come to pass and not doubt in the least bit. From this point on let us agree to take life one day at a time. Too much thinking about the past or future and you will miss the present, which is precisely where life actually happens!"

They both took a deep breath and stared at the waves rolling in from a seemingly endless sea. "Come now. Let us kneel in this place and pray before we build our shelter. If we acknowledge God in all that we do, He promises to make our path straight," proclaimed Pastor Platypus.

They both prayed right there on the sandy beach, and Porky built a small tower out of rocks at the spot where they prayed to stand as a reminder to himself of his own decision to trust God completely through this journey. The rock tower was built at the place where the trunk came ashore.

Pastor Platypus declared, "This monument shall serve as a reminder of the absolutely impossible circumstances that the Lord had delivered us from."

"Not only that, but we also have something to give us a point of reference on this beach which seems to look the same in both directions," noticed Porky.

"I'm sure in time we will learn this beach down to the last tree," continued Pastor Platypus. "But for now we will look for this tower should we get lost. We shall thank the Lord every time we see it and remember all that He has done for us. You know it is quite easy to grumble and complain when everything fails to go as planned, but this monument shall jolt us from that lukewarm mindset reminding us to maintain an attitude of thankfulness as we remember all that our Heavenly Father has already done for us!" declared Pastor Platypus as he turned to walk inland. He stopped abruptly for a moment and mumbled, "Not only that, but we shall keep a good schedule of the tides with that little tower."

Pastor Platypus started to walk inland. He looked over his shoulder to see if Porky was following, "Time to put a little pep in your step my boy, this shelter isn't going to build itself!"

He continued mumbling to himself as he turned and walked away towards the tree line, "Well at least I've never seen a shelter build itself. Not to say it's impossible. I guess there is a first time for everything."

Chapter XI

The First Night on Land

The stars were out in great splendor and the moon made the waves sparkle and shimmer as they gently rolled into the sandy shore. The sea seemed more relaxed at night and the sounds of the waves took Porky's mind to a more peaceful place. He was rather proud of the little hut they built which he thought was more like a tropical version of an igloo.

Three bushes formed a tight triangle and created a sheltered space in the middle. The admiral's trunk which they had escaped in was anchored to the back of the shelter and driftwood formed half-circles on both sides. The drift wood was held in place by being woven in between the branches of the surrounding low lying bushes, and large palm leaves were intertwined over the top of them through existing branches. There was a fire pit dug into the sand in front of the shelter's opening which faced the sea. And in keeping with his word, Pastor Platypus gathered up the six gold bars in a burlap sack and went inland to hide them in a hollowed out tree which he had found earlier.

Porky and Pastor Platypus were all nestled in on a bed of palm tree fuzz and fluff. A small fire was burning steadily just outside the entrance, and a cool sea breeze came in off of the ocean which Porky was actually happy to be sheltered from.

Porky broke the silence as they were both staring exhausted at the roof of the hut, "You know what?"

Porky took a deep breath of cool ocean air, "This is the first night I have laid down to sleep in almost a full month in which I am not bobbing up and down or rocking to and fro with the movements of the sea. It almost makes me sick as it feels like, in my head, I am still surging forth on a ship when all the while my body is still as can be."

Pastor Platypus got up to sort through some of the items in the trunk for a brief moment.

"You still have what is called your 'sea legs'. It will take some time for you to adjust to the firmament," explained Pastor Platypus. "I am quite pleased with our work today. This is a fabulous shelter, and it should keep us quite safe." Pastor Platypus went on speaking lazily with his eyes closed patting the beams next to his side, "This driftwood is quite strong and the fire at the front should deter creatures lurking about which may attempt to investigate us by means of the front door."

"Creatures lurking about!?" exclaimed Porky a bit concerned. "What sort of creatures are you making reference to?"

Pastor Platypus reassured Porky, "I'm not really expecting anything in particular. I am almost positive that we are at the top of the food chain here, but you'd hate to find out if I'm wrong the hard way!"

"I would feel a lot safer up in a tree," admitted Porky.

"I'd feel safer in the water, and I'd be a lot more comfortable back home in Wallington River," retorted Pastor Platypus. "But as you can see we have nicely met in the middle."

Porky reflected for a moment, "I'm just surprised at how unsuited these trees are for building a shelter. None of them are hollow enough and they don't have any branches, but I suppose that if we run into any real trouble that we could just hop in the trunk and shut the hatch."

Porky thought for a minute, "Hey I got an idea, what if we make some piles of shells around the hut. If anything comes by it's bound to make some noise when the creature steps and stumbles over the shells. That should be enough to wake us up so we can head for shelter."

"Yes. Splendid idea," said Pastor Platypus. "How about you head out and do just that. If you take longer than what feels like a quarter of an hour, then I'll come out looking for you."

"Alright sounds like a plan," agreed Porky realizing that the Platypus would most likely fall asleep in just moments. And with that he leaped around the fire and scurried down under the light of the moon to where the sea met the sand. Porky was awe-struck at the peaceful splendor of the sea at night. The sound that the small shells made as they rolled over each other when the waves retreated was incredible. It reminded him of a heavy rain.

Porky felt a great deal of peace in his heart and resolved to take the days and all their challenges one at a time. Like clay in the potter's hands, he becalmed his thoughts and allowed his expectations to be subject to the perfect will of God. But wisdom still directed Porky to gather up piles of shells which he set up in a circle pattern of sorts around the newly built shelter. Should any creature attempt to approach the encampment with the idea of making them a mid-night snack, at least they would have some notice first.

Porky took one last look up to the star-filled sky before turning in to sleep. He reached his hand up to the sky. It almost looked as if he could grab a clump full of stars. Porky marveled at how large and simple the heavens seemed to appear in contrast with his small and complex hand. Yet God has made them both. This gave Porky much comfort and peace on what could have been a lonely night.

Porky started to talk with God as if he was standing right there on the beach next to him, "Lord what should I do? I feel like I want to go home and yet another part of me wishes to press on to find the hidden continent of the south which of course is not hidden to you. I know you are able to guide us there." Porky took a deep breath, "Lord, watch over my family tonight on Moose Island. Surround them with your love and comfort them with your Holy Spirit. I lift up to you also the people and creatures of Australis. May you prepare their hearts for our arrival and to receive your love. And please let us not get eaten by anything while we sleep. Thank you Lord. Amen."

Porky paused for a moment to lose himself in the stars. Porky reflected upon God's word which says we were not given a spirit of timidity, but of a spirit of power. He was journaling about this very thing the morning he left Moose Island and his entire family. He reached up to the stars once more with his right hand, "I trust you Lord. I will go wherever you send me. You are my Good Shepherd."

Suddenly a streaking light dashed across the sky! It went from horizon to horizon leaving a lasting trail of light behind it as it flew. Porky swore that the shooting star even made a sound, and the most amazing thing about it was that it went right through his hand as he held it up to the sky.

92

Porky was awe-struck; he stopped breathing for a moment and eventually let out a deep sigh and exhaled, "WOW!" Then just after a moment or two, Porky realized something. His choice was either go home or carry on. He looked to where the star shot, marked the spot in his mind, and quickly ran back into the shelter. He leapt over the fire and scurried straight to the trunk. Porky quickly found the compass. Porky opened it up as he ran back to the spot where he was standing when he saw the shooting star. He lined up the compass to figure out where the star pointed to. 220 degrees southwest. Porky's home would have been north by northwest. The star shot onward in the general supposed location of the lost southern continent. It was all Porky needed to know. He was not expecting God to speak like this. Such a confirmation emboldened Porky beyond what words could express, and he knew at that moment that he would do whatever it would take to complete what God had called them to do.

Porky was extremely excited. He finished rekindling the fire in the same manner his heart had been rekindled. A deep and peaceful rest came over Porky. After a few deep breaths on his bed of palm fluff, he realized he was quite hungry and that his morning plans would consist of finding food straight away, and with that thought, he was fast asleep.

Chapter XII

Mr. Shelton Express

Pastor Platypus awoke to sun beams shining through their smoky shelter and the sound of waves thundering into shore. The waves sounded much closer and louder than the night before. Pastor Platypus figured that the tide was in. He put his bifocals on and saw that Porky was still asleep. He chuckled a bit to himself. He had always thought it was quite funny how porcupines looked like a puff-ball of quills when they slept.

He peered out at the sea and saw that they had moderate fine pleasant weather with a sea breeze at east southeast. The waves were reaching inland a mere twenty feet from their encampment. They appeared to be on high enough ground so long as the tide was at its peak. Pastor Platypus's stomach was growling, and just as he turned to go back into the hut to wake up Porky, there he saw right next to the entrance a perfect pyramid of mangos!

"No wonder Porky is so tired; he was up early this morning collecting food!" thought the platypus aloud to himself. Delighted, Pastor Platypus went in to thank Porky, "Porky my dear boy, spectacular work in collecting all the mango fruits!"

The ball of quills displayed no sign of life yet. Pastor Platypus cleared his throat, "I say, top of the morning to you Porky! Good show on collecting the mangos!"

The ball of quills opened up to roll on its back and stretch. Only Porky's starboard eye made the attempt to open.

"What is a mango? And what precisely are you talking about? I haven't been out this morning!" mumbled Porky both tired and puzzled.

"Well come and look for yourself," urged Pastor Platypus as he gestured towards the entrance. Porky worked hard to get on his feet. Once upright, he shuffled out into the light of the new day.

"Well would you look at that!" exclaimed Porky. "The circular perimeter of shells I assembled is completely undisturbed."

Pastor Platypus looked at the ground in all directions, "There aren't even any foot prints in the sand, not one disturbance to be found!"

Porky pointed at their provision, "And such a perfectly assembled pyramid of fruit would have taken many trips."

"Well, it may take us most of the day to figure out this mystery, but for now let us enjoy our mana from heaven!" concluded Pastor Platypus.

They each grabbed a mango and scurried over to a nearby rock to perch upon. It provided for them a nice view of the eastern sky.

"Praise God, this fruit is amazing. I have never tasted anything like it in my life!" Porky chomped another juicy bite. "Quite messy however," added Porky with juice running down his paws and chin.

Pastor Platypus spoke with his mouth half full, "You find these common fruits delightful on account of your lack of food for the last two watches. Eat them every meal for a few days and soon you may think differently!"

Porky replied, "I highly doubt that!"

Porky continued in thought, "If we do have a fellow guest on the island, at least we know they are friendly!"

"Yes, yes indeed," replied the platypus. "But if our guest is inclined to serve our cause, why do you suppose they keep their identity a secret!"

"Well, perhaps it is a miraculous provision from the Lord," suggested Porky.

Pastor Platypus concluded with a delighted grin, "Either way, we shall give thanks."

Porky continued in-between bites, "Last night I had an amazing moment..." Porky paused a bit with an excited gaze off into the distance.

"Go on," urged Pastor Platypus starting on his second perfectly ripened mango.

Porky spoke with great resolve, "Well, I was grappling with the feeling of wanting to return home to all that is familiar and predictable, but I concluded that this feeling was born of fear. So, I decided to replace my fear with faith, and I resolved in my heart to be certain of what it is that we hope for and to be moldable clay in the Potter's hands. God sent me a sign last night in the sky. It filled my heart with peace. Though I didn't picture it all happening like this, I firmly believe that God is directing our steps, and I am ready to do the best I can wherever my two feet are planted for the day. I am determined to find the hidden continent of the South and to be a light unto that land. I know that is what I have been created and called to do."

"Excellent!" proclaimed the Platypus tossing his mango pit blindly into the forest behind him. "Then let's get going! We have a lot of work to do! I am proud of you my boy! Now, if you are done eating, let's bring the rest of these mangos into our little shelter. Then, I suggest we pack our satchels for a bit of a day hike. If there is someone else on the Island, they might be the key to getting off and on our eventual means to the South Pacific!"

Porky replied, "Right you are! Let's get moving!" Porky stood up and as he looked over at Pastor Platypus he completely froze in fear. As the platypus was bringing fruit into the shelter he gave Porky a reprimand, "Well don't just stand there Porky, get to it boy."

Porky announced, "Um, Pastor, I think you should take a look at this!"

"What is it?" inquired the platypus. He stood beside Porky and fixed his gaze in the same direction. Pastor Platypus gasped, "Well blow down my mizzen mast, would you take a look at that!"

Porky stood frozen in fear, "So, my eyes are not deceiving me – That indeed is a giant shell moving across the beach on its own!"

"Porky, do you know what that is? It is a hermit crab! A giant hermit crab!"

Porky asked, "Do you suppose that he has been the one who provided us with our pyramid of mangos?"

"I think not Porky. Hermit crabs are intelligent, but not that intelligent. Not only that he would have left marks all over in the sand. Come along! Let's go say hello!" And with that Pastor Platypus started to walk towards the giant creature. Porky reluctantly followed.

Pastor Platypus approached the crab. Porky watched at what he thought was a safe distance remembering what his father always told him about evading the wolves on Moose Island, 'All you have to do is run faster than the slowest Porcupine'. Porky make himself chuckle a bit at the thought, and it made him long for his father to be with him. Oh how Porky wished his father could see all the wondrous adventures he had been having!

Porky had never seen anything like this before in his entire life! Pastor Platypus approached cautiously and gave it a couple friendly pats on its coiling stout cone-like shell which stood quite a bit taller than Pastor Platypus. Porky's jaw dropped when he saw the Platypus rubbing its head offering it a piece of mango which it happily gobbled up.

"Remarkable!" exclaimed Pastor Platypus. "Porky, you must come and take a look at this fellow. He is quite docile. Large, but docile indeed."

Pastor Platypus was patting his shell, walking around the friendly creature to have a closer examination of his features. He disappeared out of view from Porky hidden behind the giant shell. Suddenly Porky saw Pastor Platypus appear on top of the crab. Pastor Platypus gave it a firm double pat on the side of the shell and the hermit crab lurched forward and started down the beach with the platypus riding it as a man rides a horse!

"Unbelievable!" Porky announced to himself with increasing awe and excitement.

Pastor Platypus effectively figured out how to make it obey and turn around to head back towards Porky. The platypus ordered it to halt just before reaching Porky. "Well, don't just stand there," shouted Pastor Platypus down to Porky. "Grab the supplies, and come aboard. This crab shall aid us greatly in today's exploration!"

Porky asked, "Are you suggesting that we ride that creature all day!?"

"Of course!" answered the platypus, "He is quite agreeable and will be much more effective at traversing the terrain than we would be."

"What do you think we should call him? If we are going to be with him all day, it should at least have a name!" shouted Porky.

"Well," thought Pastor Platypus nicely patting the top of the shell. "He lives in a shell, and weighs a ton. So, it is obvious to me that his name shall be Mr. Shelton."

"Mr. Shelton it is!" agreed Porky. "I'll finish closing up the encampment and collect our things."

Pastor Platypus added, "You had better disperse the stones of our fire ring and cover up the ashes with a bit of sand as to keep our hut rather hidden."

Porky did just that and brought the fruit into their shelter, sealed the chest, and collected the rest of the essential supplies into his satchel. He came out to climb upon Mr. Shelton for a grand day of exploration.

"Before you come up here, what exactly did you bring?" asked Pastor Platypus.

"I have the compass, the sextant, the West Indies map, my journal and some ink," answered Porky.

"Excellent! Take a palm leaf would you, and wipe away our foot prints surrounding the bushes here," ordered Pastor Platypus.

Porky finished closing up camp, came over to Mr. Shelton's port side, and attempted to get on. On his first attempt Mr. Shelton moved the leg Porky was trying to ascend causing him to perform an unintentional back-flip landing face down in the sand.

"This is no time for tricks Porky! Perhaps you should try to come up the crevice at the aft portion of the shell here. I believe your claws tickled him a bit."

Once Porky had situated himself aloft Mr. Shelton, Pastor Platypus was clear in his suggestion that they should make an attempt to get to the highest point possible on a half-day trek inland to visualize as much as they could about the land they had drifted upon. Perhaps they would see smoke from the fires of human inhabitants, a harbor with ships, trodden paths, or even other islands in the near distance that could possibly be identified on their map. Yes, the day proved to be a grand adventure with tremendous opportunity for discovery!

Off they set out into the sweltering hot jungle. The ocean breeze was no longer upon them as Mr. Shelton trudged through thick vegetation. They had been riding for just a half hour when Porky broke the silence. "How do you suppose we will ever know which way we are traveling if we cannot see beyond the distance which a Porcupine can spit! This is nothing like the forests back home!" observed Porky with slight frustration and concern in his voice.

"It's quite simple my dear Porky, when the ground goes up we follow it up. We shall keep a general heading on our compass opposite of the direction of the sea which would be west northwest or about 290 degrees. When we wish to find our way back home, we will be going downhill at an opposite heading. You would subtract 180 from 290 and therefore obtain a heading of 110 degrees or east southeast. When we hit the beach we will look for our pillar of stones and there you have it," informed Pastor Platypus. "And as for the vegetation, you can forget the deciduous and coniferous forests of the northern latitudes. Presently, we are much closer to the equator and nearly upon the Tropic of Cancer which is twenty-three and a half degrees. This climate provides more intense sunlight and rainfall. Most importantly there is no winter here, usually just a dry season and a rainy season."

"I see," replied Porky with new-found understanding, "So the plants here have all year to grow and that's why the vegetation is so thick and abundant."

"Precisely! I shall make a botanist out of you yet! I also think that is why we see a much greater variety of plant species than we do in the northern latitudes." Pastor Platypus stared ahead deep in thought, "You know Porky, traveling through this dense forest provides for us a good teaching metaphor."

"Let's not get our metaphors all mixed up this time." warned Porky with a silly grin.

Neglecting his navigation of Mr. Shelton, the platypus turned around to face Porky who was sitting behind him, "Here we are riding on this helpful hermit crab not able to see any further than one can spit, as you mentioned earlier. Our perspective has been blinded by all this vegetation, but you have your compass which steers you a true course. The compass, my dear boy, guides us in the direction we ought to go which, in a time such as this, we must watch almost continually! Constant adjustments in our heading are required."

"Forgive me, but…" Before Porky could finish his sentence a branch hit him knocking him effectively off of Mr. Shelton onto the forest floor.

"Hove to Mr. Shelton!" commanded Pastor Platypus pulling back on his antennae. Once stopped, Pastor Platypus stood up atop of Mr. Shelton's back with his paws on his hips holding back the sides of his vest which was laden with supplies and looked down at Porky who was lying on the ground moaning and rolling around a bit.

"You see Porky," Pastor Platypus continued, "At times our human senses fail to help us. We cannot understand where we are exactly going. That is when we must cling on to the word of God and trust what is written! Then we follow that word and do exactly as it says in just the same way that we follow our compass going precisely where it points."

Porky was just lying on his back looking straight up at the canopy and the little bits of flickering sky and sun, "The forest certainly is beautiful from this perspective."

"Yes!" Pastor Platypus was bounding now as if rallying an entire nation, "and the key to living a significant life is often found in how one recovers from his fall. Now you must get back up to your feet, pick up your compass, take a new heading, and trudge on towards the great unknown." Pastor Platypus looked down at Porky as if he noticed for the first time that he fell, "What are you doing down there? Are you looking for grubs? We did pack some food! Come along now. All aboard. Let's keep moving!"

Porky rolled his eyes and struggled himself back atop Mr. Shelton.

They climbed and trudged for half the day reaching what appeared to be a prominent ridge. The beach and the sea could be partially seen through the forest, but climbing a tree was clearly the best option for finding the best view of the area. Porky slid off of Mr. Shelton's back and bounded around a bit looking for the widest tree trunk he could find supposing that it would be the tallest.

"I think I found the grandmother of the forest!" shouted Porky gazing up in awe and satisfaction at one of the biggest trees that Porky had ever seen in his entire life. Some of its branches were bigger than the trunks of the trees back home on Moose Island. Pastor Platypus soon showed up on the scene. The trunk was wide and the bark was smooth affording no obvious grips for climbing.

Taking off his satchel and setting it at the base of the trunk, Porky looked up and assessed the tree's structure with great thought and focus.

Pastor Platypus asked, "Porky, why do you call such trees the 'grandmother of the forest'?"

"Well, my father used to tell me that an entire forest was contained inside a single acorn seed. The one acorn seed grows to become a large tree which drops many new acorns. This in turn causes many new trees to grow. In time, an entire forest is created from the first tree making it, therefore, the grandmother of the forest!"

"Porky, that is just a fantastic notion. The teachings of your parents are a wonderful treasure to keep within your heart. I also see that you have been created to be exceptionally good at climbing such trees. Just look at those fantastic claws! I continue to be in envy of them at times."

"Well," Porky replied, "I do wish that I was as good at swimming as you are. For example, a few days ago when I fell off of the yard arm into the ocean!"

Pastor Platypus laughed and also realized that he would not be able to make it up the lower portion of the trunk. Making a closer study of his surroundings an idea popped into his head.

"Alright, just like we were at sea, I'll have you go aloft and use some of these vines like rigging. You climb up, throw the vine over a horizontal branch and guide it back down to me. I will tie off. Then you jump down holding on to the other end of the vine. As you fall down, I will rise up! Then, we'll keep doing the same until we are at the top. Sound like a plan?"

"Sounds like an excellent plan! Well worth a try anyway," agreed Porky. "I'll be aloft faster than you can say 'Mr. Shelton is a merry ol' fellow'!" And at that, Porky scurried up to the first horizontal branch.

"Life is like a tree you know!" Porky shouted down to a grinning Platypus, "half the fun is just climbing it."

"It's queer that you should say such a thing," The platypus shouted back, "why, when the daughter of Captain Hood was just a wee lass, she said one day, 'Father. Life is like a peanut, half the fun is just opening the shell'!"

Porky chuckled as he loosened a vine from its grip around the tree and tossed it down to Pastor Platypus and slung the other half over the branch above him, "Well, that's just great."

"All right then, tie on and let's give this a shot!" the Porcupine shouted.

The Platypus tied the vine around his upper arms and held on tightly to the supply satchel.

"Stand by to hoist the platypus!" shouted Porky as he leapt off of the branch holding on to the other end of the vine which was draped over the branch above him. Porky plummeted to the earth and Pastor Platypus was launched toward the sky!

By the time the platypus securely positioned himself upon the branch and looked down to say, "Well done Porky!", Porky was already back up on the branch with the platypus.

"What fun this turned out to be! Come now!" shouted Porky. "We'll keep on doing this sort of vertical leap frog until we are at the top!"

"Splendid! Yes, quite splendid indeed!" pronounced The platypus who was immensely pleased, "Except this time give me a bit more of a warning why don't you."

"Alright then!" agreed Porky.

With the end of the vine in the grips of his teeth, Porky was bounding up the massive trunk to the next prominent set of branches.

Porky threw the vine over a branch just above him and hollered, "Stand fast below!"

"Permission to come aloft?!" shouted Pastor Platypus in the tone of a ship's crewman.

"Permission granted!" huffed Porky.

With that Porky jumped shouting, "Yahoo!"

The vine zinged over the branch as Porky dropped and Pastor Platypus and the supplies went up! Porky then climbed back up to his position.

After two more pulley and vine assents the bark started to get more defined and the branches closer together and smaller. "I think we must climb on our own from here. I'll take the satchel." suggested Porky.

The branches got flimsier, but they were closely networked creating considerable stability for such a location. Much to their relief the wind could finally be felt again in the higher portions of the tree canopy bringing much needed relief from the hot and humid forest floor.

Porky maneuvered to a position where he could stand up straight on what looked like the highest point of the tree. He stood up and gasped, "This is outstandingly majestic! Come up here! The view is simply amazing!" Porky felt an incredible sense of triumph. He looked down to the platypus who was just a few branches below him, "This is just incredible, you have got to see this!"

Pastor Platypus urgently asked, "What is it?! What do you see?!"

Chapter XIII

A Grand View

"Nothing!" proclaimed Porky as he looked carefully in all directions. "Not a sign of civilization anywhere! But, the view is marvelous! I've never seen anything like it. This is the most awesome view of nothing that I have ever seen!" continued Porky in astonishment.

Pastor Platypus settled himself securely in a group of branches which formed a nice supporting perch. He wrapped the straps of the satchel around a branch in between Porky and himself so that they both could access their supplies without difficulty.

"Absolutely incredible! Such views never cease to amaze me," pronounced Pastor Platypus.

At the level of the tree tops a sea breeze could be felt and seen sweeping powerfully over the land. Porky thought aloud, "Oh such a lonely wind, to have been wandering over the sea for hundreds of miles searching for land. I think I know how the wind feels."

"Who can ever know where it comes from or where it is going," reflected Pastor Platypus in awe.

The wind almost seemed eager to sweep over the tree tops making the leaves rustle and the branches bend in a collective roar. Butterflies of many different colors fluttered and dashed from tree top to tree top.

Porky could see the beach stretch on and on until it disappeared around a ridge to the south. The waves looked small. White-capped rollers met the land seeming to move in slow-motion. Porky thought it was odd to see the sea without being able to hear it.

"Alright Porky, it's time to get to work."

"What exactly did you have in mind good Sir?" asked Porky.

"Make ready your journal. I would like you to write the date at the top 'the year of our Lord seventeen hundred and sixty-eight'. I would also like you to sketch our vista presently. Also, briefly scribe how we got here and all the observations you can possibly make such as: the weather, the types of plants, the animals we meet, our location, star patterns, moon patterns, wind direction, foods present, possible locations of fresh water, and you must also name what you see in the unlikely situation that this land happens to be uncharted. We must name the coves, the mountains, the valley's…."

"I see, I see!" Porky interrupted noticing that Pastor Platypus intended to carry on for quite some time. "Hand me my ink would you. I don't think we have enough ink to write all that down," laughed Porky.

"Yes, here you are, but what will you draw with?" asked the Platypus.

Porky explained, "My quills aren't just for my dashing good looks you know! Would you be able to smartly pull a thicker one out from my hind quarters? Pull it quickly now so it won't hurt as much."

"Ah ha! Very resourceful my good fellow. Very resourceful I say," celebrated Pastor Platypus. "You get to sketching and I'll take a few readings for you with our compass, sextant, and chronometer, and I shall see also what appears in the looking glass."

Porky got to work straight away sketching the landscape quite skillfully with…. well with one of his own quills, dipping it frequently in the ink. The Platypus took to the looking glass straight away to view the sea and the horizon for any signs of masts or sails. Then he surveyed the beaches closely looking into each cove for signs of life. A French, Spanish, or English colony would be the most likely finding. Pastor Platypus also considered the presence of native inhabitants.

A bit of peaceful time passed. "Nothing," announced Pastor Platypus.

"Nothing what?" asked Porky just finishing up his sketch.

"Not a sign of ship or colony, or life anywhere. Not even an animal or a bird for that matter! All I see is water, sky, sand, and plants!" reported Pastor Platypus. "Quite interesting actually," said the platypus as he tapped his bill.

They watched the sea sparkle in the noon-day sun as they sat perched in thoughtful consideration. Porky broke the silence with some cheer in his voice. "Salvation Cove", announced Porky turning to Pastor Platypus with a disproportionately large smile plastered to his face.

"What did you say?" asked Pastor Platypus.

"Salvation Cove! That is what I am naming the pleasant little place that we have built our encampment within," announced Porky with great pride in his voice as he compared his drawing to the magnificent back drop of their present view. Porky continued, "Can you tell if we are on an island? What do you see? Want me to write anything specific down in our journal?"

Pastor Platypus sounding more like a captain of a ship replied in stern British candor, "Shipwrecked at Salvation Cove, supplied only with the contents of a Spanish Admiral's trunk, a refreshing sea breeze from the east northeast at a moderate gale. No sign of the Scorpion or its crew as of yet. Fruit bearing trees have provided adequate nutrition and often appear at our encampment in pyramids with no evidence of the deliverer." Pastor Platypus was carefully adjusting and fixing a reading on the sextant, "Presently at twenty-one and a half degrees north latitude, most likely on a land mass in the West Indies quite near the Tropic of Cancer. No signs of advanced civilization at our present location, but there is a harbor looking as if it might support the anchorage of ships to the northeast by north at six leagues distance from our present location."

The Porcupine interrupted, "Alright, slow down for just a moment while I get the last few parts, and what do you mean when you say 'northeast by north'?"

"You see, Porky, the compass is divided commonly into 32 points with each point being 11 and ¼ degrees from the other. In this case, northeast is directly betwixt north and east. Northeast by north is 11 and ¼ north of northeast. Does that make sense?"

"About as much sense as the two of us sitting in this tree!" laughed Porky.

"Well, we'll practice boxing the 32 compass points when we get back to camp where we have some sand to draw in," proposed Pastor Platypus.

111

"That would be splendid," accepted Porky continuing on a bit with his documentation and landscape sketch.

The Platypus collected his last observations and continued after Porky gave him a nod, "An ample source of fresh drinking water has not yet been found. We will consider methods of collecting rain. A more extensive exploration of the land with the aid of Mr. Shelton, who is possibly a new species likened to a giant form of Petrochirus Diogenes, will be made in the hopes of finding an English ship bound for the horn."

Porky replied, "That better be all or I will be needing a new quill! - And what exactly do you mean when you say 'bound for the horn'?"

"The horn, my good fellow, is the southern-most point of the South Americas. It is the only way to get to the Pacific Ocean where many have searched for the lost southern continent. The horn, however, is a fearsome place with angry seas. It is a graveyard for ships I am afraid. But if God has called us through, we shall pass around the horn without any hindrance of the sort!"

"Well then," responded Porky, "The grave yard of ships!? That sounds like an interesting place to sail. How about we just worry about getting down out of this tree for now? I am getting thirsty. I will definitely need quite a bit of coconut water when we return to the forest floor."

"Well then, let us collect ourselves here and see if Mr. Shelton has decided to wait for our return! Yes, quite an interesting creature isn't he?" announced Pastor Platypus not really expecting an answer.

Porky replied, "I think he is a little odd in appearance, but quite useful."

Pastor Platypus chuckled a bit, "You're not so normal looking yourself!

"Hey, watch it!" Porky retorted, "I make being odd look good!"

They both laughed. "Alright," Pastor Platypus motioned with a wave of the arm, "let's get out of this tree before the wind blows us out of it!"

Good use of the vines was made to complete the task of descending the enormous tree. Soon Mr. Shelton came into view.

"Would you look at that! Our friend remains!" announced Pastor Platypus. With one last slide down a vine they were on the ground at last! Porky walked up to the giant shell and did a quick lap around it. A puzzled look beset his face, "He's left us! Only the shell remains!"

"My dear boy, you must remember, we are dealing with a genus of crab that retreats into his shell from time to time. Just give it a bit of a knock and he will appear," suggested Pastor Platypus as he was unbinding their supplies from the vine rigging.

Porky gave the shell a bit of a cheerful knock and spoke as if trying to wake a small child, "Mr. Shelton, we have returned."

The shell suddenly lifted up and out emerged the giant hermit crab. "He doesn't look happy with me," noted Porky.

Pastor Platypus placed upon his bill his bifocals and took a closer look at Mr. Shelton, "No, I'd say he looks a bit crabby to

113

me!" Then he burst out laughing at his own joke as he slung the supply satchel up onto the shell.

Starting to climb up the shell, Pastor Platypus looked over his shoulder, "Well, let us get under way. I would like to propose going a bit north before we descend again to the beach. There is a portion of land over a ridge to the north I was not able to visualize even from the top of the tree."

"I don't see any reason why we shouldn't. With the help of Mr. Shelton and your jokes, the time should quickly pass us by!" replied Porky with a sarcastic grin.

They crawled north for a bit quite satisfied with their accomplishments for the day. Lying on their backs watching the trees pass above Porky commented, "All those frogs croaking and chirping is sure pleasant. Reminds me a lot of the nights back on Moose Island." The two remained silent as a few more trees passed above.

"Did you say frogs?" Pastor Platypus asked coming to a sudden realization. Pastor Platypus sat up with urgency in his voice, "Is that what that sound is? Those indeed *are* frogs!"

Porky answered with on odd look on his face not quite understanding where the platypus was going with this, "It is as you say. Frogs they are indeed. It's a sound this porcupine will never forget; of course they sound a bit different here, but..."

Before Porky could finish, the platypus tucked their compass into his vest, slid down the side of Mr. Shelton, and dashed off running in the direction of the frogs.

"Hey, wait for me!" Porky shouted as he charged after him atop Mr. Shelton striving to keep up. Porky could not actually see the platypus, but he keenly followed a path of briskly moving leaves and branches which Pastor Platypus jostled as he ran. Porky did not realize that a platypus could move so quickly across the terra firma! Mr. Shelton crashed through the underbrush, downhill in pursuit. Then Porky heard a joyous shout, "YAAAA HOOOIE", which was followed by a tremendous 'SPLASH!'

Porky and Mr. Shelton soon came upon Pastor Platypus leaping, jumping, and flipping in a bustling fresh water stream!

"Frogs, frogs! Thank God for frogs! May they croak proudly all their days! Drink up, my boy, drink up!" celebrated Pastor Platypus. They both were thrilled and had their fill of water.

After resting a bit in the cool rushing stream, Porky turned to the platypus and challenged, "I'll bet you that with me running upon the land atop of Mr. Shelton and you swimming along in the stream that I can beat you to the beach!"

Refreshed with new strength the platypus answered back in a proud English accent, "I accept your challenge, but I do believe you have grossly underestimated the power of my swimming abilities!"

"I'll carry the supplies", offered Porky with a keen look in his eyes.

"Alright then, best of luck to you!" and the platypus was off and swimming down-stream with a magnificent diving entry in an obvious attempt to get a head start on his spiky friend. Porky tore off after him bounding skillfully through the forest atop his crabby steed. It was almost as if Mr. Shelton knew they were heading for the beech and took the liberty, when reaching a hill, to lift up his legs and slide down on the belly of his shell to hasten their progress towards the sandy finish-line.

The stream made for easy navigation. Pastor Platypus had the swift current and his powerful swimming abilities on his side. Perceiving his commanding lead, he turned to float on his back allowing the current to carry him so that he could watch and taunt Porky as he ran right beside him struggling to keep up. Porky looked up ahead to plot his course, and his heart suddenly sunk in his chest.

"Waterfall!" Porky shouted, "Pastor, a waterfall!"

It was approaching quickly. Pastor Platypus turned to look over his shoulder and made a helpless attempt to swim towards the river bank. Without a further thought Porky left the supplies atop the shell and leapt off of Mr. Shelton assuming the 'cannon ball' position and shouted, "I'm with you!" Porky recovered from his cannon ball entry and was able to just barely take one breath before they both went swiftly over the falls.

It all happened so quickly. Porky found himself tumbling round and round in circles at the base of the water fall unable to locate the surface. All was dark, and Porky was growing desperate for air.

Suddenly Porky's satchel strap wedged tightly under his arm pits, and he was swiftly pulled to the surface by Pastor Platypus! Porky gasped and caught his breath, "Thank You!" Pastor Platypus shouted over the rapids, "No problem at all. Let's ride this out until we get washed out into the sea. It shouldn't be much longer. Are you alright?"

"Yes, I think I'll make it." answered Porky with a nod.

Soon the river got slower and wider as it became poised to empty into the ocean. Pastor Platypus ordered, "Come now, let us swim to the river bank. If there are crocodiles in this river, this is the portion that they'd be in." And at that, Porky beat Pastor Platypus to the river bank!

They scurried along past some stately coconut trees refreshed from their swim, and for the first time in quite a while Porky was actually quite thrilled to see the salty sea again. It meant that they were safe and that rest and replenishment was just ahead.

"Well, I suppose that we just head south from here," suggested Porky.

"Indeed! And I want to commend you for your bravery back there," commented Pastor Platypus wiping the water from his face.

"You are welcome, but I feel quite foolish in that you ended up saving *me*. I know you are an excellent swimmer. I don't know what came over me. I saw you were in trouble, and for some reason I felt the need to jump in to be with you."

Pastor Platypus gave Porky a nod and a wink, "My boy! That is true loyalty. Sometimes it is better to go down a waterfall knowing you're not alone!"

They walked for a way in the shade of the trees which cast long shadows over the beach as the sun was starting its decent towards tomorrow.

"Look who decided to rejoin us!" pointed Porky behind them with his thumb. Pastor Platypus immediately saw Mr. Shelton crawling out of the tree line.

Porky walked up to their new friend, "And look, our supplies are still atop the shell! This guy is a lot smarter that we think!"

"It looks as if we have gained a loyal friend!" stated Pastor Platypus with great satisfaction, "Well, all aboard, lets ride him back to the encampment."

Just before Porky climbed on, to his great surprise, he spotted another giant hermit crab in the shade of the tree line! Porky carefully snuck around the back of Mr. Shelton's shell as not to be detected by Pastor Platypus, and scurried back in the direction of the massive hermit crab. He mounted it without difficulty and approached Pastor Platypus' blind side. He could see the platypus looking all around for him.

"Race you to the encampment!" shouted Porky as he took off running atop his new hermit crab steed.

"Not a chance, victory is ours!" retorted Pastor Platypus as he jolted Mr. Shelton into a canter.

Pastor Platypus and Mr. Shelton quickly caught up to Porky and his less-than-trained hermit crab which was zig-zagging wildly across the beach in what looked like an effort to get the Porcupine off of his shell. Porky was holding on for dear life. He gave the crab a hard command to starboard and rammed Mr. Shelton a bit.

Porky regained some ground and could hear Pastor Platypus shouting to him from behind, "Oh I see what kind a race this is! Temporary gains, Porky! Temporary gains!"

Porky finally gained control of his giant hermit crab and had him in a straight-line run towards their pillar of stones which was now in view. Porky stood up and opened wide his arms to let

118

the wind against his face enjoying the feeling of imminent victory.

Just then Pastor Platypus and Mr. Shelton appeared on Porky's port side. He looked over to see Pastor Platypus smiling while holding a coconut over his head. "What are you going to do with that!?" shouted Porky.

Pastor Platypus then smashed the coconut against Mr. Shelton's shell and threw the two halves right in front of Porky's hermit crab.

Being one of their favorite snacks, Porky's hermit crab stopped dead in its cantor to eat his new treat. When he stopped, Porky kept on going. Porky flopped and tumbled a bit through the sand regaining his focus in time to see Mr. Shelton and Pastor Platypus shoot past the finish line.

Pastor Platypus dismounted Mr. Shelton and waited for Porky to catch up on foot. "Well, you did get second place. That's not at all bad," encouraged the Platypus.

"It's bad when there are only two competitors!" retorted Porky.

"Suit yourself Mr. Sand Ball."

They walked for a bit towards their bush encampment when Pastor Platypus broke the silence, "Well blow down my main mast and call me a landlubber, is that not another pyramid of coconuts and mangos up ahead by our shelter!"

Porky replied with excitement in his voice, "Well, at least we know it's not Mr. Shelton!" And off Porky ran to take delight in their new provisions.

Chapter XIV

War Drums

"Well would you look at that!" proclaimed Pastor Platypus.

"Not even a single foot print," added Porky.

"And it was just what we needed, at precisely the right time," celebrated Pastor Platypus.

"Praise God! There has to be fifteen coconuts here! This would have taken us hours to collect!" calculated Porky.

"Actually Porky, being that this coconut stack is a perfect pyramid and having a base with three coconuts per side, mathematically that would give us fourteen coconuts. You know, we really should focus on your arithmetic skills in all of our spare time here."

Dismissing Pastor Platypus' remarks as jest, Porky walked around their encampment to look for further evidence of their provider.

Pastor Platypus figured, "Whatever kind soul has been doing this must be keeping a close eye on us, knowing when we leave and where we are all the time, or be it the very hand of God which might explain why there are no foot prints. Either way, we have been given what we need plus a little bit more!"

Porky shouted from the other side of the beach hut, "A little more is right! There is a pyramid of mangos on this side too - fourteen to be exact!" Porky chuckled to himself, humored by his own comment.

"Very funny Porky, I see your geometry is improving already!"

The two spent some time moving the supplies inside their encampment in preparation for nightfall.

That evening Porky had a hard time falling asleep. Every sound he heard seemed amplified one hundred fold. It made Porky's mind wander to all sorts of images of a helpful yet mysterious all-seeing something or somebody that was lurking around watching their every move!

Helpful as it was, it still gave Porky an eerie feeling that they were being watched all the time. Porky was in and out of sleep smothered by the sounds of a chorus of nocturnal insects and frogs. The platypus called across the hut in a strong whisper, "Porky, are you asleep?!"

Porky's mind was awake, but he still struggled to open his heavy eyelids. Pastor Platypus could see Porky tossing and turning on his bed of palm leaves. In a yelling whisper, the platypus tried to get Porky's attention, "Porky! Are you asleep or aren't you!?"

Porky replied in a fatigued and irritated tone of voice, "No, not really. I can't sleep well with the constant pounding of those war drums!"

Porky nestled himself under a palm leaf trying to bury his head to cover his ears. He appeared to have immediately fallen back asleep.

"Porky, did you say that *war drums* were keeping you up!?"

Porky didn't reply, so Pastor Platypus lay back down and stared at the moon light beaming through the loosely thatched roof of their shelter. He strained to sort out the sounds around him trying to listen through the ocean waves and chorus of insects. Then he heard it! It seemed he could feel it more than he could hear it. It was a faint, 'BOOM – boom – boom – boom – BOOM – boom – boom - boom'.

Pastor Platypus' stomach churned in fear realizing what it could be. "Natives!" he whispered aloud to himself. Just as Pastor Platypus was about to sit up, Porky shot up from under his bed of leaves. His eyes were open wide finally realizing in his mind what he was hearing.

"Please tell me I'm just dreaming," Porky pleaded.

"I'm afraid I hear it too Porky lest we are having the same dream," reasoned the platypus with great seriousness in his voice.

In the next moment, the drumming stopped.

Porky was bothered by the silence. Fear crept slowly into his heart as his imagination started to consider the worst.

Pastor Platypus was clearly focusing on an action plan, "There are reasons both good and bad why the drumming has ceased."

Before he could explain himself, the drums started up again with even more intensity. They were still far off in the distance, but the drumming was slightly louder and faster. Starting in a new more intense rhythm, 'BOOM boom-boom BOOM boom-boom BOOM...' and on it went.

Calming his fears with a bit of reason Pastor Platypus noted, "Porky, if you listen closely to the 'booms' it does give me the impression that there is only one drum."

122

They listened a bit more together at the doorway now. Porky agreed, "Yes, I think you are right Pastor…one drum for sure."

Pastor Platypus went back in and opened the admiral's trunk digging around a bit in the supplies. A great clamor was produced as the platypus searched out the trunk's contents. A bit worried about the pastor's plans, Porky reluctantly asked, "What do you have in mind? You're not thinking of going out there are you?!"

Pastor Platypus popped his head out of the trunk, "Well, Porky, it just doesn't make any sense." He disappeared again into the trunk.

Porky tried to clarify the Pastor's thought process, "*What* doesn't make any sense?"

Pastor Platypus aptly replied, "If it was a native people bent on war, tradition has it that there would be *many* people playing on a great number of drums." Pastor Platypus popped up from the trunk handing Porky a few things, "Not only that, but the natives of these parts war only during the day, so this is clearly ceremonial drumming."

Porky asked, "*Ceremonial?*"

The platypus continued, "Precisely! Ceremonial. They quite possibly are recognizing a festival, moon phase, or even a successful hunt. Often times these traditions are for storytelling to pass down the history of their people."

Porky interrupted, "Yes, Pastor, but *one* drum?"

"It makes sense doesn't it?" asked the Platypus.

"What makes sense?" asked Porky.

123

"Don't you see my boy!" Straining and drawing out his words a bit more to get his conclusion across Pastor Platypus continued, "We would have clearly noticed an entire group of people if there was one on the island, but *one* person would be able to do such a thing as to sneak upon our dwelling and leave us exactly what we need with no trace left behind. This person is one who obviously knows the island quite well to have achieved observing us without us observing him…. or her."

The platypus filled the pockets of his own exploring vest and handed Porky a fully supplied satchel, "It makes sense that this inhabitant would have their own dwelling place, and that this drumming will lead us right to it! We shall take advantage of the moon light and sneak up upon the drumming to see if we have in our midst a friend or a foe."

Porky replied in slight apprehension and fear, "I certainly hope we find a friend, but must we go at night? Can't we wait until day light?"

Pastor Platypus straightened up and with a commanding voice answered back, "My dear boy, at this time let us recall the words of our passionate Minister George Whitefield who drew crowds of hundreds of unchurched in the parks and squares of both England and the American Colonies alike. He said once in my hearing, 'We are immortal until our work on earth is done!'"

"Is that supposed to make me feel better?" asked Porky.

"Quite simply, yes it is! It is meant to bring to your heart and mind a degree of peace which will allow you to proceed into the unknown with confidence!" Pastor Platypus looked at Porky with encouragement in his eyes, "Minister Whitefield means to express that we shall remain under the Lord's protection until we have completed that which we were created to do in this life!"

Porky just stared at the ground trying to bolster his spirit.

"Porky, does it not say in the second book of Timothy, 'For God hath not given us a spirit of fear, but of power, and of love, and of a sound mind!' We are sneaky creatures, and we shall use what God has given us to our advantage. I welcome you to adventure! Now let's get going!" And with that they set out by the light of the moon honing in upon the sounds of the drumming.

Porky felt encouraged and comforted by the platypus' wisdom and bravery. They moved swiftly and stealthily across the forest floor as their nocturnal instincts took over. The two stopped intermittently to listen for the drums and kept on proceeding in their general direction.

The platypus stopped and reported in a faint whisper, "I believe we are a ship's length away. Let us go out and around a bit on this ridge to our left and see if we can approach the drumming from a position of greater height. This will give us the advantage."

They scurried along the ridge circling around until they were facing the drumming in a downhill direction. They stopped at a large stone and concealed themselves at its base.

"If anything should happen to go wrong, we shall meet back here at this rock," relayed the platypus.

Porky nodded in understanding.

Pastor Platypus continued, "If for some reason we are pursued by a hostile people, we make a mad dash back to the beach and take our trunk back out to sea. Got it!?"

Porky confirmed, "Got it."

The platypus ordered, "Before we advance, climb up this tree and tell me if you see anything."

Porky agreed, "Alright. *That* I can do."

Just as Porky took off the satchel, the drumming gave way to silence, and Porky could hear his own heart pounding in his chest! Before they could react, the drumming started up again in yet a different beat.

"Alright, up you go, quickly and quietly now!" ordered Pastor Platypus.

And with that Porky gave a nod and up he went disappearing from the pastor's sight. He was completely quiet and undetectable, and as a result the pastor himself felt more alone and vulnerable. Porky seemed to be gone forever. Pastor Platypus was looking over his shoulder when suddenly an out-of-breath voice spoke just behind his head, "We're definitely close."

The platypus jumped, "Good heavens, you scared me half to death! I didn't even hear you come down!" "Well, you told me to be quiet," retorted Porky.

"Well, what did you see my boy?" asked the platypus.

"The flicker of a flame. It was approximately a musket shot away from our current position. The smell of smoke was strong too. I couldn't see anybody through the leaves and branches," reported Porky.

The pastor asked, "Could you hear any voices, chanting, or even singing?"

"No Sir, nothing of the sort," confirmed Porky.

"Alright, let's move forward now," ordered Pastor Platypus grabbing his telescopic looking glass. They moved down the hill with the speed of a sloth carefully considering each step. They soon came to a bit of a clearing in the underbrush and a large fire came into view. Pastor Platypus lay down and extended his looking glass resting the end on a root for stabilization. His eyes widened at the sight. He looked back to Porky handing him the telescope, "You are not going to believe this!"

Chapter XV

A Captain of a Different Feather

Porky grabbed the looking scope, "Lord have mercy, would you take a look at that!" A bit of a grin started to creep onto Porky's fuzzy face, "It's a dancing bird! He's quite colorful and large as far as birds go!" Looking a bit more closely with the telescope Porky noted, "He is wearing what appears to be a captain's hat of sorts!"

Pastor Platypus took his turn at the looking glass, "That my boy is a macaw, one of the grandest and most magnificent of all the tropical birds ever created by the hand of God! Just look at those colors! An impossibly perfect assembly of red, yellow, and blue! And he appears to be doing a native dance of sorts."

Porky chimed in with a more relaxed whisper, "If you ask me, the dance looks quite odd. What a silly creature, to have such a moment all to himself."

Pastor Platypus adjusted the telescope a bit to take a closer look at the area around the macaw who was dancing wildly around a large drum. "Ah ha!" exclaimed the platypus.

Porky asked, "Ah ha what!?"

Pastor Platypus explained with great satisfaction, "We've found our helper. Look just past the Macaw at the large tree behind him. Pyramids of fruit everywhere! Clearly this is how he stores his food!"

Porky also concluded, "He certainly is the friend that has been bringing us much blessing! He doesn't look like much to be afraid of."

"Not at all," replied Pastor Platypus with great cheer, "In fact this macaw is precisely what and who we have been looking for!"

"How so?" asked Porky taking back the looking glass to view the pyramids of fruit and the creature's dwelling.

"You see," explained Pastor Platypus adjusting his bifocals, "the macaw's shelter is quite advanced in its establishment. It appears that he has collected supplies from ship wrecks. His entire shelter is made from washed up pieces and parts of ships. Just look at all the random rigging, barrels, oil lanterns, books, trunks, and for heaven sake that captain's hat! This macaw has been here for some time. Certainly he knows the island, and without a doubt the location of any harbors which are frequented by the British Navy. Come now, we must get his attention carefully, birds scare easily you know."

And with that, the platypus scurried down the hill towards the macaw's encampment. Porky hesitated and felt more comfortable just watching a bit through the looking glass. In no time at all Porky suddenly saw Pastor Platypus sneaking up to macaw as he was dancing around the drum.

Porky said to himself out loud in absolute astonishment, "My goodness, the pastor is dancing around the drum with the macaw, and the macaw thinks nothing of it!"

Clearly there was no threat. In fact, Porky thought it looked quite fun, so he scurried down to join the two. Porky set his satchel at the edge of the encampment and joined in the tribal dancing behind Pastor Platypus and the Macaw.

Porky did exceptionally well in his dancing having watched on many occasions the ceremonies of the natives around Moose Island. They were all dancing quite close to one another in circles around the large drum. Pastor Platypus had a mallet in his hand and was also contributing to the drumming with the macaw who seemed completely indifferent to his new friends joining him.

Pastor Platypus handed Porky yet another mallet, and Porky joined in the drumming too! All three were drumming together in a perfectly tremendous rhythm, 'BOOM boom boom boom BOOM boom boom boom...'

The macaw, every so often, would shake his wings up in the air then strike the drum sharply with some thunderous off-beats as the platypus and Porky continued in the baseline rhythm!

Suddenly the macaw jumped up atop the drum beating out a finish to the dancing with an intense triplet. With the final kicker beat which he slammed down, he threw his wings up in the air, tossing the drumming stick blindly into the air behind him. The macaw froze perfectly still atop the drum with outstretched wings and eyes closed. Porky and Pastor Platypus also froze not knowing at all what to expect next. All that could be heard was the crackling of the campfire wood and the stick which the macaw threw finally hitting the ground and bouncing a few times before coming to rest somewhere in the dark shadows behind them.

Then his head snapped to look at Pastor Platypus. An odd second or two passed in which the silence of no drumming actually seemed quite profound. Then the macaw let out a sudden and ear piercing squawk, "Welcome! Captain Marty the macaw at your service!"

And with that Marty removed his stately hat and gave Porky and Pastor Platypus a swooping bow. He stayed bowed long enough for Pastor Platypus to realize he was waiting to be invited back up.

"You may rise Captain Marty", ordered Pastor Platypus feeling a bit awkward at the honor the macaw had given them. Marty rose and placed his oversized captain's hat back on his red and white feathery head.

Pastor Platypus continued, "I am not accustomed to having a captain bow to me, but it is a most delightful pleasure to make your acquaintance. My name is Peter, Pastor Peter Platypus from Portsmouth England, well I was born at sea in the South Pacific, but on an English ship. I was adopted you see, but that was a long time ago."

Porky then introduced himself, "And I am Porky the Porcupine of Moose Island in the North American territories. I am under the mentorship of Pastor Platypus."

The platypus continued with a smile, "Precisely. I do hope you have not taken offence to our barging in on your……well, on your celebration."

"SQUAWK, No problemo! I am thrilled to have guests! I have been alone here for many moons. Visitors, SQUAWK, It's great to have visitors! Come on now, come on, we mustn't keep our tea waiting. Will you stay for mid-night tea or will you not!?" asked Marty quite thrilled.

131

"We will stay of course! We would love some tea!" answered the platypus.

"Yes, tea would be great," agreed Porky.

Marty replied, "Excellent, the water just came to a boil! Come along now, follow me, SQUAWK, follow me!" Captain Marty grabbed a small pot filled with water by the fire. Using a cloth to grip the handle, he took flight up to his lofty tree house. A light flickered dimly through the windows, enough to barely illuminate the branches and leaves around the tree home.

Pastor Platypus and Porky followed. They arrived at the base of the tree and circled it a couple of times before they realized there was no obvious way up. Recognizing that their new found friend seemed to believe that he was a captain, Pastor Platypus shouted up with a stern English accent, "Ahoy there, permission to come aboard for a spot of tea!?"

"SQUAWK! Permission granted, permission granted!" responded Captain Marty, and with that Marty the macaw pushed down, with his large beak, a rope ladder which Pastor Platypus and Porky scampered up with ease.

"Have a seat gentleman. Have a seat!" Marty pointed at two half broken chairs which were obviously from an old ship. They sat down feeling quite worn out from the excitement and anticipation which the night provided. Pastor Platypus looked in slight astonishment at the place settings for tea which had already been set around the table to serve exactly three. Pastor Platypus whispered to Porky with growing caution, "It's almost as if he had been expecting us ahead of time."

Marty turned around briskly after grabbing with his beak an emptied coconut which had been filled with coarse sugar. "What was that?!" he asked.

"Yes," answered Pastor Platypus trying to hide his whispering conversation, "Yes, we think a bit of sugar will be just the thing we need. Thank you kindly Captain Marty."

The macaw's tree house resembled that of a captain's quarters and was filled with many great artifacts from what appeared to be English, French, and Spanish ships. A tattered pirate flag in the corner caught the interest of Pastor Platypus the most. He had encountered pirates before. Men at their very worst they are; men willing to do any sort of evil to gain temporary treasures. He knew that pirates answered neither to king nor to God. They obeyed only their own impulsive desires.

Marty sat on a perch adjacent to the table and poured the tea in a well-coordinated movement with his head while holding the tea pot with his beak. "Thank you good sir," said Pastor Platypus.

"Yes, thank you, the tea smells wonderful," complimented Porky.

"Perhaps my curiosity is getting the best of my manners, but would you mind sharing how it is that you came to acquire such things to build this fine dwelling?" asked the platypus.

"Not a problem at all good sir, not a problem at all. It's actually quite a fantastic story," answered Captain Marty. He took a careful sip of tea and savored the flavor. Marty answered carefully, "I found these things."

133

Pastor Platypus and Porky looked out of the corners of their eyes at each other. The moment was quite strange as they expected more of an interesting story.

Pastor Platypus spoke up in a friendly tone of voice to bring a little clarity to the answer, "Captain Marty, as I'm sure you recognize, your dwelling is comprised of some fine artifacts from sailing ships from many different countries and from many different decades past. If you don't mind me pointing out, many of the books, lanterns, maps, and pictures seem to be untouched by the sea. Please forgive my forwardness, it just appears that there are a great many wonderful stories to be told here, but if you are not inclined to share we will not take offence. We are just pleased to be well received as your guests this fine evening."

Captain Marty continued without debate, "I was born on this grand island the Spaniards call Hispañola. Well, I think I was born here. It is the first thing I am able to remember anyway." Marty sipped up a bit more tea. Porky had a hard time focusing on Marty the macaw's story because he kept on noticing all sorts of new trinkets and artifacts in Marty's lantern-lit tree hut.

Marty continued, "My Father flew for a privateer captain, or 'pirate captain' as some say, chasing after Spanish gold. The treasure hunting got the best of him. He left for sea one night while I was asleep and never came home. Mother spoke often of the terrible things the Spanish and the privateers both did chasing after 'oro' from the mainland. She told me never to go to sea on a ship with those types of men.

"Wait, oro? What's oro?" asked Porky

Marty answered politely, "Gold. That would be Spanish word for gold. SQUAWK! I spent some time with the English at their colony on the north side of the island of Jamaica helping them in their efforts. They are gentlemen, not pirates. They enjoy finding riches, but they seem to mostly be driven by a deep obligation to obey their king with honor in all they do."

Porky spoke up with excitement, "I've heard about the usefulness of parrots at sea. How incredible to finally meet one!"

Marty loudly squawked in protest, "I am not a Parrot! I am a macaw! Two very different creatures you know!"

"My deepest apologies", replied Porky surprised a bit by his response.

Pastor Platypus chimed in, "Yes, please forgive my apprentice. He has never traveled outside his home island in the far north, and he is quite unfamiliar with tropical plants and creatures."

Marty continued, "Very well then. Now you know. Now you know! SQUAAAAWK!"

Porky gained the courage to ask another pressing question in his mind, "Captain Marty, will you serve under the flag of Spain again, or even that of England?

Captain Marty considerately replied while refreshing everyone's tea, "I am now under the service of no flag! Not again I say lest it is for a truly noble cause!" Captain Marty continued to explain, "They are cruel to their own kind. Just on the north side of this island, the Spanish take their own kind, that of a darker color, and treat them harshly to grow and collect sugar cane. They even subject the natives of this Island, the Taíno tribe, to very harsh labor. The humans of lighter color keep all of the profits and share not one bit with the ones who worked for it! My English master in Jamaica never did approve of this method.

"Jamaica. Is it far from here?" asked Porky.

"Too far for me to fly to," answered Captain Marty. "But I shall never offer service to any other Spanish captain! He threatened that if I did not help observe the working humans of dark skin from the air on the sugar plantations that he would pluck my feathers out one by one and make a hat out of em'! In reply, I left a large dropping on his hat as I flew away. I then flew among the darker humans who were working in the sun beaten fields, and I looked for those that were bound with rope. I cut the ropes with my beak and told them to run for their lives! The Spanish soldiers started shooting at me…" Marty paused to take a closer look at his quiet newfound friends, "forgive me, I am probably boring you with all the details."

Porky replied, "No, not at all! P-Please continue." Pastor Platypus nodded in agreement, "Do go on."

Marty fluffed up his neck feathers a bit as he took a deep breath to finish the story, "I retreated to this portion of the Island well south of all the plantations which grow sugar, coffee, cocoa, and tea. This portion is far less explored by the humans. Over the many years a great number of ships have wrecked and have been disabled from battle. The currents and tides have washed ashore many wonderful and useful items."

Pastor Platypus inquired further, "That was a brave and noble act you performed in releasing the slaves and refusing to tolerate their horrible treatment. I have traveled great distances in search of creatures such as you. Few are the number who dare to take action against such evils, and many are the number who simply talk and complain about the world's ills without responding in any way! It just amazes what people will do to accumulate wealth for themselves. Longing for more money is a thirst which can never be quenched."

Pastor Platypus took another careful look around the room, "It seems that a lot of these items have never seen a drop of sea water. These Navigational books here for example and those rolled up carts over in the corner. Might I ask how they...."

Marty interrupted with a loud 'SQUAWK' and leaned a bit more over the table turning his head sideways to look Pastor Platypus right in the face with one beady unblinking little eye. There was an uncomfortable pause before he spoke, "Not all of those ships have floundered by proper battle you see." His wings were keenly folded behind his back as he continued to look the Platypus right in the eye. Pastor Platypus noticed a more sinister tone in Marty's voice. The platypus expressed his presumption with slowly spoken words, "Are you suggesting that you have directly played a role in the floundering of some of these ships?"

Marty placed his captain's hat, which was trimmed with stained gold tassels, back on his head and he sat back with proud mischievous authority, "If cutting the rigging, disabling tiller ropes, ripping sail stays, sinking compasses, or making charts disappear credits me to disabling a ship, then yes, I may have had something to do with it!"

Marty flew to the corner of his tree hut and hung up his Captain's hat on a pole holding a pirate flag. Now Porky and Pastor Platypus became a bit uneasy, Marty's back was facing them for longer than they would have liked. Pastor Platypus set down his tea in apprehension. Marty suddenly unsheathed a long sword which was kept behind the jolly rodger. Porky looked for a quick exit and Pastor Platypus stood to his feet. It became quite apparent that a creative escape plan was quickly needed.

Chapter XVI

The Plan

Marty quickly turned around to face Porky and Pastor Platypus. Then he suddenly thrust his sword up into the air and used it to reach a book that was lying flat on the top of some shelving. The book fell to the ground. Marty tossed the sword aside like it was a piece of rubbish and brought the book to the table.

Noticing that Pastor Platypus and Porky were standing up without even finishing their tea, Marty asked in a squawky inquisitive voice, "I'm sorry Pastor, do you two need to be somewhere?"

Pastor Platypus came up with a quick answer, "Ahhh, no. We have nowhere to be. I was simply stretching. I got a little sore from trying to sneak up on you earlier……that's all. Do go on."

Marty continued, "No, I'm not like my father. I refuse to serve any master who senselessly takes the lives of others for the sake of treasure, or who works to sell the dark skinned people as property. I do not like how they cry and become sick from want of food."

Captain Marty slid the book across the table with his beak, "After reading this book, I discovered that I needed to do something to stop the terrible things that have been happening on this island!"

Pastor Platypus asked, "What book is that you have?"

Marty answered, "It says 'Santa Biblia' on the front. I found it on a Spanish ship which keeled over on a reef just north of here, and after reading the bit that I could understand, a sense of duty came to my heart to put a stop to the sufferings I have seen."

And with that Marty fluffed out his feathers, shook them out a bit and continued, "I tell you at this moment my friends." Marty was raising his voice a bit more now, "I have no Idea how some of those commanders continue to do what they do after having read this book!"

Pastor Platypus replied, "Agreed! Did you say 'Santa Biblia'?! That would be the Holy Bible! It speaks of how we all came to be, how we ought to use the lives given to us, and how we have been loved and forgiven. My friend, are you able to read Spanish!?"

Marty allowed a bit of silence and broke it proudly "Si, por supuesto!" Marty hopped up onto the top of the table and started an intense Spanish dance which involved a generous amount of tail-feather shaking. He spun around over and over with one wing covering his face so just his eyes showed over the top. Marty's feet were doing what looked like a speedy tap dance which made the dishes on the table also dance. Ending with a grand 'OLE!', Marty stopped as suddenly as he began and calmly returned to his perch to sip on his tea like a dapper English gentleman!

Pastor Platypus was beginning to see that Marty was quite silly, but he continued with the point, "Impressive my friend! I see that you are sort of a cultural chameleon able to mimic well those around you which would be in keeping with how you have been created."

Pastor Platypus saw that their new feathered friend became easily distracted and tried to get back to the point, "My honorable friend, it is our calling to bring this great message found in your Santa Biblia to the peoples and creatures of this world! God's word saves us, guides us, and helps people find their purpose in life. It encourages the broken hearted, and it mends wounds of the mind and body!"

Porky chimed in, "Yes, that is why we are here with you. Well, sort of. We are on our way to find the hidden south continent! Things went a bit wrong, but glad I am they did, otherwise we could not have found ourselves in your company on this fine night. In fact, I have a feeling that this is all part of God's plan!"

With a flighty hop, Marty flew to the back of Porky's chair. With his tail feathers almost straight up in the air, head down and turned sideways a bit, Marty matched his beady little eye with Porky's and said with a crackly, slowly spoken, and deeply mysterious parrot-like voice, "Plan? What do you mean by plan?"

Porky was a bit stunned by Marty's proximity to immediately respond.

Pastor Platypus informed, "You see…"

Marty side stepped to the back of the platypus' chair, "Yeeees". Marty's eye was almost touching Pastor Platypus' eye.

Adjusting to Marty's proximity, the platypus went on, "You see, we have not been created by accident. We have been created with a purpose. We all have been given special gifts and abilities which God wants to use to do His work here on Earth, making things the way they ought to be among the peoples of all nations and tribes. God has a plan for Porky and me. It is most likely much more grand than we realize, but for now we feel that we have been called to the people and creatures of the Terra Australis Incognido, the lost southern continent, which at this moment we are not even sure exists. Our faith tells us that it does. As you can imagine, it is quite difficult at times to travel to a land that has never been found afore now."

"I see," Marty squawked, "and how does Captain Marty become part of this plan?"

"I'm quite certain that you already are a part of this plan," replied the platypus with a grin. "Captain Marty, I can tell you have many wonderful gifts from your Creator. How would you like to join us on our adventure and use those magnificent abilities to love and serve others for the King that is above all other nations and kings?!"

Marty apprehensively asked, "Does this King of Kings make people slaves to gain wealth, because if he does, I will serve no such king!"

"Not at all Captain Marty", reassured Pastor Platypus, "This King of Kings has his throne in heaven! The entire world exists because he created it! This King sent his son Jesus to earth to find the lost, to heal the sick, to love the lonely, to forgive us and set us all free! He guides us, he protects us, and he renews our strength daily! When our bodies die, we will dwell with this King of Kings forever and ever. In heaven, where his kingdom is, there is no more death, no more tears, no sickness, and no broken hearts!"

Marty outstretched his large wing and tucked it under his belly and gave a bow, "Captain Marty at your service. May this King of kings be also my King!"

"Excellent!" exclaimed Pastor Platypus.

Porky the porcupine said, "This will be terribly exciting, and before I forget, we also want to thank you for the food you…"

Porky suddenly stopped speaking as Captain Marty flew to the window to look out at something that caught his eye. Pastor Platypus and Porky went to the window as well to look over Marty's wing. Marty was turning his head one way and then the other to allow each eye to get a clear look at whatever was outside. Captain Marty was moving his head up and down to catch the depth and distance. "The stars are breathtaking tonight," pronounced Peter Platypus.

"Yes, and look at those stars on the horizon, how they move!" noticed Porky.

Pastor Platypus adjusted his glasses, "Those aren't stars. Those are lights moving across the sea!"

Marty squawked quietly, "A ship bell, I thought I heard a…" Marty was sharply interrupted by the sight of three quick flashes of light, then BOOM…… BOOM, BOOM!" The crack of the cannon blasts echoed through the forest.

Chapter XVII

Thunder on a Starry Night

"Cannons! They seem to be firing at our encampment down at the beachfront!" noticed Porky with great distress.

Pastor Platypus ordered, "Marty, fly down there quick and see what is happening!"

"Yes Sir," Captain Marty replied, "and while I scout it out, gather what you think seems essential onto the table! We may soon have to abandon ship here!" After two powerful flaps of his wings Marty was in a rapid and silent dive down the hillside skimming over the tree tops into the darkness.

Porky turned to Pastor Platypus and remarked with a sinking feeling of fear in his stomach, "You don't suppose the Spanish are after the trunk we drifted off with do you?"

The platypus replied, "Oh I don't see why not, we only have but a few bars of gold, their navigational instruments, maps, charts, and a secret locked chest."

"Great, just great! We better get moving," suggested Porky with an overtone of uncertainty in his voice.

Both Pastor Platypus and Porky were frantically arranging supplies on the table when they were startled by a loud "SQUAWK!"

"Good heavens you scared us!" retorted Pastor Platypus.

Marty fearfully blasted, "San Carlos! San Carlos! SQUAWK!"

Porky tried to clarify, "San Carlos what?!"

Landing on the back of a chair Marty informed his friends as he caught his breath, "It's the Spanish man of war San Carlos! I saw it being built at La Habana harbor in Cuba years ago! I perched on the yard arm of the mizzen mast and overheard both Captain Don Pablo Cádiz and Admiral Luis de Córdoba."

Pastor Platypus interrupted, "Córdoba! You saw Admiral Córdoba! I'm quite certain we used his personal trunk to escape that very ship which we thought was sinking at the time! They must have made quick to repair her!"

Porky interjected, "Why are they firing? How could they possibly see the chest and know where our encampment is?"

Marty continued, "They are not firing at your encampment. They are blasting warning shots at a señorita, a lady in a skiff rowing frantically towards shore!"

"A Lady!?" Pastor Platypus exclaimed.

"Sí!" Marty the Macaw squawked, "I couldn't understand all the frantic Spanish above the cannon blasts, but I get the impression that she is trying to escape because they are loading an assembly of armed sailors into another skiff to go after her! They were being lowered into the water when I flew back here!"

Porky insisted with brave resolve, "We have got to help whoever that girl is! One lady against an entire first rate Spanish ship of the line! Come on! Let us run down to the beach at once before those Spanish pirates get to her!"

Marty shouted, "Espere! Wait! Take the supply line down to the beach! Quick now jump in the sack!" Marty pulled open a burlap sack with his beak. The sack was attached to a rope which ran out the window. The rope spun around a secure pulley fixed just above the window. Marty explained, "This line leads right to the beachfront where you have your encampment. It is how I brought all the fruit down to you! The lady will be close by. Porky, you go first. We will send down a supply sack, then I will load and send Pastor Platypus! I shall follow in the sky!"

Pastor Platypus practically pushed Porky into the sack, "Now go! And stand by at the bottom to catch and detach the supply sack!" Porky was going to ask how to stop once he reached the bottom, but right at that moment Captain Marty pushed him out the window.

The whir of the pulley soon turned into a high pitched zinging which reverberated down the rope. Porky could hear himself flying past tree branches and leaves. He was feeling completely out of control. Back up at the tree house Pastor Platypus asked Marty as they were filling up a sack full of supplies, "So, how *do* you stop?"

Marty replied after pausing for a few more cannon echoes to pass, "Not sure Pastor, Not sure. But I do know that when I send fruit down it does eventually stop. I've just never seen how." And with that, Marty let go of the supply sack and down it zinged!

Before Porky could even think about how his trip down to the beach would end, he heard the pulley loudly hit something. Porky forcefully ripped through the bottom of the sack as it came to a sudden stop and was violently thrown into the sand of the beach below him!

As Porky cleared his senses from the impact, he could hear another zinging getting louder and louder. By the time he realized what it was, the supply sack also slammed against the end of the line, had torn off of the pulley, and was tumbling toward Porky. Porky curled up in a ball just as the sack came to rest quite forcefully on top of him. He was quite stunned. The next thing Porky perceived was Pastor Platypus standing above him.

"Good heavens, there you are! I thought I heard the supply satchel moaning. Are you alright?! Come along now! Quickly!" instructed Pastor Platypus. As Porky, Pastor Platypus and Marty gathered together in a covered place where the trees meet the beach, they could see the girl in the skiff rowing hard to ram the bow of the boat into the sand. Three more shots of cannon exploded all around her. Water and sand was flying everywhere and glistened in the moon light.

The girl jumped out of the boat and started running down the beach towards the tree line. She cut quickly into the palms out of sight and was making a terrible noise clambering through the thick vegetation as she ran in the dark.

Another dinghy full of about fifteen Spanish marines were rowing hard towards shore and were all armed with muskets. The marines were ordered to amass quickly in two lines once they reached the beach. The first line knelt down blindly taking aim into the darkness toward the trees and bushes.

The commanding officer raised and sharply dropped his arm, and all the muskets fired in the general direction of the girl's escape. Porky could hear the musket balls ripping through the leaves. The girl let out a short scream and went silent.

Chapter XVIII

Royal Company

The unit of Spanish marines was about ten leagues down the shore to the South. The commanding officer gave the order to cease fire.

Pastor Platypus shouted in a whisper, "Come on, let's move!" Both Porky and Marty seemed to know what he meant. They rushed down the tree line and cut in towards the girl's location. They came upon her moaning on the ground holding her arm. The girl, disguised as a Spanish deck hand, could feel someone binding up her arm. She didn't have the strength to worry about who it was or why they were helping, but the next thing she heard was a voice say, "We are of service to you. Come with us and we will keep you safe. Now get up! We must go now!"

The girl was having trouble finding the strength to stand, that is until she heard the voices of the Spanish marines closing in on their position. Realizing this was her last chance, she struggled to her feet. A macaw barely lit by the moon light gave a quick and sharp command, "Follow me Señorita! Stay close!"

They all quickly moved inland away from and above the beach up a rocky incline. Marty hopped from branch to branch leading the girl through the terrain. They zig zagged up a steep hillside which hosted more cacti than was convenient.

Looking back over her shoulder the girl could see the lanterns of the Spaniards moving in various directions through the forest below. Marty lead them up to the summit of the small rocky cliff and made his way over to a triangular opening at the base of two large rocks. Landing on the ground next to the entrance, Marty shouted in a raspy whisper, "In here, rápido! Crawl in!"

Marty went in first, then the girl. Porky and Pastor Platypus followed. Marty instructed, "A bit further now, just a little more!"

After crawling for about a minute or two, the girl, much to her relief, felt the tight crawlspace in the rocks open up. The sounds of the gravel as she shuffled along the rocky floor began to echo more cavernously. She stopped to lean up against a wall to catch her breath. For the first time the girl, disguised as a Spanish sailor, felt safe. Usually the dark was something to fear, but now it was apparent that the dark was doing the protecting.

She heard the sound of a match strike and the cave lit up as Porky lit the top of a small torch made of palm tree bark scruff which Pastor Platypus had assembled in haste. The girl let out a small scream and quickly covered her mouth to control the sound. Her eyes remained wide open, startled and staring at her three rescuers in astonishment.

Porky handed the lit torch to Pastor Platypus. Pointing his wing towards the entrance, Marty squawked to Porky, "Cover the opening!"

Porky scurried over and made a quick pile of medium sized rocks up to the top of the narrow entrance. Scooping up wads of earthen sand, Porky went back and forth throwing and packing the rocky soil into the cracks between the bigger rocks. Marty wobbled over to the blockaded entrance. His long red tail dragged in the sandy floor behind him leaving a winding trail. Captain Marty held his wing outstretched in front of Porky's cave blockade, and felt no breeze moving his feathers.

Porky called to Pastor Platypus, "The entrance is secure! No wind is coming in and…"

Marty finished Porky's sentence with a smile of relief, "And no light will be getting out!"

A bit of silence passed as they all relaxed observing their cave of refuge illuminated by the flickering torch light. Comforted by her new found fortress, the girl spoke up in a delicate but intelligent voice, "Muchas gracias mis queridos amigos." *[Thank you very much my dear friends.]*

Marty, Porky, and Pastor Platypus all looked at each other in slight bewilderment.

The girl continued, "I wasn't expecting - well, I wasn't expecting creatures to come to my aid, but I am thankful to God that you have!"

Rubbing her wounded arm, the girl with a gentle Spanish accent tenderly introduced herself forcing a smile through the pain, "My name is Clementine. Might I have the pleasure of knowing who my rescuers are?"

Marty shuffled up first and stood proudly before Clementine, who had now discarded her disguise to reveal a beautiful yet worn dress and fine long flowing hair. She was a young lady with smooth brown skin weathered no more than twenty kind years which contrasted the tattered appearance of her clothing.

Marty folded his large wing across his chest and took a grand bow, "I am Captain Marty the macaw at your service señorita Clementine."

Porky stepped forward, "And I, ma'am, am Porky the porcupine from Moose Island in the Great Waters of the American colonies, at your service."

The platypus came along side of Porky in the flickering cave light and introduced himself in a gently spoken thick British accent, "I, Pastor Peter Platypus, am pleased to make your acquaintance. Are you hurt badly Ms. Clementine?"

"I believe I will recover in due time," said Clementine with a smile. "My heart is filled with much joy and thankfulness for such willing and brave servants to answer my prayers by coming to my aid! What are you all doing here?"

"We are on a bit of a journey," continued Pastor Platypus, "to find the lost southern continent, Terra Australis Incognito, and to bring the hope of God's love to the people of that land. Things went a bit wrong according to our expectations, but we are discovering that this journey is just as much about the works done along the way as it is about finding the lost southern continent. Does that make sense?"

"I understand perfectly," reassured Clementine with a warm smile. "You are servants of the King of Kings sent on a great and honorable mission it sounds like. Only by His provision and your courage could we have found such timely refuge. My ears tell me that you are English! Your accent tells me so."

"Yes, forgive me Señorita Clementine. Indeed, I was adopted and raised by officers of the British Royal Navy, born in the South Pacific, educated in Portsmouth, but mostly I grew up on

English vessels at sea. I do not know where my ancestors are, but I do know that some great and glorious day in the future we shall all be together again."

Porky was caring for Clementine's wound as they talked a bit more. Interrupting Pastor Platypus, Porky got Marty's attention, "Fetch me some water would you?"

Leaning over towards the Pastor, Porky spoke as a surgeon in an operating room, "Pluck one of my thinner quills if you please." Porky winced a bit as it was pulled out. He took the quill and dashed it through the flame of the torch a couple of times.

Porky looked at Clementine, "Sorry to interrupt." He poured the water over her wound. Tying a thread from the supply satchel around a notch in his quill, Porky placed a couple of stitches in Clementine's arm. "I apologize for any discomfort," sympathized Porky.

"I know this must be done. Gracias, my little friend," reassured Clementine. She grimaced occasionally during the procedure.

"I must leave this open a bit to drain to allow the bad humors to come out," informed Porky. "I will wrap your arm tightly, but if it does not stop bleeding we may have to apply a little fire from the torch for just a quick moment. The musket ball seemed to get a hold of only muscle, but thank God no bone!"

Pastor Platypus adjusted his glasses and looked at the ground rubbing his bill in thought, "Clementine. Clementine...Why does that sound familiar?"

Porky pointed at Pastor Platypus having a sudden realization, "The box! The small locked chest inside the Admiral's trunk, it had 'Clementine' written on the bottom!"

The girl became intensely serious, "My chest! You know of my security chest! How can this be?!"

Porky explained, "Well you see Miss, we were captured by the San Carlos, and we escaped during a fierce storm inside the Admiral's trunk which we pushed overboard. Just before the storm hit, Captain Don Pablo was attempting to take our merchant vessel as a prize. When our Captain, Esek Hopkins fought back, we were captured and nearly sent to the bottom."

Pastor Platypus continued, "Yes, you see the Admiral's chest was in Captain Don Pablo's quarters and a small locked box with 'Clementine' written on the bottom was inside it along with all of our other supplies." The girl took a long stare into the distance as she put all the pieces of the puzzle together in her mind.

"I guess I should tell you a bit more about who I really am," continued the girl. She hesitated a bit looking at the ground and back up again, "I am Princess Clementine of the Canary Islands."

Porky's eyes widened in astonishment. Marty didn't seem to be paying any attention as he was back in the cave a bit further. For some reason he was sifting through the bag of supplies with his beak, and he got his head somewhat stuck within the bag in the process of trying to take hold of something. He was pushing it across the cave floor frantically with his tail feather straight up in the air and his head in the bag. Marty was shaking it intermittently trying to release its hold which made quite a ruckus.

Pastor Platypus approached her with the courage that his maturity afforded him and gave a deep bow and simply said, "Your Majesty."

Porky turned around in disgust at Marty's behavior, "Hey Captain Feather Butt! Front and center! We are in the company of Royalty!"

"Royalty!? What do you mean by royalty?!" asked Marty with a muffled voice from having his head stuffed in the supply satchel.

Porky responded impatiently, "Clementine! She's a Princess!"

Marty quickly scurried over and gave a stately bow. With the sack still over his head, he proudly introduced himself, "Captain Marty at your service your Majesty!"

Embarrassment swept over Porky, "Take that thing off of your head at once!"

"Either it's stuck on me or I'm stuck in it!" replied Marty.

Porky pulled Marty away from the princess, "Please excuse us for a moment your majesty." Porky and Marty scuffled a bit in the background.

Pastor Platypus interjected, "Forgive my friends, they are…"

The Princess gently smiled and finished Pastor Platypus' sentence, "Wonderful. They are wonderful."

"Wonderful wasn't quite the word I was looking for," replied Pastor Platypus, "If you don't mind me asking, how did you end up aboard the Spanish Man of War?"

"I was captured by Admiral Luis de Córdoba who is currently in command of the Santisima Trinidad, Spain's massive flagship. A few days ago his ship intercepted another Spanish vessel, the San Carlos, which was badly damaged in a storm. The Admiral's crew has been helping Captain Don Pablo recover his ship. I was also transferred to the San Carlos as not to be left out of reach of the Admiral who has been looking frantically for his trunk.

Captain Don Pablo reported seeing the admiral's trunk floating away in the storm that nearly sank the San Carlos a few days ago, as you already know. Admiral Córdoba will stop at nothing to get that trunk. Apparently the contents were enough to get the full attention of Spain's two most powerful ships."

The Princess continued, "Admiral Córdoba and Captain Don Pablo have been searching the Atlantic for me ever since I made my escape from Trafalgar before their attack. They finally caught up with our ship. We were no match for them. My father, the ling of the Canary Islands, has dispatches of the highest importance which are intended for King George of England. Because of the increased Spanish patrols off the coast of Spain, our direct route to England was cut off. So to avoid the Spanish patrols, we set a course for Kingston, the British port in the West Indies. We were hoping to find a Captain of a well-armed ship there who could provide for us safe passage to England. The fate of my home, the Canary Islands, lies within my security chest marked 'Clementine' which must have been in the admiral's trunk! I remember now. It all makes much more sense. After I was captured and brought aboard the Santisima

Trinidad, I saw the Admiral move his trunk to the faster ship, San Carlos, which would be able to more quickly get my dispatches to the Port of Habana. That is where the Spanish have their primary fort in the West Indies. But, it sounds like the storm and you fine creatures put a stop to all of that!"

Pastor Platypus tried to clarify, "What could possibly be in such a small chest that is of such great importance that Spain would send its best ship after it.... if you don't mind me asking."

The Princess hesitated, "I'm sorry, but I can't tell you."

Pastor Platypus bowing his head slightly continued, "Forgive me for being intrusive. If its contents are that important, God help us, we shall retrieve it for you, no questions asked."

Pastor Platypus continued, "Your security box is concealed within the admiral's trunk in our encampment which is in a cluster of bushes near the area of the beach where the Spanish marines landed. It won't be easy to get to undetected. They are sure to find our encampment by sunrise. We must retrieve it before the light of day breaks!"

Princess Clementine was touched to find such loyalty and service in such a lonely place. There was a twinkle of hope in the darkness. Clementine spoke up after taking a deep sigh, "Before he was taken by the Spaniards, my father told me that all the darkness of the night time sky could not overpower or overcome the smallest light of the stars. You, my friends, are those stars sent by God to come to my country's aid. Since you are willing to risk your lives for our cause, I will tell you the contents of the chest and everything that we are striving for this night."

Chapter XIX

One Hour to Rescue a Nation

The voices of Spanish sailors could be heard close to the entrance of the cave. Porky ran the torch around a rocky corner to hide the light the best he could. He was tempted to blow it out, but was afraid that the smell of smoke would give them away. The voices faded as quickly as they appeared. They all moved back deeper into the cave just to be safe.

After settling themselves comfortably in a secluded rocky nook, the princess, poised with leadership, gathered her newfound friends in close, "Alright, this is why we must do everything we can to get that chest."

Princess Clementine continued with great focus in the flickering light of the torch, "My father, the king of the Canary Islands, knew that the Spanish were coming to our island, and not for friendly reasons. They were going to influence my father, by force, to hand control of our peaceful Islands over to the crown of Spain."

The princess continued with more intensity, "The people of our islands live together in peaceful unity. All Spain wants is gold, control over the people's lives, and control of the oceans. They will also stop at nothing to secure all of the crops and resources of the West Indies. They are chopping down the forests around Habana as we speak to continue building up their war ships with no regard for the natives of the land."

"The people of the Canary Islands have decided upon independence from the oppressive throne of Spain. Within that chest down at your beach encampment is the only signed Declaration of Independence of the Canary Islands. My father signed it the night before he was captured and forcefully removed from the throne." The princess wiped away a tear from her eye, "I fear the Spanish have done the worst; That they have taken his life and plan to take over our islands. I am the only heir to the throne. I am to be queen."

The princess took a deep breath and maintained her focus, "Also within that chest are the plans to many Spanish ships of war built in the Habana Harbor, revealing both their strengths and their weaknesses. Perhaps most importantly, there is a document detailing the layout of their ship yard and a massive fort being built called La Cabaña.

We have no navy of our own so I am to get these documents to the English as soon as possible to ask for help defending our islands, and to assist England in removing the Spanish from their position of power in the West Indies.

My father had some spies working in the Habana ship yards who gave their lives collecting this information. Before I was snuck out of our islands on a merchant ship, he gave me much gold to help initially fund the effort. When Admiral Córdoba intercepted our vessel to take it as a prize, I offered him the gold to set us free. He agreed, but in the end took our gold, me, *and* my ship as a prize. The Admiral recognized me and made an extensive search of our ship and found the chest containing all of the secret documents. Once he had what he wanted, he sent our ship to the bottom of the sea. Tonight, I managed to escape in an unattended skiff which they had hanging over the side of the San Carlos for painting. I disguised myself as a Spanish sailor and pretended to paint. I eventually lowered the skiff into the water and rowed for my life. If it were not for you all, I would have failed in my efforts."

Porky chimed in with urgency, "We must come up with a plan to get that chest at once! The sun will be upon us in just a couple of hours!"

The Princess clarified, "And we need to deliver it to the English as soon as possible!"

Getting right to it Captain Marty recalled, "English ships. Yes, now that you mention it, a few days ago I saw the masts of two English ships in the next harbor southwest of here at la Boca de Yuma where the river enters the sea. SQUAWK!"

Porky gave Marty an odd stare, "That is fantastic! Let us hope they have not yet set sail. Next time let's not wait so long to remember such things."

Pastor Platypus walked up to the princess and put his hand on her uninjured shoulder, "You are not going to believe this, but we also have your gold hidden in a satchel in a hollowed out tree close to our encampment. Five bars to be exact!"

"All this news is just so wonderful!" The princess exclaimed as she gave Pastor Platypus a giant hug, "My hope is entirely renewed!"

Using a stick, Pastor Platypus began drawing a small map in the dirt on the cave floor, "Well, let us make a plan to get these treasures back in our possession!" Pastor Platypus continued pointing with his stick, "Now we are here. Our encampment with the admiral's trunk containing your dispatches are approximately here, and the cove with the English ships is over this tall ridge to the south. Our friend Marty here has a forest encampment straight west from the beach up the hill about a cannon shot from shore with an ascending and descending zip line on pulleys that leads to and from his tree house nearly to our beach encampment."

Porky pressed forth with an idea, "Suppose Marty flew into the tree tops above the beachfront to keep watch. Pastor, since you are a fantastic swimmer, perhaps you should make your way towards the encampment from the sea. I shall come in through the woods."

"Yes, excellent!" celebrated Pastor Platypus, "Once we secure the chest we will send it up to Marty's tree house by way of the pulley and zip line. Marty, you be our scout since you can move quickly. If the route is clear, bring the princess to your tree house, then fly to the beach front from there while we move into position."

Porky commented, "What if the Spanish have surrounded our encampment?"

Pastor Platypus replied, "Marty, you will have to do your best to distract them and draw the Spanish sailors away from our location."

"SQUAWK! I will do my best."

Pastor Platypus added, "I'm not sure if we should send the princess over to Marty's encampment. Clementine is exactly who the Spanish are looking for, they know she is here, and will most likely send search parties to scour the forest until Clementine is found. It's too risky. We should leave her here in the cave where we know she is safe."

"Right you are!" agreed Porky, "No matter the situation, we shall rendezvous back here once Clemente's documents and gold have been obtained?"

"Yes, exactly," confirmed Pastor Platypus with urgency building in his voice.

Marty added, "These caves lead right out to the other side of this mountain ridge. Lots of mining has been done here. SQUAAWK! Lots of mining. The harbor, where the English ships are, should be in clear view once we make it through this maze of tunnels. We can then follow the river down to the beach front."

"Perfect!" said Pastor Platypus, "We can send the chest and gold up the zip line in our supply sack. Then we will move the chest from Marty's encampment across the hillside back to the cave. We can spend the daylight hours of the coming day moving through the caves, and by night fall we will work on getting onboard the English ships. Let us pray that they are still at anchor!"

Porky turned to address the Princess, "Perhaps, Your Majesty, you should rest here. You look terribly exhausted."

The Princess reluctantly agreed, "I think you are right Porky. The Spanish questioned me day and night and have kept me in a small cell not fit for a rat! I will regain my strength here. I know that God will go with you. Be brave and courageous my friends. The Lord will give you strength and wisdom in this mission. The fate of many people is in your hands now. Be strong and very courageous!"

Chapter XX

Surrounded

Pastor Platypus assumed command and spoke to Marty so that the princess would not hear, "Marty, take the princess further back in the cave to an even safer place; Should the Spanish break in, I want her to be well hidden."

"Yes Sir!" Marty proudly saluted with his wing.

Pastor Platypus turned to Porky, "Alright then, let's move!"

Porky and Pastor Platypus carefully removed the rocks at the top of the cave entrance. Fresh warm night air blew briskly in through the hole. They made an opening just big enough for a critter to squeeze through. Porky the porcupine scurried through first, and waited at the opening for the platypus. The air was filled with the sounds of bugs chirping and the high pitched whooping of frogs. The sounds where overwhelming after being in the perfectly silent cave for some time. Both Porky and Pastor Platypus waited at the entrance of the cave calculating their next moves and keeping a silent look out for any Spanish Marines in the area.

"You do realize we could be killed in this effort and never accomplish that which God has called us to do!" added Porky as he mentally processed their odds of survival against the full force of the Spanish Navy.

Pastor Platypus looked at Porky with calm peace-filled eyes, "Have I ever taken the time to tell you about George Whitefield?

"No I don't believe you have," Porky recounted.

"He is a fantastic preacher of God's word. The Church of England never gave him an official pulpit to preach from, so he simply went out to where the people were to preach to them in the open air. He gathers crowds of thousands in the town squares, almost all of whom would have never stepped foot in a church. That short cross-eyed man has effectively brought hope, salvation, and purpose to the masses. Such a great man! Oh, how I envy him."

Porky paused for a second, "I'm sure he is a fantastic individual, but what does he have to do with our facing the entire crew of the San Carlos,...again!

"Ah yes, forgive me." Pastor Platypus tensioned his eye brows in refocusing thought, Mr. Whitefield once said, "We are immortal till our work is done!"

Porky looked off in the distance to process the phrase repeating it softly to himself in an attempt to bring forth comprehension. Then he looked back at Pastor Platypus as if desiring clarification.

"You see Porky, the Lord has set apart, for each of our lives, certain works or callings which have been prepared for us since the beginning of all things. God will see us through anything, until the work he has for us is brought about to completion. So until that time, we are immortal!"

Porky looked at Pastor Platypus taking a deep breath as he processed the interpretation.

Pastor Platypus finished, "Porky, with God all things are possible. Especially when those things are what he has called us to do! Look at how far we've come! Look at all that God has done to protect us thus far. Whatever work God starts in a person, he will bring about that work unto its completion."

Pastor Platypus reassured Porky, "You see, sometimes God will call you to one thing, or to a particular purpose, but lead you to many works along the way. We are clay in the potter's hands. It could be that a key purpose of our mission to find Australis is to do this very thing in the process thereof, and look at how important it is! If we get these documents, the maps, the Declaration of Independence, and the detailed plans of the Spanish ships from the Habana ship yard to the English, we could drastically change the future of the West Indies and liberate the Canary Islands. In fact, I find it quite an honor that such fates have been trusted to rest on our shoulders!"

Porky replied nervously, "That's what worries me!"

Marty emerged from the cave and shook the dust from his feathers and said with great eagerness and excitement in his voice, "Alright amigos, what's the plan!"

Pastor Platypus again laid out the operation at hand, "Marty, you take to the air and be our lookout. Open wide both wings atop a tree if the cost is clear to move in on our beachside encampment. Porky make your way around to the upper ridge and approach the encampment from the hillside. Take to the low branches of the trees if possible."

Pastor Platypus gestured with his hands more expressively, "Porky, you must imagine yourself to be a squirrel and move about as they do. This will give you a slight advantage over the troops on the ground."

Porky responded nervously, "Just great! Me, move through the trees like an agile squirrel!? That should be entertaining. I might as well prance through the forest shouting 'LONG LIVE THE KING'!"

"Aright, perhaps a squirrel wasn't the best analogy," snuffed Pastor Platypus growing impatient, "Do what you can to proceed as stealthy as possible. I'm just saying if you found a way to go along the canopy it might be best."

Marty was chuckling as he pointed at Porky, "You! A SQUIRREL! Yes, a new species has been discovered, the great and rare northern spiked behemoth squirrel! Ha Ha Ha!" Marty cackled uncontrollably in laughter rolling on the ground kicking his talons up into the air.

Porky doubled in size as he raised all of his quills in a show of protest, "Hush that beak of yours! And not only that, be quiet!"

Pastor Platypus buried his face into his hands and took a deep breath. "Gentlemen! Please!" The platypus grumbled from within his hands, "might I remind you that we have a mission of extreme importance to accomplish here!"

Straightening up a bit Pastor Platypus began to direct the situation, "I'll take to the sea. Once we get Clementine's chest up the zip line to Marty's tree house, we will gather some last minute supplies from Marty's encampment for our trip through the caves. We, most importantly, will need oil for his lantern so we can find our way. Then rendezvous at the cave entrance as soon as possible. Does everyone understand!?"

Working hard to subdue their laughter, "Yes, yes we understand", Porky and Marty replied.

"Attention!" commanded Pastor Platypus. Both Porky and Marty snapped to attention with a regrouping of focus. "Dawn is quickly approaching! Let's move out!" ordered Pastor Platypus.

Away they scurried into the darkness. Captain Marty immediately took to the air and swooped down the hillside towards the sea gliding silently over the tree tops which was a little trick he had learned from an owl when he was a young Macaw.
From all the mornings that Marty delivered fruit to his shipwrecked friends, he knew exactly where their beachside encampment was. Marty glided in silently just above the concealed beachside hut atop an overhanging tree. He immediately heard the voices of Spanish Marines conversing in haste. Moving in slow motion Marty carefully inched his way down a branch to gain a better view of the beach. Marty gasped and whispered to himself, "Well pluck out my tail feathers and call me a chicken! The Spanish Captain himself has set up his beachside command right in front of the Pastor's beach hut!"

The encampment Porky and Pastor Platypus built was well camouflaged in a cluster of bushes. It did not appear that the Spanish captain and his men had seen the encampment or the large trunk within, but he was sure that once the sun came up that they would see it very clearly!

Marty crawled back up the branch into the cover of the leaves to where he could see the ocean clearly. The sea was calm. The silhouette of the massive Spanish ship, San Carlos, could be seen clearly against the horizon. It twinkled in many parts with the dim glow of lanterns. There were two dinghies, one full of men rowing from the ship to the beach, and another heading back relatively empty.

Marty became quite anxious when he realized how many men the Spanish had brought onto the beachfront to search for Princess Clementine and their missing bounty. Marty could hear the voices of men as well as twigs and branches snapping all throughout the forest behind him. Even though Marty was a creature of the air, he began to get the feeling that he was surrounded. But he had the cover of night and the chorus of insects and frogs to mask his movements giving him the advantage.

Marty started to look out at the sea for signs of the platypus. He thought for a moment that he could see the silhouette of another ship far off in the distance. Marty decided to wait a few more minutes, and went back down to the low hanging branch to sneak another peak at the encampment.

The Spanish captain and his officers were close enough to spit on. They were giving orders to the marines as they came to shore, ensuring that their search was well executed. Out of the corner of Marty's wee little eye, he saw a brown blob scurry up from the sea and curl up on the sand next to a messy pile of neglected coconuts.

"Ah Ha!" Marty thought to himself, "The little coconut-looking lump is Pastor Platypus!" Hoping the Spanish officers would move or leave, Marty waited for what seemed like forever. No signs yet of Porky. Marty was sure he was well hidden somewhere nearby. Marty's heart began to pound in his chest as the sky started to lighten up in the east. Ever so gradually the eastern stars were retreating. He had to do something before it got any lighter and he had to do something quick!

Chapter XXI

A Narrow Escape

Concealed in his pile of beachside coconuts, Pastor Platypus was growing more and more anxious as dawn approached. He could see Marty in the tree looking down at the Spanish officers that were collectively scheming to find and capture the princess. They were so close to the encampment, Pastor Platypus thought that if it were daylight, the Admiral's trunk would certainly be in clear view. Worse yet, it looked as if Captain Don Pablo intended to remain there as a staging point for the search!

Captain Don Pablo shouted impatiently as he paced the sandy beach, "The San Carlos will remain anchored here until the Princess and my chest are recovered! Understand?!"

"Sí Capitan", they all answered in unity.

Captain Don Pablo motioned for his men to gather around a map he had opened, lit by the light of a lantern, "According to my calculations, the admiral's trunk should have drifted and landed here somewhere along this shoreline. After we re-capture la princesa, I want all available men to comb this beach until it is found! Our flagship Santisima Trinidad is on its way to help as we speak and should be at anchor by the end of the morning watch! I do not care if it takes three weeks! We will find that trunk and the princess! Now go!"

The Captain and the officers moved away from Porky and Pastor Platypus' hidden encampment for a moment. Pastor Platypus saw that his chance had come. He had what seemed like quite a bit of open beach to cross. He looked up at Marty. Marty spread his wings wide open giving the 'all clear'. The platypus left his coconut pile of concealment and began to creep slowly and steadily up the beach towards the bushes.

He was in! The Platypus went right to the admiral's trunk which was hidden in the cover of three bushes overgrown together. He opened the trunk and crawled in searching quickly and carefully for Clementine's smaller security chest.

He found it! It seemed heavier and more awkward to carry than he remembered. Pastor Platypus was looking frantically for the best way to carry it out through the branches without making too much noise. He set down the chest to dig a little into the sand in an attempt to crawl under a larger branch which would bring him out of bushes on the side of the tree line in order that he might be able to make an escape under the cover of the forest vegetation.

Just as he was about to start pulling the chest through, Captain Don Pablo and his officers came back towards the encampment and had Pastor Platypus surrounded! It would be impossible to escape with the chest into the forest unnoticed with all the Spanish officers so close! He could hear the officers debating rather intensely with the ruthless and proud Captain.

Pastor Platypus was trapped and surrounded. He was thinking of making a run for the sea to float the chest and swim it down the shoreline to safety. The contents could be damaged slightly by the salt water, but at least they would not be in the hands of the Spaniards.

Suddenly he heard the Spanish men shout in fright. Pastor Platypus could not believe his eyes! Marty had swooped down and landed on Captain Don Pablo's shoulder! Pastor Platypus could see the captain quickly cover up his surprise with an over inflated pride and casualness. Captain Don Pablo stood up a bit taller. "You see my amigos, even the parrots on this island recognize authority and greatness when they see it!" announced Captain Don Pablo.

Marty cringed at being called a 'parrot'. Captain Don Pablo continued overseeing his search and capture efforts as if having the macaw on his shoulder happened every time he set ashore on an island.

Pastor Platypus could see that Marty was playing dumb, pretending to be more wild than not. Marty let out a large dropping on the back of Captain Don Pablo's jacket as his first order of pretending to be wild. Pastor Platypus was relieved that the captain did not notice it drip all the way down the back of his jacket!

Marty waited patiently, and at the first mention of the princess by Captain Don Pablo, Marty loudly screeched "PRINCESSA, PRINCESSA!" Captain Don Pablo grabbed his ear in pain.

The other officers commented, "El loro speaks as if he has seen her!"

"Dónde está la princessa!?" they asked Marty.

Marty shrieked "Allí Allí!" He pointed down the beach with his wing.

"Vamos!" the Captain shouted. Marty flew just in front of the Captain. His officers ran following Marty down the beach to the north away from Pastor Platypus and the secret encampment.

172

"Brilliant!" celebrated Pastor Platypus with great relief, "What a fantastically brilliant macaw!" Pastor Platypus pushed Clementine's chest along the ground out the back side of the encampment and ran with it into the tree line.

It seemed as if not a soul was around. Pastor Platypus moved in the direction of where he thought the zip line terminal was. He was making more noise than he liked by moving quickly, but he knew Marty's distraction wouldn't last forever. Dawn was approaching, but still Pastor Platypus knew he was lost within the thick vegetation.

By the grace of God, he remembered back on Moose Island how Porky and his father would find each other in the woods. One would whistle the call of the North American Cardinal, a fantastically impressive masked little red bird. Before Pastor Platypus got himself more lost wandering through the thick intertwined vegetation, he whistled the song of the cardinal. To his astonishment he heard the call of the cardinal come right back to him! It was faint and off to his right! Porky must have positioned himself at the zip line having also taken note of the situation. It felt so refreshing to be completely unified! The platypus made a course adjustment and did the best he could to head towards the call. After trudging a bit, he stopped and whistled out the cardinal call in an effort to refine his heading.

But this time, no response. Pastor Platypus took a deep breath to let out the call again and just as he was about to let the melody fly, a paw slammed over his mouth from behind.

"Shhhhhhh, Pastor. It's me! There is a search party close by." Porky whispered intensely, "let's move quickly and quietly!"

Pastor Platypus whispered back, "I am certainly glad to see you Porky! Well played! I'll follow you to the zip line!"

Off they scurried. Porky whispered back, "I've got the gold! Do you have the chest?! I was almost ready to head back to the cave! What took you so long?"

"Never mind that", answered Pastor Platypus, "I'll explain later. Marty is providing a bold distraction, and we shouldn't assume that we have much time. How did you know where the gold was?"

Porky quickly replied, "Never mind that, I'll explain later. Now follow me if you can keep up with my squirrel-like speed!"

"Very funny Porky, let's go!"

Porky soon stopped at the base of a large tree which supported the lower anchoring of the zip line and pulley.

"Excellent!" proclaimed a relieved platypus, "Let's get these things hooked up and out of here!"

Porky scurried up the base of the tree to secure a large sack to the line with the small chest inside, "Now hand me the gold bars."

"Are you sure that this satchel won't tear away under all of this weight?" asked Pastor Platypus quite concerned.

"No, I'm not sure," replied Porky, "but I did double the thickness by placing one burlap sack within the other. It should hold. It's the only option we have."

Porky continued, "You finish loading up these bars. I'll climb up the rope and when I get to the tree house, I'll find something heavy to hook up to the pulley. You hold on to the line as if your life depended on it because it does! I'll zip the counter weight down, and you, the chest, and the gold should zip up! Understand?!"

Pastor Platypus confirmed, "Sounds great! Now hurry! I can hear men approaching! Climb for all your worth Porky!" Porky replied with a smart smirk on his face, "Like a squirrel?"

Pastor Platypus responded urgently, "Yes, like a squirrel! Now go!"

With all of his agility and might, Porky scurried up the rope hanging upside down! Pastor Platypus could see the rope shaking from Porky's climbing which brought him some comfort, but he could hear Spanish voices coming closer which took that comfort away.

Pastor Platypus could even start to see the flicker of their lantern. The Spanish sailors seemed to be on course to find both him and the zip line system.

Porky had finally reached the tree house. He quickly attached a canvas sack to the descending rope of the zip line. Then he scurried with all of his might filling the sack with as many coconuts as he could. The sack was completely full of whole coconuts, and Porky gave the line three strong tugs.

Pastor Platypus felt the three tugs in sequence just as the Spanish marines arrived at the lower zip line apparatus. The light of their search lanterns completely illuminated Pastor Platypus and the sack with the chest and gold in it. The Spanish marines stopped a bit startled and surprised at the sight.

Pastor Platypus taunted, "Looking for something?" Then he gave a little wave, "Adios amigos!"

Just then Porky had released the satchel of coconuts and in a flash the Platypus and the prized chest and treasure zipped out of sight up the hill into the darkness of the forest!

The marines were quite tired from their long night of patrols. They were rubbing their eyes and checking with one another to make sure that what they just saw was real. Some thought it was just fatigue and too much grog the night before. But a couple of the Spaniards examined the rope a bit closer which was zinging and whining loudly around the pulley fastened to the tree. The keenest sailor of the bunch yelled, "Cut the rope! Cut the rope! After him! Vamos!"

The front man drew his sword and poised himself to chop the line. Just as he began to thrust his arm down to chop the rope, a high-speed delivery of coconuts had arrived which briskly smashed into the Spanish sailors sending them tumbling down the hillside both mentally and physically battered!

Pastor Platypus arrived just as briskly and violently at the top. Both the platypus and the burlap sack flew off of the line crashing onto Marty the Macaw's tree house floor!

"This is no time for lying around Pastor! Come along now! Let's get back to the cave!" exclaimed Porky. "Impeccable timing on the zip line operation my friend," thanked Pastor Platypus, "now let's gather a few supplies before we retreat to the caves. It won't be long before the Spaniards follow the zip line up to our location."

Porky warned, "We best hurry, the sun is nearly cresting the horizon!"

Pastor Platypus started to grab supplies. He set a lantern and a canister of oil on the table, a casket of water, some fruit and small sacks of tea and sugar.

"Any signs of Marty?" asked Porky throwing the things into a canvas satchel.

"Not yet, but he knows where we are going to be. Last I saw he was leading Captain Don Pablo and his men down the beach away from our encampment to the north," answered Pastor Platypus.

"I beg your pardon?" inquired Porky with a look of disbelief on his face.

The platypus also reluctantly informed, "*And* it is possible that a squadron of Spanish sailors saw me with the chest and the gold just before I arrived here in the tree house. I trust your counterweight delayed their pursuit."

Fear took the words right out of Porky's little mouth. Pastor Platypus was halfway down out of the tree house when he shouted up, "Well, let's not just stand around and wait for them!"

Off they scurried half-dragging the heavy satchel of supplies behind them. Porky dragged and Pastor Platypus pushed. Dawn finally broke with the sound of musket fire erupting down by the beach.

"Oh, well that's just great! I have a hunch that the Spaniards have caught on to Marty's deception. Would you mind giving me a hand with the satchel?" requested Porky having noticed that Pastor Platypus had stopped pushing.

The platypus now nearing a full canter speculated, "You don't suppose they are doing their morning target practice do you?"

They ran a bit more being greatly assisted by the downward slope of the terrain.

Pastor Platypus encouraged Porky, "I think you are doing a splendid job with the supplies! Don't give up now. The sooner we get there the less we will have to run!"

Porky had trouble figuring out that statement through the fog of his fatigue. "Are you laughing?!" asked Porky with a bit of irritation, "perhaps this would be going a little quicker without the tea and sugar rations."

Pastor Platypus celebrated, "Look Porky! We have arrived at the entrance of the cave!"

"See. There it is my boy!" said the Platypus pointing towards a rocky outcropping.

"I'm not seeing it," huffed Porky readjusting the large sack of supplies behind his back.

"Oh come now Porky, it's the only rock with the Macaw in front of it! Now how may rocks have Macaws waiting in front of them? Must I explain everything! Let's get going, I'll take the satchel from here. Just follow me!"

Porky rolled his eyes and followed feeling about thirty stone lighter. Marty greeted them with great relief and joy, "Squaaaawk! Mission accomplished!"

"Mission accomplished", smiled Pastor Platypus, "I trust you had a good morning. I see you are missing a few feathers!"

Marty shook his wings out a bit, "Not too bad. I still have most of them. Folks might mistake me for a red chicken for a few days until my tail feathers straighten out again!" Captain Marty shook his tail trying to straighten them out, "Capitan Don Pablo figured out after a bit that I wasn't helping when a group of marines reported that they spotted a critter with Clementine's chest heading the opposite direction. Next thing you know; the musket balls were a' flyin'!"

Pastor Platypus declared, "Well, you look great! Thank you for your courage Marty."

Captain Marty bowed his head slightly, "It was my pleasure."

Pastor Platypus motioned towards the entrance of the cave, "Come now we had better get inside and tend to the Princess." They all shuffled into the narrow rocky corridor entrance working to shove the supplies through an opening of the dirt and rock blockade which lead into the cave.

Just as they were about to crawl in they could hear the sound of men approaching. There were loud shouts in a language which they had never heard before. Marty, Porky, and Pastor Platypus did not have time to squeeze into the cave when the men passed by the entrance. Still in the tunnel of the entryway, they disappeared as far back into the rocky crevice as they possibly could. "Freeze! Not a sound now!" directed Pastor Platypus in an urgent whisper.

Chapter XXII

Rescue or Run

Marty was the only one who had a view of what was happening outside the cave entrance. Pastor Platypus and Porky were crammed back into the rock too far to see out.

"It's Captain Don Pablo!" whispered back Marty with urgent intensity, "he's coming up the hill and…"

Pastor Platypus interrupted, "Quick, into the cave!" Porky squeezed through the opening first and rolled to the side, Pastor Platypus slid through, and Marty followed with ease.

"Porky, close off the entrance straight away!" ordered Pastor Platypus.

Porky got to work. Marty turned to Pastor Platypus patting the dust off of his feathers and calmly informed, "I don't think you have much to worry about."

"What do you mean by that?" he asked.

"Well you didn't let me finish a moment ago," said Marty.

"Well, go on. What is it?" asked Pastor Platypus.

Marty informed, "I reported that Captain Don Pablo was coming up the hill, but he wasn't walking! Squaaawk! Hanging tied to a pole he was, being carried up the hill by the Taínos."

As Pastor Platypus lit the oil lamp from their satchel of supplies from Marty's house, Porky asked, "Taínos!? Who are the Taínos?"

"They are the people that lived on this island before the Spanish and English came on their sailing ships. They were peaceful, they were kind, but many became ill after the sailing men came. Many of them died. Those that remained have been harshly worked as slaves in the haciendas to produce sugar and coffee for Europe. One small tribe remains free and un-captured. Unfortunately, their hearts have become hardened against the Europeans. They have been working hard and doing all they can to make the Spanish leave this island, and I am afraid they have resorted to behaviors that are quite uncharacteristic of their culture."

Pastor Platypus asked, "Why didn't Don Pablo's men come to his rescue with a force of marines?"

Marty replied, "For one, the Spanish sailors do not help because they are very superstitious of what they call the Taíno Phantom Tribe. These Taíno have become stunningly accurate with poison tipped arrows. The Taínos will attack and disappear again completely undetected. The sailors take them to be evil spirits of those who have died as slaves."

"I don't believe it! His own men won't even put up a fight for their commanding officer!? What will become of Captain Don Pablo?" asked Pastor Platypus.

"They will most likely offer him up to their gods with fire; They don't know of the God of the Santa Biblia," informed Marty. "In fact, I don't know what they will exactly do," clarified Marty, "They are an elusive people who are always on the move and out of sight……. even for a Macaw."

Porky asked Marty with slight disbelief in his voice, "You mean to say the Taínos will burn him as an offering to a god that doesn't even exist! Well, at least he won't be bothering us anymore! Come on now and let's go find the princess and get to those English ships!"

A lovely and gentle voice emerged from the darkness just beyond the glow of the lantern, "Señores, are you there?"

Porky responded with joy and relief in his voice, "We have returned to Princess Clementine! We have the chest and the gold! Are you well?"

"I'm well. That is fantastic news Porky! I'm simply thrilled," Clementine reported as she emerged from the darkness into the light, "I became worried when I heard the musket fire. Is there now still reason for concern?"

"Squawk, not at all Princesa, not at all," reassured Captain Marty.

"I beg to differ," interrupted Pastor Platypus with somber intensity in his voice. "Are Captain Don Pablo's men not even going to attempt a rescue?" asked Pastor Platypus looking Marty squarely in the eye with his bill nearly touching Marty's beak.

Marty took a big gulp and stuttered as he struggled to tell the platypus what he did not want to hear, "N...No Sir. I believe the fear and superstition of the Taínos will outweigh their loyalty to their capitan."

"Senselessness!" shouted Pastor Platypus, "What kind of men would abandon their commanding officer!? I'm going to put a stop to this!" growled Pastor Platypus in disgust.

182

And with that he started to dig frantically at the dirt and stone which was blocking the entrance of the cave. Porky grabbed Pastor Platypus' shoulder and pulled him back from the blockaded entrance. "What in God's name are you doing?! Do you want to get us all captured and offered up as sacrifices with fire! Me and poison darts don't agree. We have the princess and her treasury; it is time to move on!"

Pastor Platypus whipped Porky's hand off of his shoulder and sharply rebuked his quill-covered companion, "God's Name! What do you know of God's Name!? Have you forgotten about the Cross?! Have you?!"

Pastor Platypus spoke with deep compassion, "Remember the criminal at Jesus' side as he hung there for you and for me…. for Don Pablo. Jesus hung there to save that criminal, and even the lives of those who pounded the nails into his hands and feet! 'Today, thou shalt be with me in paradise.' Do you not recall!!"

He softened his voice, but the intensity remained, "The obedience of Captain Don Pablo or lack thereof to the Word of God shall not disqualify him from receiving grace and the salvation of Jesus Christ. It is easy to love and fight for those who love you back, but we have been called to love and serve our enemies. That is when true love happens. Jesus loved and laid down his life for the very people that crucified him." The Princess, Marty, and Porky were frozen in deep reflection in the flickering light of the cave. Porky's gaze was towards the ground as he searched his heart.

Pastor Platypus continued with deeply British candor, "Gentlemen, when it is within our power to do good, we shall not withhold that power for personal gain or comfort. You all must remember we are servants to God. Jesus came to earth to serve, not to be served, but to give his life as an offering to the lost sheep among us. Who needs a doctor? The sick or the healthy? Jesus offered up his life for people like Captain Don Pablo. I will not allow a man to be senselessly burned alive, having been abandoned by his men, when it is within our power to stop it!"

Porky, hesitated slightly, "I know that God offers his grace to the sinner, but this man tried to kill us!"

"This Captain", clarified Pastor Platypus with great focus, "lives to obey his master, his admiral and king. His authority was given to him by God. His title must be honored whether or not Don Pablo has brought honor to the title. We have the opportunity to save this man physically and in heart."

Pastor Platypus took a deep breath, "It is God's to judge! We are not the judge! We have been called to administer the grace, love, and the forgiveness of Jesus. Human judgment is not my master, God is, and I will attempt to rescue Don Pablo as Jesus rescued me!"

Pastor Platypus took a deep reflective sigh, "I recall in one of my visits to the American Colonies the words of a fantastically passionate Methodist preacher by the name of John Wesley. I will never forget these words he spoke, he said, 'Do all the good you can, by all the means you can, in all the ways you can, in all the places you can, at all the times you can, to all the people you can, as long as ever you can.'"

Everyone was silent for a moment.

Princess Clementine spoke up with authority blanketing her voice, "Pastor Platypus has chosen the way of honor." She pleaded gracefully and powerfully with Marty and Porky, "Do you recall David, the second king of Israel? We must follow David's example in his dealing with Saul. The sun was setting on Saul's time as King. Saul's jealously and greed fueled many attempts to take David's life, but when David had the opportunity to kill Saul in a cave just like this, he instead cut off a corner of his robe. Later when David presented the corner of the robe to Saul, King Saul realized David had honored Saul's God-given place as King by sparing his life. Saul's heart was subdued by grace, and the judgment was left in God's hands. Saul ceased his efforts to take David's life. Now go my friends and do what is right! Go quickly!"

Porky was humbled and refreshed by God's word. In submitting to God and to the Princess' judgement, Porky dropped to one knee with a humble heart and answered softly, "Yes, your majesty." Porky now comprehended the gospel like he never had before and knew also what needed to be done. He stood and turned to Pastor Platypus, "Please forgive me. I'm with you. I'm prepared to lay down my life for this man who has wronged us."

Pastor Platypus grinned ever so slightly. Warmly grabbing Porky's shoulder, "Romans chapter five tells us that it is hard enough to find someone who will lay down their life for a good man. Only Christ has done so for the sinner. Porky, *now* you are sounding more like a man saved by the cross of grace. Jesus died to save us while *we* still lived for evil. We are called now to save others in the same way. Should my life be asked of me, I consider it a privilege to die for this man in Jesus' name."

Tears welled up in Porky's eye's and he struggled to speak, "Me too."

Princess Clementine kissed both Pastor Platypus and Porky on the cheek, "Now go quickly! Be strong and very courageous!"

Pastor Platypus ordered, "Marty, take the Princess and her treasury through the caves to those English ships!" Marty looked distressed that they would be separated. "Go!" ordered Pastor Platypus, "God willing, we shall all be on the same quarter deck by this time tomorrow!"

And with that Porky and Pastor Platypus slipped through the opening Porky had made. The Princess, with a lantern in one hand and a heavy satchel of supplies over her shoulder, disappeared with Marty the Macaw in the depths of the tunnel, and all was still and silent in that place.

Chapter XXIII

A Leap of Faith

The smell of smoke immediately hit the noses of Pastor Platypus and Porky. Pastor Platypus' heart sank in his chest, "I hope we're not too late, Porky. Can you track the smell?"

Porky closed his eyes with intense focus sniffing the air and feeling the wind against his face. "I think I've got the general direction. Follow me!" Porky began to run uphill through the vegetation, ripping through giant leaves and leaping over logs and rocks with great agility. Porky could feel focused power ebbing through his body. The Platypus was struggling to keep up.

"Pastor, are you with me?!" Porky shouted back.

"Go on! I'll catch up! Just go my boy! Go!"

Porky suddenly slid to a stop, sniffed the air once, and took off down a small trail. Porky stopped just long enough for Pastor Platypus to catch a glimpse of the change of direction. Porky was galloping down the Taíno's path grunting with each pull of his legs. The power of a lion was within him. He could now hear the shouts of Captain Don Pablo, "Dios mío, Ayuda me! ….Por Favor!!" [My God, Help me please!]

Porky could hear the wild shouts of the natives. The camp came into view as the trail neared its end. He could see Capitan Don Pablo tied to a post with flames climbing around his feet. Porky ran straight through the dancing Taínos with unshakable focus, and leapt through the flames right onto the post. It was enough for Don Pablo to notice through all of the panic and pain.

Porky clawed his way around to the back of the post. The native's song and dance halted just as Porky chomped right through the ropes binding Captain Don Pablo's hands. With his free hands the Captain unfastened his chest straps while Porky slid upside down and chomped off the ropes binding his legs.

Just then the platypus ran into the camp and shouted with a war-like battle cry, "WAAATUMBAAAAAA!"   He didn't know what it meant. It's just what came out! And it was enough to startle the Taínos causing them to turn away from Captain Don Pablo and Porky to look for the one who gave the battle cry.

Porky saw their chance. "Run Captain Run!" Porky shouted to Don Pablo motioning him to follow. The Taíno's turned back just in time to see Porky and Don Pablo disappear into the forest which is exactly when Pastor Platypus ran off into hiding as well. For a moment the natives didn't know who to chase. Their chief shouted an order and the Taínos shot their poison darts blindly into the lush forest in the direction of the Captain and Porky.

Capitan Don Pablo was struggling to run on his burnt feet. Darts whizzed past ripping sharply through the leaves and sticking into the trees all around them. Suddenly two poison darts hit Captain Don Pablo in the back causing him to cry out and fall to the ground. Pastor Platypus arrived to the Captain just as he fell and immediately pulled the darts from his back.

The Captain rolled onto his back and saw the platypus. "Get up and run for all your worth!" shouted the Pastor Platypus. Captain Don Pablo quickly stood picking up Pastor Platypus and began to move as fast as he could through the forest following his porcupine rescuer. The Taínos were fast and by the sound of their yells and cries they appeared to be gaining. At least it seemed, for now, that they had run out of darts.

Captain Don Pablo could feel himself becoming dizzy. He struggled to keep his eyes in focus and working together. The sounds of the Taínos shouting started to get muffled as if he was underwater. The poison was setting in. Nevertheless, he kept clamoring through the forest trying to put distance between him and the natives. The terrain suddenly dove down and revealed a small, but quickly moving stream. "Come on! This way!" Porky called to the captain who was still carrying the platypus clumsily slipping and sliding down a muddy and rocky hill towards the river.

Captain Don Pablo was extremely relieved to place his feet in the water as it greatly abated the pain from his burns. The platypus jumped into the water just as soon as he was over it. It was deep enough for him to float so that he could use the current as an aid for escape if needed.

There were wide and smoothed over stones on the sides of the river free from snagging vegetation which Porky and Captain Don Pablo used to speed their movements downstream.

The Taínos seemed to move like jaguars though the forest. They were swift and their shouts and commands could be heard up both sides of the banks in the gorge behind them. Porky knew in his mind that they were attempting to overtake them on the lofty hillsides above the rushing stream and feared that they would close in from both in front and behind. The water in the stream was quickly picking up speed and intensity.

Captain Don Pablo was stumbling and falling more from the short exposure he had to the poison darts. Pastor Platypus was praying in his mind on behalf of Captain Don Pablo against the effects of the poison as he floated down the stream alongside of Porky and the captain on the river bank. Pastor Platypus could tell that if the effects of the poison got any worse that the captain would no longer be able to walk. Then they'd *all* soon be on their way to meet their Creator!

Pastor Platypus stopped atop a smooth boulder in the middle of the stream. He was considerably further downstream than Porky and the captain due to the increasing speed of the current. Pastor Platypus looked down off the other side of the rock to see the water disappear as it fell approximately the distance from a crow's nest to the sea, about 75 feet, down into a deep half-circle opening of the gorge.

Pastor Platypus turned back to alert Porky "Waterfall! Waterfall!!" Porky soon caught up to look over the edge. It was a horseshoe shaped cliff with long rectangular formations making up its sides as it dropped slightly backwards into the gorge below which was well covered by a canopy of trees.

"The water level is far too low to survive the jump!" noted Porky panting for air. The Taínos could now be seen in and along the waterway upstream closing fast.

"Look, there is a small underwater kettle right where the water is falling into. It looks to be at least two men deep in the middle. If we hit it just right, we might survive the jump!" reasoned Pastor Platypus.

"It looks like at least a 60-foot drop, like a leap from the top of a mainmast into the sea!" shouted Porky over the sound of the rushing water. Captain Don Pablo was crawling on all fours now about halfway between the waterfall and the Taíno warriors. Pastor Platypus urgently pointed out, "Porky! Look! The captain!"

"He'll never make it!" Porky thought quickly, "I'll run back and jab him with one of my quills and see if that will get him going."

"It's too late Porky! The Taínos are nearly upon him!" shouted Pastor Platypus over the raging waters.

"We made it this far! I must at least try!" argued Porky.

Just as Porky was going to run upstream towards Captain Don Pablo, a massive chorus of ear piercing loud screeches suddenly commanded the attention of Porky and Pastor Platypus causing them to turn and look to the canopy beyond the vast opening past the waterfall and cliff.

"Ha HAAA!" shouted Pastor Platypus raising an arm and fist up into the air in celebration.

Just them Marty the Macaw folded back his wings falling out of the sky into a screaming dive towards the peak of the waterfall where Porky and Pastor Platypus were standing. And behind Marty a tremendous flock of deafening Green Quaker Parrots also folded back their wings to dive rapidly down to the level of the stream. They each opened their wings to pull out of the dive just above the heads of Porky and Pastor Platypus. A cloud of green attack angels zipped past their heads in a blur of speed upriver towards the Taíno tribesmen with Captain Marty at the spearhead screaming "BONZAAAAIIII"!

Captain Don Pablo was barely moving as he was attempting to crawl down the river bank in a clear state of delirium.

A Taíno warrior stopped to take clear aim at the captain with his poison dart gun and took a grand inhale for Don Pablo's final blow. Marty opened his air brakes, stuck his talons out in strike position landing squarely atop the long dart gun. He let out a grand squawk and sharply pecked the warrior in the forehead with his tremendous beak causing the Taíno to fall down into the river. The Quaker Parrots split up dashing through the forest like green bolts of lightning in every direction in pursuit of the Taíno warriors.

They cut through the bushes and trees with the speed of a musket ball. Their ear piercing squawks echoed throughout the forest with devastatingly disorienting dissonance. The sound was enough to disable any man's focus. The Taínos were in a state of disorder and chaos.

Porky and Pastor Platypus perceived well their rescue and were not about to waste it. They managed Captain Don Pablo to the edge of the falls using the current to thrust him upon the last rock in the middle of the river just before the water spilled over.

Pastor Platypus looked sharply at Porky and instructed, "Just jump within the falling water and we should land in the deepest possible spot." Captain Don Pablo struggled to his knees. Porky shouted "We're jumping Capitan! Hold your breath!" They couldn't tell if he understood. He was barely holding up his own head.

"I'll jump first so I can help him out of the water as soon as he lands!" shouted Pastor Platypus. And with that, he jumped.

Porky was frozen for a moment in awe of his leap. He took in a deep breath and pushed the weary captain over the falls hanging on to his overcoat as they fell. Everything for a moment went quiet. The water seemed to stand still as Captain Don Pablo and Porky plummeted into the unknown.

Chapter XXIV

Humility and Freedom

Captain Don Pablo and Porky the Porcupine plunged into the water; The water was deep enough to slow their descent, but they still hit the rocky bottom with considerable force. It was enough to startle the Captain back into consciousness. He swam instinctively for the surface. Two things shined causing him to strain his eyes and focus his mind; the sun reflecting off of the water and the smile on the face of Princess Clementine who was reaching for him with an outstretched hand.

"Tome mi mano Capitan. [Take my hand, Captain]," invited the princess as she waded into the water to assist the Spanish Captain who had been chasing down the Princess the night before. His heart was overtaken with humility as he comprehended the situation. He was as good as dead, nearly burned at stake, and now he had been saved by his adversaries.

Captain Don Pablo required the princess's strength just to make it to the firm ground of the river bank. The princess helped the captain out of the water and sat him down on a smooth and large rock which was nicely warmed by the sun.

At that moment, Porky the Porcupine and Pastor Platypus arrived beside Princess Clementine. The Captain realized he had just been rescued by the very ones whom he labeled as his enemies. His hands began to shake and his head dropped low. Pastor Platypus gave a firm pat on the captain's knee, "We made it!" he exclaimed with a slight chuckle. Porky turned to the princess, "Your timing was fantastic! Well done Your Highness!"

"My pleasure Porky, it was our great fortune that Captain Marty was able to navigate the caves so well. He insisted on doing everything possible to help with the rescue."

Captain Don Pablo lifted up his head just as Marty the Macaw swooped down and landed on Princess Clementine's shoulder, "SQUAWK! The Quakers should hold those natives off for a bit." Screeches and squawking could still be heard echoing in the canopy above muted by the sound of the waterfall.

Seeing all of his rescuers before him together, his mind suddenly flashed back to a time earlier that morning. The macaw was the same one that had landed on his shoulder down at the beachfront misdirecting his attempts to capture the princess. Yet, he would be dead if it were not for his efforts.

Captain Don Pablo wiped the water from his face with a single swoop of his large hand which was worn and weathered from years at sea. He sat up straight and took a deep breath, "Thank you for rescuing me; my life is indebted to you all."

The Princess firmly replied, "You're welcome Captain."

The captain looked down to Porky and Pastor Platypus, "Mis pequeños amigos, Capitan Don Pablo is forever at your service. You both have shown me more faithfulness in one day than my officers and men have given me in all my days at sea. If it were not for all of you I would have died in a most unpleasant way. I am now at your service. You may do with me as you wish."

Pastor Platypus bowed his head giving honor still to Don Pablo's position as captain and answered, "Today, Captain, love and grace have won both our battles."

Marty interrupted with feathers fluffed up doing a little dance on Clementine's shoulders, "Squawk! Los Loros Verdes - The Parrots are saying to me that we don't have much time. Down the river with us, down the river!"

Clementine stood up, "Alright then, let's keep moving." The Princess, Captain Don Pablo, and Porky took to the side of the stream. The platypus went with the flow of the water and Marty hopped and flew from branch to branch above them looking ahead for any potential problems.... or snacks for that matter. Rescuing captains does create a great deal of hunger in a macaw.

The Captain's feet were still a little singed from the fire earlier, but for some reason not fully understood by himself, the effects of the poison he was exposed to seemed to help by numbing the pain.

They all moved quite swiftly for the next half hour or so. The sea was near. It could be seen through small openings in the forest before them. And much to their relief a fresh sea breeze was blowing up stream. After nearly one half hour of trekking seaward, they all stopped for a moment to rest. Marty left to rendezvous with the Quaker Parrots to see how things were going with the Taínos and whether or not they had given up their pursuit.

"I'm going up ahead a bit. Please excuse me, I need to relieve myself," informed Captain Don Pablo too exhausted to be embarrassed. He found a secluded spot downstream and into the woods to answer to nature's call. Afterwards, he returned to the stream to freshen up and get a drink.

The stream was much more wide and calm at this point as it was nearing the end of its journey to the sea. He took a moment to enjoy the lizards that were running across the top of the water. Captain Don Pablo bent down on his knees to wash his face and drink from the stream. Upon hearing a twig snap, he looked up to find the end of a musket pointed against his head!

"On your feet! Up with you at once! Turn around!" a stern voice commanded. Don Pablo thought urgently to himself, "It's an English Marine".

Their red coats and white cross straps were unmistakable. Not to mention the English accent. Don Pablo was thinking to himself as he was being escorted down-stream towards the beach that he was at least excelling at being captured. Twice captured in one day was a new achievement for him.

Marty flew in landing on a rock next to his friends squawked out a report, "The natives have been slowed down but are still heading down stream to find us. Also, it is good that you like to rescue people!"

"What happened!?" asked the Princess.

"English Marines! Red coat marines led Don Pablo down towards shore with a thunder musket to his back!"

"English! Are you sure!?" the Princess exclaimed not really giving Marty time to respond. The Princess was both excited and quite apprehensive to hear that there were English at the shoreline. She was certain there would be a ship too! She was also urgently concerned for the Spanish capitan's welfare.

"I'll grab the satchel. Let's get going friends. We must explain all this to the English officers before they suppose too much", urged the princess.

"Marty, why don't you fly out ahead of all this a bit and see what can be done", suggested Pastor Platypus.

"Not a chance!" squawked Marty, "I've dodged enough musket balls for one day! I'm staying with you Princesa! I know the English are gentlemen and they will not fire upon this fine lady whose shoulder I shall remain soundly upon!"

Pastor Platypus let out a frustrated sigh, "Alright then. Let's get moving!"

The English sailors were loading the last of their barrels into their skiff which they had resupplied with fresh water from the stream. They were also coaxing the rope-bound Spanish captain into the boat as well.

Two proud English frigates waited at anchor in the harbor. The 32-gun fifth-rate HMS Lowestoffe and the 28-gun sixth-rate HMS Hinchinbrook; both seaworthy ships, clearly weathered from many years at sea, yet well-kept enough to make it back to their port of call.

"Wait! Stop!" shouted the princess. The English sailors and marines were startled. They were not expecting company, and especially not the company of a lady. The Marines' arms became weak under the weight of their long heavy musket rifles, for the sight of a fine lady was not one they had beheld for not less than three months.

The princess kept running across the beach toward the English skiff with a macaw on her shoulder. "Stop! Release him!" she shouted between heavy breaths. Porky was by her side now. The platypus got washed out to sea a bit and was struggling to get back to shore through the surf.

"Apologies my lady, we have orders not to release captured officers until they are questioned by our commander," the English Marine informed.

"You may bring him *and me* to your Commander, but I order you to unbind his hands and mouth!" commanded Clementine sternly.

"My lady, you are not in a position to give orders. Are you accompanying this Spanish officer?" asked the commanding marine with raised suspicions.

"I am not", replied Clementine straightening out her dress a bit, "But if it's of any interest to you Sir……..?" She waited for a reply of formal introduction.

"Shipton, Corporal Shipton", answered the Marine.

"If it's any interest to you Corporal Shipton, I have been sent by my father, who happens to be the king of the Canary Islands, and I require that you take me to your commanding officer at once!" Reaching into the supply satchel, she pulled out a large bar of pure gold with the seal of King George III impressed upon it, "Compensation awaits you and your crew for your troubles, and there is plenty more where this came from."

"SQUAWK! Tainos! Tainos!" alerted Marty as a small angry hoard of natives appeared from the tree line about two ship lengths away.

Corporal Shipton sprang into action, "In the boat my Lady!"

The marines helped her in and sat her down next to Capitan Don Pablo. The English Marines were too distracted to notice the Porcupine that joined the Princess. Marty remained on her shoulder. Pastor Platypus dove back into the sea and disappeared into the depths.

The Marines shoved off and the dinghy lurched up into the air with the breaking surf.

"Row for all your worth!" ordered Corporal Shipton. Just after they cleared the breakers, Clementine was about to say something to Don Pablo when the muskets broke out with a thunderous explosion. The English Marines were deterring the Taínos. It was a terrifying sound, but the princess's mind was finally at rest. She at last felt safe. Safer anyway.

Pastor Platypus swam swiftly along with the skiff and about one fathom below it. The musket fire sent muffled concussions through the water.

"Row! Row!" shouted Corporal Shipton as he could now see that many of the natives where about to enter the water. Only four marines were firing to defend the boat. The Corporal could see that the skiff had taken on a bit of water in the departure from shore and that it was quite bogged down with their barrels full of fresh water and their two new unexpected passengers. Shipton ordered two of the marines to bail leaving only the two on the stern to fight. Clementine grabbed an ore on her own initiative and started to row with all the strength left in her.

Chapter XXV

His Majesty's Ship

"Well, Mr. Dowling, I am going to race you to the masthead, and I beg that I may meet you there!" challenged 1st Lieutenant Nelson with playful yet firm resolution in his voice.

The Midshipman, William Dowling, a boy of 12 years old, was ruddy and not more than five feet from heels to head. His face had never been shaven and appeared quite smooth and unweathered much unlike some of the old salts which he was in command of. In his eyes one could see that he had taken on the responsibilities of a man.

Though it was only mid-morning, sweat beaded heavily on Mr. Dowling's brow. He wore a smartly fitted blue overcoat giving him the appearances of a young English gentleman. It proved much too warm for the tropics, but was required as a midshipman.

Having yet to conquer his fear of heights, Mr. Dowling looked his lieutenant in the eye and gave a hesitant nod in acceptance of his challenge to race to the top of the mast.

The Midshipman ran for the starboard mast shrouds. Lieutenant Nelson scuffled over to the larboard shrouds, and they both began to climb for all they were worth. Nelson could see that the slack in the ratlines was slowing the boy a bit more than he liked. The midshipman had never made it past the futtock shrouds which awkwardly leans a seaman sharply back over the deck as one made his way up to the top platform.

Nelson waited to coach the boy up the small section of futtock shrouds. The midshipman was clearly flustered. The boy's feet slipped causing him to hang momentarily by just his hands with absolutely nothing to catch his fall other than the well-scrubbed deck of the HMS Hinchinbrook.

"Swing your legs up and make tension with your feet as you climb Sir," instructed Nelson, "That's it! Now climb!"

The boy clumsily heaved his body up onto the mizzen top. "I wouldn't stop to rest now!" challenged Nelson as he started up the mizzen topmast shroud. The midshipman leapt to his feet and skillfully ascended after Nelson. Nelson did beat him to the masthead by just a body's length. He spoke cheerfully to the boy, "Any person should be pitied who fancies that getting to the masthead is either dangerous or difficult!"

They both embraced the refreshing wind of a beautiful day admiring the view around them. Nelson closed his eyes and turned to warm his face against the rising sun speaking aloud to the midshipman, "It is always the darkest just before dawn. I believe that sunshine of a new morning bears a prophetic glory. That light which leads us on to the object of our ambitions is indeed light from Heaven. Hence forth we shall confide in Providence and brave every danger."

Lieutenant Nelson's near-black and deep-set eyes blazed brilliantly as he looked right at Mr. Dowling who was trying not to appear terrified. Nelson held loosely to the masthead with all the confidence and comfort that you would expect from an officer who had been many years at sea. The lieutenant was fatherly and quick to smile, yet when it came to seamanship, his zeal for battle, his love for England, and his resolution to maintain the highest levels of honor were unmatched by anyone else among England's royal naval officers.

The Midshipman aboard the HMS Hinchinbrook perceived it as a great privilege and opportunity to be under the command of Nelson who was well known to be one of the best lieutenants in the Royal Navy. He didn't always follow the rules, but his adventure-filled success stories were what raised him to fame as he demonstrated a brilliant prowess for battle.

The young midshipman was still clinging on for dear life to the mast-head.

Nelson saw that he was well outside of his zone of comfort atop the mast, and he went right to testing his ability to think clearly under pressure, "Alight Mr. Dowling, name for me the thirty-two compass points in clockwise order starting from North East by East!"

Suddenly the sound of erupting musket fire in the distance captured their attention. From their lofty view they immediately perceived the situation of their marines who had been ordered to replenish the fresh water stores. Natives were pouring into the surf in pursuit the bogged down vessel loaded with barrels of water, marines, a princess, a captain, and gold.

"They'll be overrun," Nelson thought aloud.

By the time the midshipman looked away from the shoreline back at Nelson, the lieutenant was already descending the lower shrouds. Mr. Dowling could hear him shouting firm and direct orders. The intensity in his voice sent chills up the midshipman's spine and prompted him to immediately begin navigating his descent.

Nelson was never at a loss of what to do during an emergency. Neither the Hinchinbrook, nor the HMS Lowestoffe where in a position to deliver support from their side cannons.

"Man the stern swivel guns at once!" commanded Nelson, "Provide close cover to betwixt our marines and those natives!"

The captain's quarters of the Hinchinbrook sat just below the quarter deck. The explosion of the swivel cannons jolted Captain Collingwood causing him to smudge the fresh ink in his morning entry of the captain's Log.

"Bring up the swivels from the forecastle immediately!" shouted Lieutenant Nelson.

A battle-ready sergeant of the Royal Marine Guard appeared before Nelson for orders. He simply stood at attention just to the side of and just behind Nelson who stood against the back rail of the quarter deck focused on the marines rowing towards his ship. Nelson's hands were folded behind his back as he observed the directed fire of the swivel cannons. Nelson looked back over his shoulder briefly at the sergeant and ordered with calm direction, "Send your sharp shooters aloft the mizzen. Fire only if it is required to save lives."

Captain William Locker of the HMS Lowestoffe anchored in seventeen fathoms on the other side of the harbor had now well perceived the situation and directed his men to effectively employ his cannons to aid in slowing the native's attack.

Clementine could feel the cannon balls wiz and whirr over the top their heads. A wall of exploding ocean shielded the retreating supply vessel from the rogue Taíno tribe. Corporal Shipton ordered his riflemen to now all row having perceived the effectiveness of their cover fire. Princess Clementine was still pulling at an ore. Captain Don Pablo remained bound.

"What is the meaning of all this ruckus Lieutenant!" bellowed out Captain Collingwood still buttoning up his overcoat as he stepped up onto the quarter deck of the Hinchinbrook to see why his lieutenant was at the cannons.

"Apparently, the natives were reluctant to give up their fresh water Captain, more importantly, take a look at this," Nelson handed Captain Collingwood the looking scope.

The Captain strained his eyes a bit as he adjusted the looking glass, "What in God's name!"

"It looks as if we are about to have visitors Captain. What do you make of it?" inquired Nelson.

Captain Collingwood was becoming quite irritated with all of the cannon fire, "Cease Fire! The natives have retreated. Cease fire! Prepare to bring the skiff alongside!"

The captain was a well-experienced and admired officer who expressed his love for England by enforcing every sense of duty that pertains to the command of a vessel in His Majesty's Royal Navy. His face was noble and advanced in age. Captain Collingwood wore a dark blue overcoat with white facings and a white cravat around his neck. His coat was adorned with golden trim, golden buttons and cuffs, and golden epaulettes. A matching and regal bicorn hat set atop gray hair, established, without any doubt, that he indeed had unquestionable and ultimate authority aboard the Hinchinbrook.

The captain peered keenly through the looking scope, and turned to Nelson with a composed and inquisitive look upon his face, "It looks as if they have retrieved a lady *and* a Spanish officer along with our fresh water. Mr. Nelson, I believe all I asked for was fresh drinking water." Captain Collingwood handed the telescope to his Lieutenant, "Have the men remain at general quarters until we sort out exactly what the situation is here."

Nelson confirmed, "Aye Sir. We cannot rule out the presence of Spanish soldiers in the area. Not to mention the ship, or ships, they came on."

Captain Collingwood also ordered to Nelson as he was walking off of the quarter deck, "Raise the signal flag indicating to the Lowestoffe that she needs to clear her decks for action."

Nelson directed his midshipmen to raise the signal, and he himself went alongside to receive the marines and their guests. Lieutenant Nelson leaned over the edge of the rail to greet the marines as they rowed alongside the Hinchinbrook, "Greetings Corporal, glad to see you in one piece!"

Corporal Shipton shouted back up at Nelson, "Impeccable timing Sir. Your shots were well placed."

"At your service Corporal," answered Nelson, "Now come up here and explain these events at once!" Nelson turned to the deck hands and sternly ordered, "Hoist them up and mind the lady!"

Chapter XXVI

Hosting a Princess

All the marines climbed up onto the quarter deck with their newly acquired guests. Corporal Shipton stepped to the front and stood at attention to present himself to Lieutenant Nelson. The corporal was a well-built man of twenty and two years. His facial expressions and speech had the keepings of a gentleman, but his body was clearly that of a soldier.

Nelson squared up to Shipton, "Are you and your men alright?"

"Yes Sir, all men are accounted for and uninjured," reported Shipton.

"Might I inquire who this officer is that you have captured?" asked Nelson with intensifying focus.

Corporal Shipton, took a deep breath and appeared a bit nervous, "You may Sir. We have taken Captain Don Pablo of Spain. My marines found him at the river where we were drawing up the water." Nelson did not look pleased. Shipton continued, "We suspected that he would alert his crew of our presence, so he was detained Sir."

"I see," replied Nelson distressed in thought, "well done Corporal, but just the same, it won't be long until they realize that he is missing."

Lieutenant Nelson turned to one of his midshipmen and signaled to a couple of marines, "Take Captain Don Pablo below and show him to the hold please."

Clementine spoke up trying to look at Nelson from behind one of the four marines who had formed sort of a human wall around her, "I beg your pardon Sir, but this man has wounds that ought to be tended to at once."

Don Pablo stood bound with his head hanging low. He did not look anyone in the eye nor say a word. Humility had silenced him.

Nelson gave a slight nod and may have expressed a bit of confusion by the look of his eyes. The marines, one at each side of Captain Don Pablo, stopped and looked at Nelson. Midshipman Bradford came back a few steps to properly await any adjustment in the lieutenant's orders. Nelson softly changed his orders, "To the sick bay then, and have the marines stand guard until Captain Collingwood gives you further orders."

Nelson walked over to Captain Don Pablo and quickly looked him over from head to toe assessing for injuries which did not readily present themselves. His uniform was quite soaked and tattered, "I apologize for your treatment Captain. I am Lieutenant Nelson. On behalf of Captain Collingwood, I welcome you aboard His Majesty's Ship Hinchinbrook."

"Gracias Señor," remarked Captain Don Pablo with considerable fatigue.

"Our surgeon will look well after you," assured Nelson.

Nelson walked back over to Corporal Shipton who was still standing at attention, waiting to formally present Clementine. Noticing that a large crowd of deck hands had gathered around to observe their new guests, Shipton leaned in awkwardly towards Nelson. Clearing his throat, he looked out of the corner of his eye at all the deck hands whose attention was fixed on them. Nelson perceived that the corporal did not want to speak aloud, so Nelson leaned in closer. The Corporal whispered something in Nelsons ear. Nelson's eyes widened a bit. Learning of her royal status, he momentarily glanced back at the lady who was standing quite composed in the midst of all the marines who were at attention forming a wall between her and Nelson.

Nelson turned to all the gawking deck hands and bellowed, "Well don't just stand there like a flock of buzzards, unload and store these barrels of fresh water at once!"

After dispersing the crowd of weathered and stout sailors, Nelson parted the wall of marines and approached Clementine. He was taken by slight surprise at the sight of her simple and noble beauty. Her dark brown eyes demanded his attention. Clementine's dress was elegant in design. It was very dirty, yet she wore it with confidence as if it was without blemish. To make the sight all the more stunning there was a scarlet macaw that was sitting on her shoulder who was also staring directly at Nelson with an examining gaze. Over her other shoulder, she had slung a canvas sack. The durable fabric appeared to be under a great deal of stress from the weight of its contents, yet Clementine casually kept hold of it as if it was no burden at all.

Nelson hesitated allowing a brief moment of awkward silence attempting to fully perceive and comprehend the situation. Remembering his manners, Nelson properly greeted the lady, "Your Majesty, welcome aboard the HMS Hinchinbrook. Please forgive me for any mistreatment that you may have already received. I am Lieutenant Horatio Nelson at your service."

And with that Nelson removed his hat and slightly bowed his head. Captain Collingwood was watching intently at a distance from the rail of the quarter deck. Porky remained unnoticed at Clementine's side nearly blending in with the color of the deck.

Clementine spoke up in near perfect English overlain with an accent unfamiliar to Nelson, "Thank you Lieutenant. It is a pleasure to make your acquaintance. If it is not too much trouble, I will see your captain now."

"Of course my Lady, please come with me," instructed Nelson. Some of the crew unloading the barrels of water were staring and snickering at Nelson's awkward handling of the greeting. They could see clearly his gentlemanly composure unraveling in the company of Princess Clementine. Nelson gave them a glare which burned with a firm message.

The crew went back to their work, and Nelson led Clementine towards the captain's quarters with Corporal Shipton bringing up the rear, musket still in hand.

Nelson motioned with his eyes for Captain Collingwood to come off of the Quarter Deck to meet in his cabin. They had served with one another long enough where one would almost always know what the other was thinking.

Captain Collingwood, not expecting to host in his quarters, excused himself from the quarter deck and quickly entered his cabin from a side entrance. Nelson stopped at the door after trying to delay as much as possible to give the captain time to prepare for at least a few seconds. Nelson knocked, "Permission to enter Captain?"

"Just a moment if you would," delayed Collingwood who had Mr. Gaddish one of his younger midshipmen with him helping frantically to straighten up the cabin which was in no state for the company of a lady. Intermittent clamoring could be heard from behind the door. Nelson's face grimaced as he listened to all the ruckus.

On the other side of the door Captain Collingwood straightened out his overcoat, wiped the sweat from his brow and placed on himself his stately tricorn captain's hat. Collingwood whispered to his midshipman with some sympathy, "I apologize, Mr. Gaddish, for that what is about to happen."

Nelson was standing at the Captain's door, with the lady close behind and Corporal Shipton who was still at the rear facing out at attention with musket in hand as to deter the crew from approaching. His blaze red jacket with golden stripes on the arms was quite enough of a deterrence for the common crew. Lieutenant Nelson was tempted to speak with Clementine during their awkward time of waiting, but he knew himself better than that and refrained for fear of making a bigger fool of himself.

Suddenly they heard a thunderous rebuke from within the Captain's cabin which was easily heard by the party waiting to get in.

Captain Collingwood bellowed from behind the door while Midshipman Gaddish was making the final touches running around the cabin lighting a couple lanterns, "And that is precisely the reason we do not spit over the side of the quarter deck! Now return at once to your duties, and remember you are a gentleman!" Firm footsteps could be heard approaching the door.

Midshipman Gaddish looked at Captain Collingwood in mild astonishment and embarrassment, "Spitting over the quarter deck?!" whispered Mr. Gaddish looking at Captain Collingwood with perplexity.

Captain Collingwood whispered back with in apology, "It's all I could think of under the circumstances. Now, return to your duties."

The Captain refreshed the stern look upon his face and opened the door to send Mr. Gaddish out and invite Nelson and their guest in. Mr. Gaddish saluted Lieutenant Nelson as he passed by.

Captain Collingwood brightened up his face, "I apologize for the delay. Please, come in and have a seat."

Corporal Shipton had now just noticed that a porcupine was following the lady into the captain's cabin and maintained a look of bewilderment on his face in an effort to understand why this might be. Lieutenant Nelson, Clementine, and Porky stepped into the captain's cabin. Corporal Shipton closed the door behind them and remained at guard outside and took a great deep breath of relief as he reflected on the eventful morning that had come to pass.

Captain Collingwood was still a bit flustered by the company of the lady who had just entered his cabin behind the lieutenant. The large macaw that sat on her right shoulder was whispering something into the lady's ear. A porcupine, of all things, stood at her feet. And over her right shoulder was slung a heavy satchel which seemed to be of no burden at all to her. At first glance, the captain perceived her to have formidable mental and physical strength, not to mention her eyes which cast forth keen wit. Moreover, she maintained a sharply focused demeanor despite her apparent fatigue and physical disarray.

Nelson struggled to recapture Collingwood's attention, "Captain, I would like to introduce you to Clementine. She claims that her father is the king of the Canary Islands."

Captain Collingwood was now thoroughly enthralled, "Why that would make her a princess."

"That it would Sir," replied Nelson with expressed uncertainty at the captain's delay of comprehension.

Captain Collingwood mumbled in thought under his breath, "I send for water and I get a princess."

Nelson worked to regain his eye contact from the floor, "And a Spanish officer sir. A Spanish Captain at that. Don Pablo is his name Sir."

Stuttering a bit more now, "Where? Where is the captain?"

"In the sick bay, Sir, being evaluated by Mr. Morris the surgeon's mate. I told Captain Don Pablo that you would be seeing him in the hold after a bit Sir," informed Nelson.

"Please, sit down at my desk here and rest a bit," invited the Captain.

"That would be wonderful, thank you," replied Lieutenant Nelson taking a sigh of relief.

"Not you Lieutenant! The princess!" clarified the Captain with increasing irritation.

Nelson was a bit embarrassed, "Of course Sir, my apologies." Clementine took her seat and the captain set before her some water, fresh fruit, and bread.

"Thank you, Captain," said Clementine graciously as she set down her treasury and took her seat. She broke the bread giving half to Porky, then she took Marty the macaw off of her shoulder and set him on the Captain's desk before the fruit that he might have something to eat. Captain Collingwood looked a bit puzzled and was going to say something but was interrupted by the door knocking.

"Nelson, would you tend to that please," asked Collingwood.

Nelson made his way over to the door. "What is it Corporal?" asked Nelson quite irritated at the interruption.

"Well, you may not believe this Sir, but there is a strange sea creature likened a bit to a beaver having a bill like a duck that just came aboard requesting the whereabouts of Princess Clementine.

"Well, what is it Lieutenant?!" asked the captain gruffly from within the cabin.

"Ah yes, well you see sir the men are trying to chase a strange sea creature off of the deck who just happens to be requesting to see the princess," informed Nelson.

"You have got to be joking. What kind of creature is it?" inquired the captain.

Before Nelson could answer Princess Clementine spoke up, "That would be Pastor Platypus. We owe our rescue to that creature; please let him back at once. He is not to be harmed!" Nelson turned back to Shipton, "Go quickly Corporal and bring the creature here."

214

"Yes Sir," and off he ran. Nelson came back in and stood handsomely by the captain's desk. The lieutenant looked very becoming with his well decorated and stately overcoat.

Clementine sat up straight. Poised with authority, she regained the captain's attention, "Gentlemen, I am grateful to God that we have been brought into the shelter of your ship. On behalf of the citizens of the Canary Islands and my father, I thank you. Your hospitality and provision for us will not go unnoticed."

Clementine placed a loaded-down satchel on the Captain's desk with a firm thud. Just then Pastor Platypus showed up at Clementine's side. A bit frazzled and wet, Pastor Platypus did the best he could to straighten himself out and acknowledged Captain Collingwood with a nod and a salute, "Thank you Captain for sending for me."

Clementine knelt down and warmly greeted the platypus with tender affection. She gave him a piece of bread and stood up to face Collingwood, "Captain, I have a matter of extreme significance to discuss with you regarding the future of the Canary Islands and the Spanish Navy. I have with me highly sensitive information that I believe will be of great interest to England."

The tone of the princess's voice commanded and captured Collingwood's attention. The captain turned to Nelson, "Lieutenant, have Corporal Shipton ensure that we are not interrupted under any circumstance for the time being."

The captain turned back to Clementine, "England is at your service my Lady. You have traveled far and endured much. What message do you bring?"

Chapter XXVII

Papers Unravel the Spanish Navy

Princess Clementine formally addressed the English officers, "Our Islands have come under attack by Spain. Before my father was captured, he disguised me the best that he could as an ordinary sailor and snuck me out to sea in a small merchant vessel bound for the American Colonies. He entrusted me with many vitally important documents which clearly, and in detail, expose the secret strengths and weaknesses of Spain's newest ships as well as some of their key ports in the West Indies. Our spies have obtained this information at the cost of their lives. The documents and maps are in the chest which I have placed here on your desk.

"The fate of the Canary Islands and Spain's rule in the western colonies now rests in your hands Captain Collingwood. Our people are peaceful and we want to remain free. We do not want the crown of Spain to rule over our islands. Their thirst for wealth and temporary riches cannot be quenched. We have no way to defend ourselves. I have journeyed far and endured much to seek the favor and protection of the Crown of England."

"I highly commend you for your efforts of valor Princess Clementine, and I can assure you that the Crown of England has the best interests in mind for the Canary Islands. We share a common enemy and that, therefore, would make us allies and friends."

The Captain asked, "May I see what your father has entrusted to you?"

"Yes, but realize this first," warned the Princess, "before you take on the responsibility of its knowledge, Spain has sent their navy's best officers and most powerful ships to recover what you are asking to see. I barely escaped the hands of the Spanish. And, if it were not for the efforts of my new found friends, Captain Marty the Macaw, Porky the Porcupine and Pastor Platypus, this dispatch would not be before you now."

The princess continued, "Capitan Don Pablo's life is also indebted to my dear friends here. If it were not for their courageous rescue, he would have been brutally killed by the Taíno tribe."

Marty climbed up Clementine's arm to whisper something in her ear.

"Of course", she softly replied.

Clementine turned back to the captain, "Could I trouble you for a bit more fruit and bread for my friends here?"

"Yes, of course" replied Collingwood.

"Lieutenant," Collingwood nodded to Nelson. Nelson understood and began assembling more food for their guests.

Captain Collingwood continued, "Well, Princess Clementine, I honorably welcome your friends aboard the Hinchinbrook. Proper recognition will be given to them. And as for your dispatches, I will receive them and do everything within my power to come to the aid of your islands. But, understand, my influence has its limitations."

"I understand Captain," acknowledged Clementine formally handing over her chest. "I have also brought along a little something to help you get past any limitations you may encounter."

The princess reached into the satchel and pulled out a large solid gold bar and set it on the desk with an immense thud right in front of Captain Collingwood. Both Lieutenant Nelson and the captain's eyes widened at the sight. She reached into her satchel and repeated the process 4 more times, placing three gold bars side by side and two more on top making a small pyramid, and atop the gold she placed her security chest. Captain Collingwood remained in silent awe at the sight. Clementine removed a necklace from around her neck which held one key, and handed it to the captain.

"Since you were willing to help out of the goodness of your heart's convictions without payment," said the Princess, "I now present to you a gift from my father to compensate you for any inconvenience or limitations you may encounter."

"My God in Heaven," is all that came out of Captain Collingwood's mouth for a few passing moments. "This gold has the seal of King George!"

"I imagine my father recovered it from the Spanish. He wanted it returned to its rightful owner," informed Clementine.

Captain Collingwood sat up straight in his chair and opened the chest. He shuffled through the papers a bit partially opening a few. Urgency flooded Captain Collingwood's eyes. He removed his hat and wiped some sweat from his brow.

"God help us!" Captain Collingwood slumped back in his chair in astonishment. "Lieutenant Nelson, come take a look at this."

"Ship plans! These are the ship building plans of the Spanish fleet's newest and most powerful vessels most of which I believe have been built at the Habana ship yards!" commented Nelson with growing intensity. "And look at these", pointed out the captain, "These are detailed maps of some of their most fortified harbors and fortresses here in the West Indies!"

The Captain looked up to the princess, "My Lady, this is absolutely fantastic! We should now be able to well exploit Spain's weaknesses. We have lost many good officers and many good vessels to Spain's newest ships because of their speed, maneuverability, and armor which has well exceeded our own. The Admiralty will be most pleased, and I'm certain they will offer a fine blockade of protection for your Islands."

The Princess replied with a heavy heart, "My cousin served as a spy at the Habana ship yards in Cuba. He laid down his life to obtain this information. Also, you will find our written Declaration of Independence. There is only one and Spain refuses to acknowledge that it exists."

Princess Clementine took a deep breath and looked Captain Collinwood sharply in the eyes, "I will leave the actions that must follow to your judgment."

Captain Collingwood stood up, "Princess, these documents will be the undoing of Spain's influence at sea, and I am certain that the gold will help fund the efforts needed to effectively defend your islands. England is indebted to the sacrifices your family has made."

"Lieutenant", ordered Collingwood pointing to the creatures in the room, "Place upon these honorable guests the Captain's

Star so that none of our crew shall misunderstand their place among us."

"Yes Captain," replied Nelson.

"Now explain to me something a little further Princess," requested the captain, "you mentioned a Spanish ship. The one you escaped from. Tell me more about this."

Nelson meanwhile was introducing himself to Porky the porcupine and Pastor Platypus while placing a ribbon around their necks on which the Captain's Star hung close, resting with royal glory on their chests in recognition of their good deeds and their status given to them by Captain Collingwood. Nelson was doing circles looking for Marty the macaw.

"This is no time for dancing Lieutenant! Might I ask what you are doing?" inquired the Captain slightly irritated.

"I'm looking for the large bird," answered Nelson.

"His name is Marty, Captain Marty……he is a self-proclaimed captain," informed the princess with a little wink.

Captain Collingwood pointed out to Nelson, "Ha! Well Lieutenant, it seems that you have been out ranked by our feathered friend here. We will have to raise a flag for him just below mine aloft the main. Have the carpenter tend to it at once. And Lieutenant, you should consider my hat with the long red feathers sticking out the back which seems to be moving across the floor by itself!"

Porky chuckled softly at the sight.

Under the hat one could hear Marty shouting out orders which sounded muffled under the felt, "Beat to general quarters!

Hoist the main sail! Squaaawk! Clear the deck for action! Larboard battery fire!"

Nelson lifted the Captain's hat, "My apologies *Captain* Marty, but *our* captain still requires this hat." Nelson handed the hat back to Collingwood, and placed the Captain's Star on Marty as well.

The Princess went on to answer Captain Collingwood's initial question, "Yes, Captain, I suspect that there are at least two first-rate Spanish ships of war up the shore to the north-east. One has two decks of cannons and the other has three decks."

"My god," said the Captain as he rubbed his face in serious thought.

"We are quite vulnerable at anchor here in the harbor," thought Nelson aloud.

Captain Collingwood snapped back at Nelson, "Yes, thank you Lieutenant, I am well aware of our current vulnerabilities!"

The captain stared down again silently at his desk rubbing his chin a bit as he looked over the detailed drawings of the latest Spanish vessels laid down at the Habana Harbor.

The Captain ended his thoughtful silence as everyone in the room waited with anticipation, "Alright then," Captain Collingwood hit the desk resolutely with a flat hand, "Lieutenant, send communication to Captain Locker aboard the Lowestoffe informing him of hostile Spanish ships in our immediate area. Raise the signal flags accordingly for them make ready at once. Take some men and row over to the Lowestoffe and personally inform Captain Locker and Captain Locker *alone* of our situation here regarding the princess and our new assets of gold and information. Have him patrol these surrounding waters to provide some form of security while we prepare to get both the princess and these dispatches back to Portsmouth England as soon as possible! And tell him we plan to leave under the cover of night."

"Aye-Aye Captain", replied Lieutenant Nelson with a salute, and with that, Nelson left the captain's cabin tipping his hat to the Princess on his way out.

"And as for you Princess Clementine", said Captain Collingwood, "my cabin is now your cabin. It will be secured at all times by a marine just outside that door there. It is the best I have to offer."

"Thank you Captain, but where will you stay? I certainly do not mind a smaller room elsewhere on the ship", replied Clementine.

"No, I insist, Princess. England extends to you all that we are able at such a great distance from home. I do not think I will be sleeping tonight anyway. I will have my men draw up a fresh barrel of hot water that you may get cleaned up and refreshed after your long journey. There is an extra bunk in the lieutenant's quarters. I will stay there with my officers."

Clementine stood up from out of the chair and grabbed the captain's hand, "Thank you Captain for the kindness you have shown towards my father and me."

"My pleasure", replied the captain, "Your friends Pastor Platypus, Porky the porcupine, and Marty…. *Captain* Marty, will be respected as officers among the crew and they will stay with the midshipmen and take orders only from Lieutenant Nelson and me. In the meantime, I must find an officer to get started on making copies of the documents sent from your father. I think it would be best to have two copies as to ensure that they reach the admiralty in Portsmouth."

"Captain, I would be happy to complete this task for you if you think it necessary," offered the princess.

The Captain hesitated a bit in thought, "Yes, I think that would work nicely."

An idea sparked in the captain's mind, "You know, if it is not too much trouble, would you perhaps be able to translate the Spanish to English on our behalf. This may save us a lot of time back in Portsmouth if you know what I mean."

"Of course Captain, this is a wonderful idea and no trouble at all," replied Clementine smiling with delight. This in turn made the hard-faced captain grin which was a treasure in itself.

"Splendid, splendid indeed!" responded Captain Collingwood. He then ordered Marty, Porky and the pastor, "Honorable guests, I will show you to your quarters and introduce you to our fellow officers."

Marty tried to follow with the captain's hat which was sliding towards the door with a long waddling red tail sticking out of the back. Collingwood spoke up, "Marty, I will, however, be requiring my hat!"

Marty stuck his wings out the sides and managed to take off in flight landing on the captain's head! The hat's position appeared normal; however, the captain acquired a feathered ponytail! Everyone in the room laughed. Captain Collingwood bellowed a bit deeper to get through to the macaw, "I would prefer to wear my hat *without* you in it if you do not mind!"

Marty laughed from under the hat a muffled sort of cackle. And everyone else laughed even louder. The captain took it well, but he did look towards the princess for a bit of help as he removed his cap.

"Marty, that's enough fun for now. Perhaps see if the lieutenant needs any help," suggested the princess. Off he flew out to the quarter deck landing on Lieutenant Nelson's shoulder who was busy preparing a boat to row to the Lowestoffe. Believing he outranked Nelson, Marty ordered, "Alright Lieutenant, shove off now. Drop the dinghy! Take to the ores, take to the ores! SQUAWK!"

Nelson cringed at Marty's screeching loud voice. He humored him a bit, "Yes Sir, Captain Marty. I am privileged that you have chosen me to join you!"

As the others stepped out of Collingwood's cabin, Pastor Platypus turned and waved goodbye to the princess, "We'll see you in about two or three bells." And off they went following Captain Collingwood.

As the captain left the princess, he placed the gold in his safe and said, "Please don't feel like you must get started on the translations right away. Take the time to rest and refresh yourself. You and your friends will be our honored guests at dinner this evening. It will be just the officers, but afterwards you will be left alone for the night."

"Thank you Captain", replied Clementine. The captain stepped out and closed the door behind him assigning one marine to stand guard for the princess at all times.

Captain Collingwood ordered Corporal Shipton, "No one is to enter this cabin unless it is me or Lieutenant Nelson, is that clear?"

"Yes Sir", replied Corporal Shipton.

"You may change the guard once per watch," finished the captain, and off he led their new guests to their personal quarters.

The door was shut. For the first time in days the princess found herself in peaceful solitude and silence. She took a giant sigh of relief and sat in her chair looking across at the documents on the captain's desk from her father. The ship creaked as it rocked in the small waves of the harbor. Feeling safe and quite satisfied with the situation, she laid down on a bench in-between two book cases, closed her eyes, and fell fast asleep.

Chapter XXVIII

Greetings, Stories, and Fights

Below decks Porky and Pastor Platypus were well received right away by the young Midshipmen who welcomed having such fun and witty mascots aboard.

Any break from their daily routine of intense training and discipline was welcome. For some of the young Midshipmen it was their first time away from home, and they marveled at the sight of these impressive creatures which they had never seen anything of the like before.

There was a lot of laughing and introductions going on in the Midshipmen's quarters.

"Hey, take a look at this gents! Lieutenant Nelson is rowing over to the Lowestoffe," alerted one of the Midshipmen to his peers as he looked out the larboard portal.

"Is it just the lieutenant?" asked one of the other midshipman.

"No, No. A couple of marines are at the ores, and a giant parrot of sorts on his shoulder!"

"Yeah, something is up for sure," another pointed out, "Corporal Shipton has been standing guard at the captain's cabin for the entire last watch!"

Pastor Platypus spoke up to catch the attention of the eight young midshipmen, "Tell me more about this Nelson fellow. It seems you all hold him in special regard."

The most senior of the midshipman spoke up, "We could tell stories all day about the lieutenant. The chances are good that he'll make some new ones before the sun sets! There is never a dull moment with Lieutenant Nelson!"

The midshipmen all broke out in laughter agreeing with the statement.

"Remind me of your name," asked Pastor Platypus.

"Wexcombe, Jack Wexcombe," warmly answered the midshipman.

Jack continued as the room went silent in anticipation of a Nelson story, "The man who claims 'Fear, I know nothing of it' has more zeal for his duty than for life itself. He walks the deck in the most frigid weather, when your breath forms a thick cloud before you, with no jacket on of any sort. And when asked if he is cold, he claims 'My love for England keeps me warm'!"

Another young midshipman by the name Norman Gainsford spoke up, "I've never studied so hard in my life. When we're on watch, he makes us take readings with our sextant to perfect our celestial navigation, and he is constantly quizzing us on sail names, rigging names, and flag signals. When we come below deck to rest, we have piles of navigational assignments and book work on the history of England!"

Midshipman Wexcombe carried on, "Right you are, but a fine officer he'll make of you someday, you'll see."

Then Wexcombe turned back to the platypus and continued, "I've seen much action with Lieutenant Nelson. He'll break the line of battle and sail right at ships perpendicular to their lines.

Rather than making the traditional broadside passes. He'll rake their sterns and bows and board them before they even know their being attacked! God be his strength, he'll stand on the deck in the middle of action with musket balls whizzing past his head, cannon shot exploding all around, and the man won't even flinch! He'll stand calm as if nothing is happening. He pulled me aside on one occasion, with explosions all around and wounded all scattered about, and he took the time to point out specific errors of the French fighting tactics as if we were in a quaint classroom!"

Midshipman Gainsford broke back in with excitement, "Better yet, better yet," he said regaining the room's excited focus. "Remember the time when he was just an apprentice on that expedition to find the Northwest Passage. Well, you see Mr. Platypus, his ship got locked in with ice all around and they were absolutely stuck."

"I know all about ice!" said Porky, "Where I come from you don't need faith to walk on water, because it's frozen half the year!" The room broke out in laughter.

Midshipman Gainsford continued, "Well, Nelson was serving under Captain Lutwidge on an expedition to sail to the North Pole. I believe he was on the HMS Racehorse, and even though her hull was strengthened, it was no match for the ice they encountered and the ship was ice-locked in no time at all!"

Wexcombe interjected, "Go on with it, get to the good part!"

Everyone was listening contentedly. Gainsford continued, "Well one night, during the middle or morning watch, Nelson snuck off board using a rising fog as cover, and he and one of his shipmates set out over the ice in pursuit of a giant white bear!

The fog thickened and Capt. Lutwidge noticed the absence of his young sailors and became alarmed. It wasn't until morning that the fog cleared and Nelson could be clearly seen atop a frozen berg.

The captain called for Nelson to return to the ship, and Nelson shouted back, "Do let me get a blow at this devil with the butt-end of my musket and we shall have him!" The captain didn't appreciate that response and fired a musket at them startling both Nelson and the bear. The bear ran off just as Nelson was winding up to take a swing at him with his musket. He returned to the ship to find waiting for him a firm reprimand from Capt. Lutwidge, and do you know what Nelson said!?"

Pastor Platypus and Porky shook their head 'no'.

"He said", finished Wexcombe, "Sir, I wished to kill the bear that I might carry the skin to my father!'"

And the room erupted with laughter at the incomprehensible audacity of their lieutenant. Midshipman Gainsford peered out the port window at the Lowestoffe, "Gents, Gents!"

He finally got the room's attention. "The Lowestoffe let down her sails and is heading out of the harbor. I wonder what that is all about?" asked Wexcombe aloud.

Gainsford took a more careful look out the window, "The men aboard the Lowestoffe look as if they are readying themselves for action, and judging by the look on the lieutenant's face I'd say we better ready ourselves too."

Gainsford spoke up, "Let's get our things and our minds in order gentlemen. Nelson will be back to the ship soon. Clearly something significant is at hand and we all know the lieutenant will expect nothing less than our very best."

An older, but much less mature midshipman, Mr. Kensington, spoke up in hostile sarcasm as he stepped up to Gainsford's face, "What!? I suppose you think that *you* are Nelson's 'very best'!? Well allow me to remind you that you are not lieutenant yet!"

Gainsford looked back at him with a face of stone, "By god, John, have you not yet learned to restrain your tongue! Do what you wish with yourself! Make good use of your feet now and take yourself out of my way. I have better things to do with my day!"

Gainsford walked a bit into John to step past him. Midshipman Kensington, who had many times failed his lieutenant testing, sternly pushed Gainsford back. Gainsford threw his books down on the table, grabbed Kensington's collar and wound up for a punch. But Gainsford didn't throw the punch. Both stood there frozen.

Gainsford broke half smile and relaxed his fist bringing his arm back to his side, "You aren't worth the trouble." Gainsford continued with calm intensity, "One hundred lashes to the back of a fool and they still won't learn to separate themselves from their folly."

Gainsford picked up his books and turned to walk away. Kensington tackled Gainsford to the ground and began throwing punches.

Gainsford didn't fight back, but he didn't have to. Soon a pile of five midshipmen dove in to restrain Kensington!

Suddenly there was a firm pounding on the cabin door. All the midshipmen stood up and were filled with fear. Their fears were confirmed as the door opened and the late afternoon sun shone in perfectly displaying the silhouette of a man wearing a lieutenant's hat. His boots clicking against the floor as he stepped in seemed to be the only sound currently happening in the entire Caribbean Sea.

The men were silent and still breathing hard from the fight. Nelson stood still looking them over with disgust in his face and fury in his eyes. With all the tattered uniforms and the blood running down from the mouths of various midshipmen it was no secret what had been occurring. Nelson allowed a few moments of intense silence which felt like eternity to the midshipmen. They all knew punishments aboard ships of the Royal Navy were harsh and they all knew there was no going back to England anytime soon.

Most would spend the rest of their lives aboard ships, and the course of their life would often be directly related to their success as midshipmen. It was metaphorically and literally, at times, a life or death situation for the young boys serving as midshipmen in the Royal Navy.

Nelson finally broke the silence and quietly and simply ordered, "You will all present yourselves on the quarter deck in exactly ten minutes." And with that Nelson turned and walked out.

All the midshipmen began to bustle with activity talking in small conversations with each other as they went along getting their cabin in order while making proper adjustments to their uniforms and general appearance.

Pastor Platypus motioned to Porky, "Well then, it sounds as if the midshipmen will be busy. We should probably join Marty and take a bit of a rest before our formal dinner this evening in the captain's cabin. I have a feeling that we may not get much sleep tonight."

Porky looked up to where Pastor Platypus was pointing to see Captain Marty sleeping balanced upon a large wooden beam with his feathers all fluffed up and his beak tucked back in between his wings.

The ledge atop the large oak beam appeared inviting. All three were soon curled up, tucked away, and sleeping above the nervously clamoring midshipmen.

The midshipmen were rarely all called up to the Quarter Deck at the same time. They knew that the captain would likely be there. There was no verbal punishment from Lieutenant Nelson which is what worried them the most. It meant that the consequences of their actions were waiting for them on the quarter deck with the captain and the lieutenant.

Chapter XXIX

Dining in Good Company

"I haven't had a meal like this since I was home last with my family in the Canary Islands," complemented Clementine.

"Yes, this is quite the treat," commented Pastor Platypus. "Thank you for hosting us Captain Collingwood."

The captain finished taking a sip of his drink, "No trouble at all my friends, no trouble at all. We have also been refreshed by your company, wouldn't you say lieutenant?"

"Yes, indeed," Nelson nodded his head in satisfaction taking a sip from his water. "Will you have no rum Mr. Nelson?" asked the captain offering the lieutenant the bottle.

"No thank you Captain," politely declined Lieutenant Nelson, "you know how I prefer to keep a clear mind. I have a feeling we shall soon be encountering the Spanish. I would prefer to remain as mentally prepared as possible."

"I see. Duty. Yes, Good man," commented the captain as he set down the bottle. Looking up at his guests, "That is why I love serving with this fine officer. He truly is a great asset to England and will make a fine captain someday!"

The captain raised his glass, "Here's to England, and to the liberty of the Canary Islands! May the Spanish run like dogs with their tails tucked between their legs all the way back to Spain!" Everyone gave glad cheer to the toast and continued to feast and exchange stories.

Their conversation kept getting distracted by the pounding of footsteps above them on the poop deck. When the footsteps stampeded above there would be a burst of shouts and orders then all would be quiet again.

Porky asked Nelson, "Lieutenant, should we be concerned about what is occurring on deck? It seems a bit out of ordinary routine."

Pastor Platypus, Marty, and Clementine were also curious to hear the explanation.

Nelson chuckled a bit, "That would be our midshipmen." Nelson struggled to find a nice way to explain what was going on, "Let's just say they are working on building their unity and personal character. It is also highly probable that we will encounter the Spanish soon. I want them in a proper mindset when we set sail at dusk."

"Yes, well said, unity and character," affirmed the captain as he went to take another sip of his evening drink.

"Might I inquire how exactly England goes about transforming their boys into men of the sea?" asked Clementine.

Captain Collingwood smiled warmly, "Well now, I can't quite speak for England as a whole, but I can tell you how our lieutenant here does the task!"

The Captain patted Nelson firmly on the back of his shoulder, "There is not another officer I know of who trains midshipmen like this fellow here. He trains up the whole person, developing them in every aspect with a relentless zeal not likened to any other lieutenant I have had the pleasure to serve with! The young gentlemen both love and fear the man! He works them in body, mind, and soul. In the end, they all respect and adore him. Two or three of them, in fact, are scheduled to take their lieutenant examinations upon our return to Portsmouth. That's the way of it I tell you! Right when they become useful, they get promoted and reassigned."

Leaning into Nelson a bit, the captain reaffirmed, "Be it known, I intend on keeping Mr. Gainsford as 2nd Lieutenant as soon as he passes his examinations!"

Nelson was clearly uncomfortable with the captain's compliments, "Please Captain, any man would do the same if given my duties."

Clementine asked with a sparkling gleam of admiration in her eyes, "So, Lieutenant, what exactly do you have the midshipmen doing now?"

Captain Collingwood spoke on Nelson's behalf, "I couldn't believe it myself! The lieutenant here has them climb to the mizzen mast head, back down, all together up to the Main Mast head, then back down, and up to the foremast head, and then down – all the while the crew are shaking the shrouds as they climb to give them a tough time about it. After they all crawl out and touch the end of the bowsprit, they must run all the way back to the stern of the ship and report to the Quarter Deck to solve navigational problems by written exam! And they have been at it for nearly two hours now!"

Nelson interrupted as to defend himself, "They must learn to handle the rigging in high winds, they must learn to stay focused in the midst of disorderly circumstances, they must set aside their fear of heights, and, for the sake of England, they must stop quarreling amongst themselves and learn to work together to accomplish goals that would otherwise be individually impossible!"

Captain Collingwood stared at Nelson for a moment chewing his salted brisket heartily, "Outstanding Lieutenant. Outstanding indeed!"

"A spot of coffee please, a spot if you will," asked Marty.

Porky shot back, "That is the last thing *you* need Marty, more energy!"

They all laughed a bit, and Porky poured him some anyway.

"That's wonderful lieutenant that you have such purposes behind what you do and that anger does not drive you, but rather love for your country and for the men. In light of that lieutenant, we have much in common," commented Princess Clementine with a delighted smile.

Suddenly, Corporal Shipton busted open the door to the Captain's quarters sharply interrupting their dinner and conversations.

"My God man, have you no sense to knock first. What could possibly be the matter?!" bellowed the Captain. "Masts over the east ridge moving towards the harbor Sir!" announced the Corporal catching his breath.

The Captain stood up and walked towards him and asked in a low growl, "What flag do they fly?"

Corporal Shipton replied with beads of sweat running down his face and fear in his eyes, "That of Spain!"

Chapter XXX

Cornered by a Spanish Goliath

"Beat to general quarters Corporal Shipton and have some of your men stand by to cut away the mud hook!" ordered Captain Collingwood.

The Captain stepped into the doorway to look out towards the quarter deck and shouted to the quartermaster who was looking on with his telescope, "Any sign of the Lowestoffe!?"

The quartermaster shouted back, "No Captain, she sailed off on her patrol at about four bells into the first-dog watch. This Spanish ship has come in close to the coast from the northeast Sir. It would have been difficult to spot her approach."

The captain replied under his breath, "Let us pray the Lowestoffe spotted her and made a change of course to come to our aid."

Captain Collingwood dashed back into his cabin, "Corporal!"

Corporal Shipton stood at attention, "Yes Sir."

The captain continued, "Take the princess and hide her below and have three of your best marines keep close watch over her."

The captain turned to Clementine, "Forgive me for not protecting you better, but I must take you below into safe hiding for the time being."

Clementine stood up and maintained a calm peace about her, "I am not worried captain. It is clear to me that you have made the Lord the true master of this ship, he will uphold you in this hour."

"Yes", replied the captain half-distracted by a hundred other thoughts, "Did you happen to make copies of the documents?" Princess Clementine handed a thick envelope to the Captain, "These are for you and for England. I only had time to copy a few. The originals I will take below with me."

The Captain smiled brightly, "Thank you Princess." He placed the papers in a hidden inside pocket of his jacket, and the princess went below with her guards. Nelson signaled for Marty, Porky, and Pastor Platypus to accompany him to the quarter deck.

"Whenever we beat to general quarters, you all are to report to me on the quarter deck immediately, understood?" ordered Lieutenant Nelson.

"Yes Sir!" replied all three in unison.

Once on the quarter deck Captain Collingwood took hold of his brass looking scope and waited for the Spanish ship to fully appear out from behind a small hill which separated the East end of the harbor from the sea.

A massive bowsprit emerged from behind the hill. It was nearly as big as the Hinchinbrook's mizzen mast! The massive bow surged forth and came slowly into view.

Suddenly it appeared, a massive 1st rate ship with *three* gun decks.

"My God," muttered Captain Collingwood to Nelson who was standing directly to his side, "It's the Santísima Trinidad, Spain's flagship! I've never heard of it ever coming to this side of the Atlantic. They must really want what the princess has!"

Collingwood compressed his looking scope and turned to Nelson, "Lieutenant, why do you allow that bird to sit upon your shoulder!?"

Nelson replied matter-of-factly, "It is his general-quarters position."

Collingwood sighed, "It looks as if the affairs of Princess Clementine and her father are far more pressing than I first realized. For God's sake, they have sent their flagship all the way across the Atlantic after her. And now here we sit at anchor with our stern facing her completely vulnerable to what appears to be a good 75-gun broadside!"

Nelson took a look, "Córdoba, Admiral Córdoba! That is the commander's flag which is being flown above the main."

"Let us not forget about Captain Don Pablo," reminded a familiar voice from behind them.

Both Captain Collingwood and Lieutenant Nelson turned around immediately, for the comment was that of a woman's voice. They both found themselves momentarily speechless at the sight of the princess dressed in a Midshipman's uniform with her hair tucked up into her hat and a bit of dirt rubbed on her face to liken the start of a beard.

The marines ran up finally catching up to her, "Forgive us Captain, there was no stopping her."

Marty chuckled on Nelson's shoulder and turned his head sideways and lowered it to get a clear look, "Lookin' good...SIR!" and he cackled some more!

The helmsman urgently shouted, "She's opening her gun ports Captain!" There was no time to debate with the princess who maintained the look of a young midshipman.

By the time Captain Collingwood turned to look, three bright flashes were seen from the top deck of the Trinidad. Three chest-compressing booms thundered through the air. The ocean exploded just off of their stern in what appeared to be very precise warning shots.

"They want us to surrender as their prize", muttered the captain. The rest of the Trinidad's seventy starboard gun ports opened clearly signaling the implied consequences of not surrendering.

Midshipman Clementine spoke up softly behind Captain Collingwood, "I would advise bringing Captain Don Pablo immediately into full view here on the quarter deck."

The captain understood her reasoning, and turned to his marines with a deep sternness in his voice, "Get Don Pablo on deck immediately!" And the marines ran quickly to retrieve him.

"Mr. Gainsford," continued the captain, "Take six marines and Midshipman Clementine here and prepare to smuggle her to shore should they open fire upon us to send us to the bottom. Remain in hiding on land until the Lowestoffe returns. You have better chances with the natives than we do with the Trinidad!"

The captain turned back to Nelson and the bos'n, "Have the anchor at the bow cut without being seen. The tide is low. And the wind is in our favor to drift us to the north side of the harbor. Be sure no one goes aloft lest they suspect we are preparing to lower our sails and run for it in which case we would be done for in seconds. Our only hope is to get her to pursue us into the harbor towards the north side where there rests a reef. With only her bow facing us and her cannons away she will get stuck on the reef in pursuit of us! Once she is stuck we shall beat her with all cannons until the Lowestoffe returns! God help us!"

Captain Collingwood lifted his looking glass to his eye to see again if there was any sign of the Captain Locker and the Lowestoffe which there was not. He then peered to the forecastle of the Santísima Trinidad to see Admiral Louis de Córdoba looking through his scope directly back at him!

Chapter XXXI

The Best Way to Stop a Broadside

The barrels of the Santísima Trinidad's cannons began to appear as her crew pushed them out of the gun ports to take aim at the stern of the Hinchinbrook. All Admiral Córdoba would have to do now is just nod his head and the Hinchinbrook would be at the bottom of the harbor. Captain Collingwood's men were growing quite anxious.

At that moment, Capitan Don Pablo came hobbling up the stairs to the poop deck at the very stern of the ship still dressed in his uniform which clearly portrayed him as a Spanish captain. He was brought to stand next to Captain Collingwood who was still staring at Admiral Córdoba in the looking scope.

"For heaven's sake, wave! Do something!" urged Captain Collingwood to Don Pablo who began immediately waving to his flag ship with outstretched arms.

Nelson asked Captain Collingwood, "Any sign they acknowledge his presence?"

One by one the Santísima Trinidad started to close its gun ports keeping only the swivel cannons at the ready. The crew of the Hinchinbrook breathed a sigh of relief and let out a brief cheer. Lieutenant Nelson and Captain Collingwood kept their stately composure as they realized their every move was being closely observed by the Spanish Admiral.

"Thank God!" sighed Captain Collingwood collapsing his brass telescope.

Corporal Shipton was the first to report, "Captain! They are lowering a skiff into the water with the admiral and a number of their soldiers in it!"

Captain Collingwood turned to whisper in Nelson's ear, "Let us assemble on the main deck at once, but not a word of the princess. If the matter of her whereabouts is addressed, she was sent back to Portsmouth aboard the Lowestoffe with Captain Locker."

"I understand Sir. Is she still aboard or did they row her towards shore?" replied Nelson.

"Yes, I believe she is below decks at this time. She is so well disguised, there is no telling where she is at this point," concluded the captain.

Nelson gave orders to have the crew and marines prepare the deck for a formal yet secure reception of the Spanish Admiral and his men.

Nelson turned to Captain Marty who was sitting on his left shoulder watching Admiral Córdoba and his men rowing over to the Hinchinbrook, "Marty, do you have an understanding of the workings of a ship?"

Marty moved his head in front of Nelson's so that he could see him eye to eye. He paused for an anxious moment with uncomfortable closeness, "Yes I do!"

"Good", said Nelson adjusting to his closeness, "Give your captain's metal to me so that they do not spot you. I want you to stand watch as a spy on the Trinidad. Go first to the forest, then fly to her from behind. Be as unnoticed as possible. Fly towards her just above the water from the northeast. Remain

243

with the ship until we get ourselves out of this mess. Do whatever you can to delay and disable that monster the best you can to aid our escape. Once night has fallen return to the Hinchinbrook, or whenever you think it best. The wind should be in our favor for a quick escape to the west southwest after sunset. Now go!"

"Aye-Aye, Lieutenant," and off Marty flew over the main deck. Marty quickly spotted Princess Clementine among the men and flew over to her, "Good Bye Midshipman Clementine."

The Princess inquired, "Are you going over to the Trinidad?"

"Yes Princess" answered Marty.

"Listen closely Marty" urged the princess, "As I was copying the plans from the Habana ship yard, I came across a detailed drawing of the ships steering system. The tiller for the rudder is down on the second deck behind the room where the gun powder is stored. You might consider finding a way to lock it in its place once they have a course set. Better yet, if you can cut the ropes governing the mechanism, their rudder shouldn't answer to the helm. Now go Marty, I'll be praying for your safe return!"

The princess gave Marty a little kiss on his beak, and he was on his way diving off the quarter deck flying close to the sea towards land as not to be seen by the Spanish.

Princess Clementine, disguised as a midshipman stayed on the Quarter Deck looking down to the main deck where Captain Collingwood was now standing with his marines. Captain Don Pablo was waiting to receive the Spanish Admiral.

Lieutenant Nelson knelt down to speak with Pastor Platypus, "Mr. Platypus, I'll have you take to the sea and remain close to or under the Spanish skiff that is nearly upon us. Should anything go wrong on deck, do your best to try to reverse it!"

"At your service," saluted Pastor Platypus, and with that he immediately dove into the water falling about twenty feet before splashing into the sea. The platypus swam under the Hinchinbrook to where the Spanish skiff was now being brought alongside. He came up for air just at the stern of the skiff to listen to the situation as it unfolded.

"Porky," ordered Nelson "You stay close. Do your best to find and monitor Midshipman Clementine and report to me her whereabouts the next time I ask, understood."

"Aye-Aye Lieutenant," and Porky the Porcupine scurried off.

Nelson went down to be with Captain Collingwood who was waiting for the admiral to come aboard His Majesty's Ship Hinchinbrook. The marines were beating their drums as the coxswain piped aboard the admiral. Captain Collingwood and the Spanish Admiral now stood face to face and the drumming stopped. There was a tense silence. Not a sound could be heard for a few seconds other than waves lapping up against the side of the Hinchinbrook.

Chapter XXXII

Dastardly Diplomacy

The Spanish admiral keenly surveyed those aboard the English ship as if looking for somebody in particular. The admiral's overcoat was immaculate. Golden braided aiguillettes adorned his chest and golden tasseled epaulettes decorated his shoulders with authority. A stately athwart bicorn with golden embroidery sat proudly atop his head. Medals and stars from the Crown of Spain filled the left side of the off-white jacket, and a red sash came over his left shoulder and across the chest.

The admiral's face was well wrinkled from many decades gone past. His skin was dark and greatly weathered from a lift-time under the sun and at sea. Full of restrained anger, his facial expression looked as if it was chiseled from granite. The Admiral did not remove his stately hat in the presence of Captain Collingwood signifying his intention to take command of the Hinchinbrook. Ten well-armed Spanish sailors assembled close behind him.

Captain Collingwood was the first to break the silence. Bowing his head ever so slightly, yet all the while keeping his right hand resting on his sword, he greeted the admiral, "I welcome you Commodore aboard His Majesty's Ship Hinchinbrook. On behalf of King George, how might we be of service to you?"

Nelson's eyes focused keenly upon the admiral. Nelson understood that Collingwood was provoking the admiral by, for one, assuming that the conversation would be in English; and two, by calling him commodore when his rank was admiral thereby implying that his fleet was nowhere to be found; and three, speaking in a manner that boldly implied that the Hinchinbrook had the upper hand over the Trinidad.

A snarl of irritation was starting to overtake Admiral Córdoba's formal composure. A few more formal exchanges took place.

Pastor platypus was in the sea under the Spanish skiff and saw that no one was in the boat which was tied up against the hull of the Hinchinbrook. He cautiously crept into their vessel to take a look around. He noticed a number of muskets leaning up against the seats, and moved quickly to pour salty sea water down their barrels should the situation deteriorate. Pastor Platypus shoved off half of their ores into the waters of the harbor giving them each a push to help them float away. He then slipped back into the sea and remained hidden at the stern of the admiral's skiff.

Admiral Córdoba took a deep breath and spoke directly to the English Captain, "It was fortunate for you Capítan that I saw Capítan Don Pablo. I was just about to give the orders to send your ship to the bottom of the harbor."

With a defiant smirk, Captain Collingwood replied, "How kind of you to spare us for a few more moments. I will be sure to take note of your generosity in my ship log. I am actually quite surprised you and your men cared enough to rescue Captain Don Pablo this time."

"This Time?" inquired Admiral Córdoba.

"Yes", informed Collingwood, "It seems that my men came to rescue Capitan Don Pablo after yours abandoned him. Your men ran to save their own skins after he was captured by the natives of this island, whom you continue to oppress for personal and temporary gain."

"Es la verdad Capítan? [Is this the truth Captain?]", asked the admiral turning to Don Pablo.

Don Pablo responded, "Sí, I was about to be burned at the stake, and three of their crew nearly died to rescue me and bring me back here."

He said 'crew' not wanting to reveal to the admiral the identities of Porky the Porcupine, Pastor Platypus, Marty the macaw, and Princess Clementine.

Admiral Córdoba turned back to Captain Collingwood, "Well, it seems that Spain is indebted to you and your men. Is there anything we can do in return to repay you?"

Captain Collingwood confidently replied, "You can start by leaving these islands at once and you can finish by ceasing to oppress the people of the West Indies and the Canary Islands!"

"Ha! Ha Haaaa haa!" laughed Admiral Córdoba in ere defiance. Becoming angry he snared back at Collingwood, "You are in no position to tell me what I am to do! Perhaps you would like to count my cannons again! I will take Capítan Don Pablo now, and you shall also hand over to me the princess and her special cargo. Then I will decide whether or not to crush your little ship into tiny splinters!"

"Don Pablo! Into the barco!" bellowed out the Admiral as if talking to a little child. Don Pablo stepped forward answering as a son would to an overbearing father. Don Pablo stopped and faced Captain Collingwood, "From the bottom of my heart, I thank you and your men for what you have done for me," and with that he gave Captain Collingwood a long firm hand shake and a wink.

Collingwood could feel that a small piece of paper was secretly being handed to him in the handshake. Collingwood carefully closed his hand to grasp the paper slipping it back into his pocket a bit puzzled by the interaction. Captain Don Pablo descended down the side of the Hinchinbrook into the skiff along with a few Spanish sailors.

"And now Capítan, the princess if you would, por favor!" demanded Admiral Córdoba.

Collingwood flatly answered, "I regret to inform you that I have no idea what you are talking about."

"I see", said Admiral Córdoba. He began to shout loud enough for every ear on the ship to hear, "Princessa! I know that you are here! And before I sink this tiny worthless English boat to the sea floor, know this! The Canary Islands belong to Spain now, and your father shall be my personal slave until the day that he dies!"

The Admiral turned to Collingwood and muttered in a near growl, "England will be no more! And the princess with all of her stolen treasures will be of no concern to us at the bottom of the sea!"

And with that he descended into his skiff and began to row for the Trinidad. He was yelling at his men for losing half the ores which were floating aimlessly out into the harbor. Admiral Córdoba was beyond enraged at his men, "Fools! Can you not even keep the ores in the boat!"

The disguised Princess could no longer hold herself back after hearing the admiral's declaration against her father. She took off her hat and let down her hair. Still in a midshipman's overcoat, she leaned over the side of the railing and shouted at the top of her lungs at the admiral who had just started rowing back to his ship, "You ruthless pig! Your plans will never prevail!"

The sailors of the Hinchinbrook tried desperately to pull her off of the rail, but she would not let go. Princess Clementine continued, "So long as I live, my islands will remain forever free from the crown of Spain!"

Admiral Córdoba's eyes filled with madness. He drew a black powder pistol off the belt of a Spanish Marine in front of him and took aim at the princes, the future ruler of the Canary Islands.

Just as the admiral pulled the trigger Captain Don Pablo who was more towards the bow of the skiff leapt in front of the pistol's line of fire and directly received the shot that was intended for the princess. Captain Don Pablo immediately fell into the water. The princess was tackled to the deck of the Hinchinbrook for her protection.

"Let him sink! Row for the Trinidad!" bellowed out Admiral Córdoba.

The English marines now lined the deck with muskets drawn aimed at the Spanish sailors who were inefficiently rowing back with only three ores. Captain Collingwood perceived no further resistance from the Spanish men in the skiff who were rowing for all they were worth for the Trinidad, "Hold your fire men! But if one of those Spanish sailors even looks at us wrong, you know what to do."

Lieutenant Nelson threw off his overcoat and dove over the side of the Hinchinbrook plunging into the salty harbor to retrieve Captain Don Pablo who was wounded in the upper chest.

Captain Collingwood turned to the boatswain with a blaze in his eyes, "Full sail! Turn the wheel hard over to port! Get us out of this harbor!" Captain Collingwood turned to the officer of the watch, "And throw a rope in for the Lieutenant and Captain Don Pablo and retrieve them immediately." The captain made his way back up to the quarter deck.

The bos'n began to give urgent orders and in a flash the deck and rigging broke out with men in action! There were shouts and orders bellowing out in all parts of the ship.

"Port Battery, make ready to fire!" ordered Captain Collingwood to the men below deck. The other half of the crew went aloft to unfurl the sails. One by one, the sails fell to catch the brisk east wind. The Hinchinbrook had begun to lurch forward just as Admiral Córdoba was nearly to the Trinidad.

"As soon as Admiral Córdoba gets back to his ship he will give the orders to fire upon us. Get us out from the line of his port battery and turn for the sea! We can maneuver a lot faster than that 1st rate goliath!" ordered Collingwood to the helmsman.

"Aye-Aye Captain!" he answered.

Lieutenant Nelson tied a rope under the arms of Don Pablo which had been lowered down to him. Once secure, he gave the signal for the men to hoist him back aboard. Nelson climbed up the side of the ship assisting as much as he could in guiding Don Pablo aboard. Princess Clementine was close by when Lieutenant Nelson and some of the crew helped Don Pablo to lie comfortably on the main deck of the Hinchinbrook. The ship's surgeon and carpenter, Mr. Moxly, arrived at once to tend to Captain Don Pablo's chest wound.

Princess Clementine ran up to the captain, fell to her knees, and supported his head as he lay wounded on the deck. The princess' heart was overflowing with gratitude and sadness, "Gracias Capítan, you saved my life."

It was becoming more difficult for Captain Don Pablo to breath, and with all the strength he could muster he told the princess, "You have done nothing to deserve death. I thank you and your friends for saving my life." He struggled with all his remaining strength to finish, "and also for saving my soul." The princess kissed Captain Don Pablo on his forehead, a small gesture for allowing her years to continue. He closed his eyes and breathed his last. The princess closed his eye-lids with her hand.

Nelson ordered the surgeon and his mate, "Take him below and give him proper honors."

To avoid the death of every man and creature aboard the Hinchinbrook, Lieutenant Nelson had to quickly move onto his other duties to see to it that their ship evaded the Trinidad and found the open sea as soon as possible.

Fearing more musket and cannon fire, Nelson grabbed Princess Clementine by the arm and pulled her up to her feet, "Come with me princess, we must move quickly." Nelson moved the princess swiftly to the aft gun deck into the midshipmen's quarters where he felt she'd be most protected from the impending battle. He ordered three marines to stand guard giving them a stern order, "I expect and England expects you to do your duty to protect the princess and her secret cargo! If it looks like we should be captured or sent to the bottom by the Trinidad, row her ashore and go into hiding! Understood?!"

"Yes Sir!" answered back the marines who were preparing in their heart to fight with all they had in obedience to the lieutenant's orders.

Nelson returned immediately to the quarter deck grabbing two pistols for his belt along the way. Captain Collingwood was focused only on getting past the Trinidad and out to sea. Nelson reported, "We can get clear of their initial opportunity to fire, but if they are able to negotiate one quarter turn to port we'll be at the bottom in one broadside."

"Do you think I do not realize that!" snapped Collingwood.

"Marty! Don't forget about Marty!" interrupted the princess who had also made her way up to the quarter deck still with the appearances of a midshipman.

Nelson was clearly amazed and irritated that yet again the Princess got past the Marines to be a part of the action up on deck, "Princess Clementine, you do realize that I have a duty to protect you, so you must..."

Collingwood still upset interrupted, "I appreciate your optimism Princess, but I highly doubt that one macaw can destroy Spain's flagship!"

"Sir, when I saw the Trinidad come upon us, I examined her structure in detail and found a weakness which I informed Captain Marty about," pleaded Princess Clementine.

"Well, what is it?" asked Captain Collingwood not much bothered by her presence on the quarter deck.

"The tiller Sir, I instructed Marty to disable the rope and mechanism that causes the rudder to answer to the helm!"

"Brilliant!" exclaimed Collingwood, "let us hope your Captain Marty succeeds in his efforts. We shall know soon enough if he does not, but if we ever get out of this mess Princess, I myself will defend your Islands with *my* very life as you will have well saved ours!

The Hinchinbrook was coming across the Trinidad's bow with full sail aimed straight for the outlet to the sea. The Trinidad was letting down her sails and raising her massive anchor.

"They are turning their wheel hard over to port Captain", reported Collingwood.

Nelson boldly reiterated, "One quarter turn and their starboard battery has us."

"Shall we clear the decks for action Captain?" asked Nelson.

"No, keep the men on those sails and get us out of this harbor! The wind is in our favor. We run for the open sea *now*!" ordered Collingwood.

"Nelson!" shouted Captain Collingwood with a new order, "Have our Marine sharp shooters lay down fire on the Trinidad's forecastle gun ports so their men cannot organize a shot against us!"

The wind now filled the Trinidad's sails and it began to lurch forward with promising momentum. The English marines were firing heavily into the Trinidad's fore gun ports which prevented the Spanish sailors from being able to load their cannons. Nelson looked keenly through his looking glass to see if the Santísma Trinidad would answer to the helm. He watched their helmsman frantically turn the Trinidad's wheel to port. Nelson shouted to the Captain Collingwood with great excitement,

"She's not answering to helm Sir, and she's headed straight for shore under full sail!"

With all of his men up in the rigging, Admiral Córdoba was not able to drop his anchors in time. The Hinchinbrook passed in front of the Santisima Trinidad's great bowsprit out to the open sea. The great Santísima Trinidad continued to slowly lurch forward towards shore under full sail! Her crew was frantically trying to stop her advance, but it was too late. The wind filled the Trinidad's sails and the massive ship rammed into the shore of the harbor. The wind subsequently heeled her over to lee causing the flagship to come to rest at quite a distressful angle resting nearly on her beam ends.

Captain Collingwood worked hard to hide a grin as the men of the Hinchinbrook erupted with cheering, "Take us with full sail out to sea Mr. Nelson. With the wind three points on the quarter, make a heading of southwest by west."

"Yes Sir!" answered Nelson, his voice quivering with excitement. Nelson echoed the orders from the quarter deck to the Officer of the Watch. Captain Collingwood walked slowly across the quarter deck to look off the stern at the Trinidad which was likened to a beached whale. He reached in his pocket and felt the paper handed to him by Captain Don Pablo. Unfolding it he read, 'Captain, I owe my life to you, the Princess, and her creature-friends. I will return the favor the next chance I am afforded. May God's will prevail!'

Princess Clementine calmly approached the stern railing and stood next to Captain Collingwood removing her midshipman's hat to embrace the wind which was so swiftly pushing the Hinchinbrook out into the safety of the open sea. She pointed at the sea between them and the beached Trinidad. Captain

Collingwood strained his eyes to see that which the Princess was pointing out. Then he saw it. A brightly colored macaw swiftly flying with outstretched wings just over the top of the sea toward the Hinchinbrook.

The Captain turned to Princess Clementine and smiled, "Our colorful savior approaches."

Chapter XXXIII

Burial at Sea

The Hinchinbrook and its crew sailed all night to the southwest under the cover of darkness. The men readied and recovered their ship returning to it order and balance. At the first light of day not a ship was in sight in any direction.

Marty the Macaw arrived from out of the rigging somewhere above landing swiftly upon Captain Collingwood's shoulder giving him a good startle.

"Goodness Marty! Back from your morning patrol already! You sure make quite the entry," commented Collingwood. "England salutes you, and I salute you for your valiant actions yesterday. You saved our entire ship! And for that Captain, you shall be given the Royal Navy's highest honors which I will be sure to note in my reports to the Admiralty in Portsmouth upon our return."

"Squawk! Thank you Captain!"

"Any sign of the Lowestoffe Marty?" asked Collingwood.

Marty shook and ruffled up his feathers to air them out a bit and gave them a rearranging fluff, "Captain Locker has been informed of the events that have taken place. He sends his apologies, and made a change of course to intercept our ship in two days' time."

"Does he have the secret orders?" asked Collingwood.

Marty answered promptly, "He does, and instructs you to proceed to the agreed upon location just off of the coast of Nicaragua."

Captain Collingwood replied, "No further word of this until I address my officers. You may carry on and report to Lieutenant Nelson for your accommodations and duties."

The captain gave the orders to turn into the wind and hove to. The sails remained unfurled, but the ship was positioned so that the wind would not fill them.

Captain Collingwood approached the boatswain, "Assemble the crew for the burial of the dead."

"Aye-aye Captain.".

The body of Captain Don Pablo, still in his Spanish Captain's Uniform, was placed on an eight-man table at the entry port on the starboard gangway.

Captain Collingwood turned to Porky on the quarter deck, "Mr. Porky, climb up the mainmast and let fly the black pennant." Porky saluted, "Aye-aye, Captain."

Pastor Platypus, Marty the Macaw, and Princess Clementine came alongside the body of Captain Don Pablo to wrap him in a canvas shroud. Porky returned from aloft the main and used one of his own quills to ceremonially sew the canvas shut around the honorable Captain Don Pablo. Princess Clementine placed two cannon balls at the feet of Don Pablo within the canvas.

There was some debate as to whether or not the captain's body should be covered with the Union Jack or the flag of Spain, but no Spanish flag could be found. Lieutenant Nelson stepped forward and quickly put to rest the dispute, "Captain Don Pablo laid down his life on behalf of the interests of England! Lay over him the Union Jack."

The Boatswain called out, "Ship's Company! Off hats!"

At this, the crew assembled in formation beside the canvas wrapped body of Captain Don Pablo covered by the laid-out Union Jack. The Captain and other officers removed their hats.

Pastor Platypus stood atop a barrel to officiate the service, "The book of Psalms chapter thirty-nine, 'Show me, Lord, my life's end and the number of my days; let me know how fleeting my life is. You have made my days a mere handbreadth; the span of my years is as nothing before you. Everyone is but a breath, even those who seem secure. Surely everyone goes around like a mere phantom; in vain they rush about, heaping up wealth without knowing whose it will finally be. But now, Lord, what do I look for? My hope is in you! Save me from all my transgressions; do not make me the scorn of fools. Hear my prayer, Lord, listen to my cry for help; do not be deaf to my weeping.'

Pastor Platypus closed his bible, removed his bifocals and stood up straight to address the men and officers, "Gentlemen, Captain Don Pablo had a transformation of heart and chose to lay down his life for a worthy and honorable cause. In the book of John, we are told that 'Greater love hath no man than this - that a man lay down his life for his friends.'

Pastor Platypus continued to implore the men, "Let us now live lives worthy of Christ's sacrifice and worthy of Captain Don

Pablo's sacrifice, for their lives were not lost in vain, but for a greater purpose that should outlive them towards eternity!"

Captain Collingwood spoke aloud, "In the sure and certain hope of the resurrection to eternal life through our Lord Jesus Christ, we commend to Almighty God, our shipmate, Captain Don Pablo and we commit his body to the depths. Ashes to ashes, dust to dust. The Lord bless him and keep him. The Lord make His face to shine upon him and be gracious unto him. The Lord lift up His countenance upon him, and give him peace."

And with that all hands said, "Amen".

Princess Clementine and Lieutenant Nelson lifted up the body of Captain Don Pablo and it fell out from under the Union Jack down into the depths of the sea until the day of resurrection.

The boatswain gave the command, "On hats! - Dismissed!" And with that the crew dispersed. Captain Collingwood approached the bos'n, "Bring us about to our former heading and sail us three points large to accommodate our moderate northeasterly gale, and keep a sharp first watch until we lose the light of day, these waters are teeming with potential visitors."

Collingwood then ascended the quarter deck, "Quartermaster! Bring us about two points south of west if you would please."

There was a tinge of uncertainty in the quartermaster's voice as he knew this heading would bring them further away from the Atlantic, away from home, and into the heart of the Caribbean where many Spanish ships lurk about, "Yes, Sir. Two points south of west it is Sir." And the helmsman obediently turned the wheel away from England.

Chapter XXXIV

A Bold and Secret Mission

Lieutenant Nelson well perceived the change of course though he was not on the quarter deck. Nelson made his way up to Captain Collingwood with concern flooding his mind, "West Captain?"

Captain Collingwood did not even look at Nelson as he approached. He continued to look forward over the ship, "Have the officers assemble in my quarters including the midshipmen. Include also Captain Marty, the Porcupine, Pastor Platypus, and Princess Clementine."

"Yes Captain," and Nelson immediately carried out the captain's request.

In just a few moments all the officers and special guests were formally assembled in the captain's quarters.

The conversations immediately hushed and the officers all stood up at attention as Captain Collingwood entered the room, "Please, take your seat." The Captain took his place at the center of the room, "Gentlemen and honored guests, I am sure you are all wondering why we have changed course to a westerly heading as opposed to turning back to Portsmouth."

Captain Collingwood continued to pace slowly across the room before his silent and attentive listeners, "We have received secret orders from Governor General Dalling at Port Royal Jamaica to slice the Spanish settlements in half cutting off all communication and supply exchange between North and South America. We will proceed down the Mosquito Coast of

Nicaragua directly to the mouth of the San Juan River, make passage up the river, capture the Fort of San Juan, and gain control of the cities of Granada and Leon! Thanks to the efforts the princess and the people of the Canary Islands, we now have detailed maps of these Spanish fortifications!"

The men cheered in unison at the bold new orders.

Nelson spoke up first, "With all due respect Captain, our marines alone could not complete such a task."

"Right you are Lieutenant!" grinned Collingwood, "Major Polson of the Royal American Regiment will be in command of the ground efforts and will have at his disposal nearly three thousand men who will be assembling at the proposed location in the weeks that approach."

"Three thousand men! Good heavens!" exclaimed one of the officers. The room erupted in small conversations.

"Gentlemen! Gentlemen!" Captain Collingwood regained their attention, "These soldiers will be made up of the Liverpool Blues, the Royal American Marines, The Royal Jamaica volunteers, and the Royal Batteaux Corps. Lieutenant Nelson, I want you to oversee this mission. You will be the highest ranking officer present ashore. Technically your authority will be limited to Naval Operation, but I want you to keep a close eye on Major Polson. Lieutenant, you are held in higher regard by the men, but you must do your best to make the major feel like he is the one in command."

Nelson grinned, "I understand Captain."

"Attention!" shouted Captain Collingwood. The officers all stood up around the table.

"Now make ready your men, and be at the ready to eliminate any Spanish obstacle we might encounter en route to the Mosquito Coast of Nicaragua. Dismissed!"

After everyone left the cabin, Lieutenant Nelson questioned the captain, "Sir, with all due respect, shouldn't we bring the princess's documents directly to the Admiralty in Portsmouth?"

"Oh, come now Lieutenant, do you have any idea how long it would take for all of those over-inflated egos to arrive at a consensus as to how we should respond. Admiral Córdoba now knows that we have the documents and it won't be long before he sends word to all of his constituents as to our upper hand. We need to carry out the governor's orders before Admiral Córdoba is able to alert the officers at the fort of San Juan. Once the men are offloaded, I will have Captain Locker run the dispatches and the princess back to Portsmouth."

"Fantastic plan, Captain," agreed Nelson.

That night during the first watch there was a great celebration below decks among the crew. In lieu of their narrow escape from the Santísima Trinidad and of their bold new mission, the crew had reason for a night of music, singing, and dancing.

As the sun set giving way to the stars, the winds remained in their favor, the sea was becalmed, and a waxing gibbous-moon provided a pleasant light. Not a ship was in sight. The joyous singing of men sounded out from below deck.

The helmsman could hear them quite clearly on the quarter deck, "Shall I silence them Captain?"

The Captain stared proudly out over the sea taking a deep breath, "Let them sing Mr. Bickham. I fear many of them may never see England again; tonight their joy shall not be taken from them."

Porky the Porcupine, Marty the Macaw, Pastor Platypus, and Princess Clementine were just finishing their evening meal in the midshipman's quarters enjoying a nice warm night-time breeze coming in through the portholes.

They sat quietly for a moment each taking the time to reflect on the day. Porky broke the silence first, "Pastor, what do you suppose we will do when we get to the mouth of the San Juan River? Do we wait and look for another ship that is bound for Cape Horn, or should we support the English in their efforts?"

Pastor Platypus shuffled across the room to the porthole and let the wind blow against his face as he considered the days to come, "Porky, I believe that sometimes the whispers of God's voice come riding on the wind. The reasons for our being alive are upon us. All we need to discern is the next best step. We should do what obedience leads us to do in each day. Then we will not be like waves tossed around in the wind. We will not be moved in a different direction by every feeling and circumstance."

Pastor Platypus patted his hand against a sturdy oak beam, "We must be like this ship and set a steady course. Terra Australis Incognito will be found by learning to hear the voice of our Good Shepherd. Porky I suggest that we take a moment to clear our hearts and minds tomorrow morning at the end of the bowsprit or atop the main mast. We must take time to listen and to remember."

"Listen and remember," repeated Porky, "as I did atop Grandmother Pine on Moose Island. I did a whole lot of hoping and dreaming up there too."

Clementine chimed in, "My father always used to tell me not to be afraid to dream impossible dreams. Dream so big that only God could make them come true. You three have a beautiful calling upon your lives. With your abilities alone, your task is impossible, but with God all things are indeed possible. I believe we are all born with destines placed within our hearts that will come forth through faith; hope, courage, and love."

"Yes indeed, yes indeed!" squawked Marty the Macaw, "faith, hope, and love are like big coconut seeds that you plant into the ground, then up comes the dream tree!"

"The dream tree?" questioned Porky thinking that Marty was being just a tad on the strange side.

"I see! The dream tree! That is well put my feathered companion," encouraged Pastor Platypus. "If you plant the seeds of faith, hope, and love in the soil of your day, in time, a dream fulfilled will come forth, a dream come true, a tree that bears much fruit for others to enjoy and live upon! Well put Marty, I say well put!"

"Thank You Pastor!" replied Marty with a bow.

Pastor Platypus stood up and walked towards the door, "Well, are you all going to sit around all night!? Enough worrying about tomorrow, it isn't even here yet! Let's join in the festivities and celebrate with the crew! Let tomorrow worry about itself!" Pastor Platypus walked towards the door and shouted before walking out, "Tonight we celebrate life and the victories we have had!"

Porky and Captain Marty looked at each other a bit uncertain, and the princess stood up at once with an excited smile on her face, "Wait for me! I will join you Pastor!"

"I'm in too," agreed Porky.

"I'm already halfway there!" declared Marty. And they all rushed down to the gun deck and mess hall laughing in excitement as they went.

There were two men playing the fiddle and others were atop the tables clapping and stomping their feet! Dishes and cups were all over the floor and a united chorus of men singing overwhelmed the air.

As Porky, Pastor Platypus, Captain Marty and the princess entered the room, the men erupted in cheer and a toast was made by Mr. Christian the Boatswain, "Long live the princess, may her radiance shine on forever! And to our new mates Pastor Platypus, Porky the Porcupine and Captain Marty!"

The room erupted in cheer, "Huuzaaaa!" The fiddles came to life again, and the dancing was joyous. The princess laughed and spun around dancing with the crew. Marty was dancing atop the fiddler's hat singing and squawking without restraint.

In a crowd of England's happiest and bravest sailors, Princess Clementine picked up Pastor Platypus and Porky, one in each arm, and spun and sang.

Suddenly the princess tripped over a man crawling on all fours across the floor through the ruckus crowd. To her great surprise it was Captain Marty the Macaw riding Lieutenant Nelson like a wild horse! She was absolutely taken back that an officer would be so undignified and humble to celebrate in such a way among the crew. He stood up equally surprised that he had caused the princess to fall down. They both lay on the deck together surrounded by dancing feet. Lieutenant Nelson laying on his side reached over to grab the hand of Princess Clementine who was also still lying on the deck. "Mind if have this dance my lady?" asked Nelson kissing lightly Clementine's hand.

Clementine replied with a beautifully bright smile, "The pleasure would be all mine Lieutenant."

"Horatio, my lady. Please, just call me Horatio."

Clementine stared into Lieutenant Nelson's eyes with delight, "Alright, Horatio it is."

The fiddle struck up an exhilarating tune and the sailors erupted with shouts, clapping, foot-stomping, and singing. Horatio and Clementine danced the night through as the Hinchinbrook bounded west towards the San Juan River under a clear star-lit sky.

Pastor Platypus and Porky retreated from the festivities and made their way up to the rail up by the bow sprit. "Pastor, do you suppose this is how we were intended to make our way to the lost southern continent? I feel at times we are heading in the wrong direction."

"That, my dear friend, is how moving forward sometimes feels," reflected Pastor Platypus as he watched the moon-lit sparkling sea flow around the bow of the Hinchinbrook.

Marty the Macaw flew up landing on the railing. "There you all are! Quite the day! Quite the day!" squawked Marty. Noticing his friends admiring the sea, Marty closed his eyes and embraced the breeze coming across the bow.

"Pastor," asked Porky, "Do you suppose Captain Collingwood will bring us around the horn after they accomplish their mission in the San Juan?"

"I believe they will make their way back to Portsmouth England with the princess and her valuable dispatches. We will most likely have to remain in Central America and wait there for another vessel bound for Cape Horn."

Marty the Macaw chimed in, "There is another way."

"A way to what?" asked Porky.

Marty resumed his thought, "There is a much shorter way to get to the South Pacific."

Marty looked keenly towards the Western horizon, "We cross the land bridge! Many years ago, I was in the land of called the Rich Coast, or Costa Rica. I was soaring high in the sky trying to get a better view of a smoking mountain, which I had never seen before."

"A smoking mountain?" inquired Porky.

Pastor Platypus clarified, "He is speaking of a volcano."

Marty continued, "I saw the most incredible thing in the far West. Another Ocean! The Pacific Ocean to be exact!"

"Of course! We could skip rounding South America entirely!" realized Pastor Platypus. "Marty, would you happen to know how far west the San Juan river will take us across the land bridge?"

"Nearly three parts of four. The Spanish fort Captain Collingwood seeks is on a great lake which feeds the River San Juan. A trek to the Pacific Coast from there would be but a few days."

"That's fantastic!" celebrated Porky.

"Well gentlemen," resolved Pastor Platypus, "That settles it! We'll simply walk to the Pacific and see if we can find for ourselves a ship of exploration that might be bound for the south seas in search of Australis!

With hearts contented and minds settled by their newly proposed plans, they took a deep breath of fulfillment and watched the Hinchinbrook plunge resolutely westward through the moon-lit Caribbean Sea.

To Be Continued..........